"Forgive me if I sound like a typical reporter,"

Elizabeth said. "But you sound like a man who has something to hide."

Jonas clamped his lips together to keep himself from saying anything too quickly. Damn, she was one vexing woman. She stepped a little closer to him, close enough for him to appreciate the sparkling gleam in her warm brown eyes and the rich shine of her honeyed hair.

"What are you hiding, Mr. Bishop?" she asked with the husky chuckle that had taunted the edges of his memory last night. "You promised me an answer to one question."

Jonas folded his arms across his chest and looked directly in her eyes. "Come in, Ms. Reporter," he said, holding open the gate, "and I'll tell you something you might not want to hear."

Celeste Hamilton

has been writing since she was ten years old. The broadcast media captured her interest in high school, and she graduated from the University of Tennessee with a B.S. in communications. From there, she began writing and producing commercials at a Chattanooga, Tennessee, radio station. Celeste began writing romances in 1985 and now works at her craft full-time. She lives in East Tennessee with her policeman husband, and they enjoy traveling when their busy schedules permit.

Celeste Hamilton

MAN
WITH A
PAST

Silhouette Books

Published by Silhouette Books
America's Publisher of Contemporary Romance

Special thanks and acknowledgment to Celeste Hamilton for her contribution to the Montana Mavericks series.

Text and artwork on page 8 is reprinted with permission from NEVER ASK A MAN THE SIZE OF HIS SPREAD: A Cowgirl's Guide to Life, by Gladiola Montana. Copyright © 1993 Gibbs Smith Publisher. All rights reserved.

 SILHOUETTE BOOKS

ISBN 0-373-50175-7

MAN WITH A PAST

MONTANA Mavericks

*Welcome to Whitehorn, Montana—
the home of bold men and daring women.
A place where rich tales of passion and
adventure are unfolding under the Big Sky.
Seems that this charming little town has some mighty
big secrets. And everybody's talking about…*

Elizabeth Monroe: Investigative reporting has taken the place of facing her own troubled past. But it'll be more than just another story when she uncovers the mystery behind the infant abandoned at the Kincaid ranch…

Baby Jennifer: She's found a home in the hearts of the townspeople. But her true identity may just about rock Whitehorn to its foundations, especially her new parents…

Sterling and Jessica McCallum: Wedded bliss was complete when they officially adopted Jennifer. Then tragedy followed close on the heels of happiness when Jennifer was suddenly kidnapped. Could this have something to do with…

Mary Jo Kincaid: As if the rumors swirling around her weren't enough, now she has to contend with a pesky reporter asking too many questions. And just when she was so close to her plans being realized, she faced the formidable lawman…

Clint Calloway: This cowboy cop hoped things would settle down around town, but now a whole new hornet's nest of trouble is abuzz. He'll do whatever he has to to protect the town—as well as his own secret.…

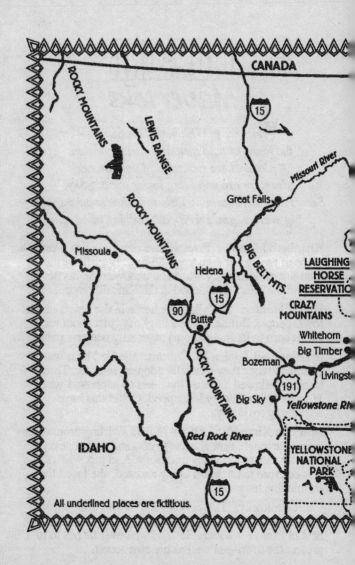

All underlined places are fictitious.

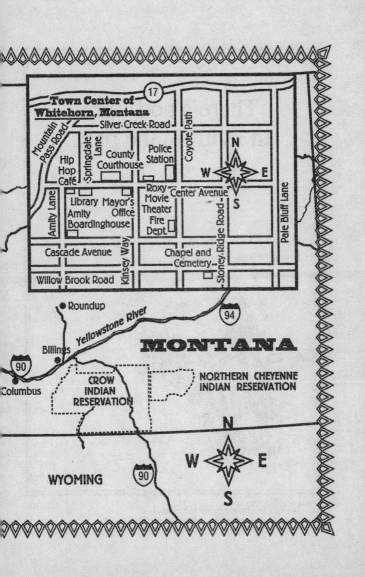

Town Center of Whitehorn, Montana

17

Silver Creek Road

Mountain Pass Road

Springdale Lane

County Courthouse

Police Station

Coyote Path

Hip Hop Café

N
W · E
S

Amity Lane

Library
Amity
Boardinghouse

Mayor's
Office

Roxy
Movie
Theater
Fire
Dept.

Center Avenue

Stoney Ridge Road

Pale Bluff Lane

Cascade Avenue

Kinsey Way

Chapel and
Cemetery

Willow Brook Road

● Roundup

Yellowstone River

94

● Billings

MONTANA

90

● Columbus

CROW
INDIAN
RESERVATION

NORTHERN CHEYENNE
INDIAN RESERVATION

N
W · E
S

WYOMING

90

There's no future in livin' in the past.

Quote and Illustration from:
NEVER ASK A MAN THE SIZE OF HIS SPREAD,
by Gladiola Montana. Illustration by Bonnie Cazier.
Copyright © 1993 by Gibbs Smith Publisher.

One

Whitehorn, Montana, was the last place Elizabeth Monroe would expect to find a funky-looking little restaurant called the Hip Hop Café. A town like this, a speck of civilization amidst ranches and wide-open spaces, was supposed to be filled with eateries called Mom's or the All-You-Can-Eat Canteen. But here in the heart of Whitehorn, the neon-lit Hip Hop appeared to be doing a brisk business. A family of four was coming out the door, while two men in cowboy hats and faded jeans paused beside an easel that advertised grilled salmon and quiche *primavera* as the specials of the day.

"Small towns have obviously evolved," Elizabeth murmured to herself as she surveyed the busy scene. This definitely bore little resemblance to the tiny part of Colorado she had fled from some fifteen years ago. She could almost imagine she was in Denver, the cosmopolitan sprawl she now called home.

The aroma of grilled meat and fresh bread wafted through the cool evening air. Her stomach rumbled in response, reminding her she was hundreds of miles from Denver and hours from the sandwich she had grabbed on her way to the airport earlier today.

Inside the Hip Hop, the smells were even more delicious, the atmosphere even more of a surprise. The walls were jammed with an eclectic mix of art and memorabilia. Cool jazz spilled from the stereo speakers, harmonizing with the laughter and conversation. Tables formed a palette of primary colors. Every table and booth was occupied. In fact, Elizabeth spotted only two empty chairs, one each at a pair of small tables situated close together near the front. A busy waitress thrust a menu into her hands, calling over her shoulder, "It'll be just a few minutes," before dashing off in the direction of the kitchen.

Elizabeth's stomach rumbled again, loud enough for anyone close by to hear.

"Do you want to share?"

Turning, Elizabeth stared into the bright blue eyes of the bleached blonde who sat alone at one of the small tables. She looked to be fiftyish, but was dressed much younger, in a rhinestone-studded T-shirt with gaudy green-and-purple earrings to match. Her smile was friendly as she added, "You can join me if you want."

"Why, thank you," Elizabeth said. "I'm so hungry, I wasn't sure I wanted to wait."

The woman chuckled. "The food here is worth waiting for. Please sit down."

Elizabeth took the offered chair gratefully, depositing her heavy purse at her feet and shrugging out of her tweed blazer. After traveling most of the day, she was happy she had chosen jeans and a light cotton sweater over more professional attire. As it was, she still felt grubby and tired, and hoped her dinner would be served quickly, so she could find her accommodations and get some sleep.

While she was settling in, the man at the small table beside theirs glanced up from the newspaper he was reading. The paper's familiar masthead, *Denver Free Press,* caught Elizabeth's attention, and she smiled. Though the man nodded, no warmth touched his dark eyes before he turned back to the pages in front of him.

The blonde leaned toward Elizabeth, lowering her voice a few degrees, although it was by no means a whisper. "I've never understood why a person would want to read at the dinner table when they could have a good conversation."

Murmuring something noncommittal, Elizabeth slanted another glance at the attractive man at the next table. He seemed to be absorbed in his reading, but she noticed the telltale quirk of one corner of his mouth. He had heard the comment. Her guess was he had been invited to join the blonde before Elizabeth arrived. And maybe the fact that he had chosen to eat alone and bury his head in a newspaper meant he knew something about the older woman that Elizabeth didn't.

"I'm Lily Mae Wheeler." Half an armful of silver bracelets jangled as the woman extended her hand. "And you're not from around here."

"I'm from Denver. I flew into Billings this afternoon and rented a car."

"And drove this way? Where are you headed?"

"Here."

The unmistakable gleam of a true busybody had come into Lily Mae's eyes. "Vacationing or visiting family?"

Before Elizabeth could reply, the waitress arrived with her companion's dinner and took Elizabeth's request for a glass of white zinfandel and the grilled-salmon special.

The minute the flurry of activity was over, Lily Mae leaned close again, her rhinestone earrings swinging forward like two exclamation points on either side of her animated features. "Now who is it you're visiting?"

"Actually, I'm working," Elizabeth said, amused by the woman's excitement. "I'm a reporter for the *Denver Free Press*."

"A reporter?" Lily Mae's voice rose to an excited squeak. "A reporter from Denver? Tell me your name. Do you write for the women's section?"

The waitress brought the glass of wine while Elizabeth introduced herself to Lily Mae and explained that she usually wrote articles that focused on state and regional government issues. She felt, rather than saw, the man at the next table look at her as she answered her companion's questions about the paper. She glanced his way, and for a moment their gazes locked, but he quickly turned toward the passing waitress and asked when his dinner would be ready. His voice was as deep, as rich as the midnight black of his eyes and hair. As smooth as brandy-flavored coffee. Elizabeth frowned, wondering at her whimsical comparison, before her attention was once again captured by Lily Mae.

"What in the world would a Denver reporter want way up here in Whitehorn, Montana?"

"We cover news from all over the Rocky Mountain states. The paper even publishes a regional magazine-style section every week—"

"I read it every Sunday," Lily Mae said. "But what would Whitehorn—" She broke off in a startled gasp and her blue eyes widened. "I bet you're up here to do a report on Dugin Kincaid's death."

"Dugin Kincaid?" Elizabeth turned the name over in her mind, wondering why it sounded so familiar.

"Jeremiah Kincaid's son," Lily Mae offered, as if that was all the explanation needed. "Everybody's talking about the tragedy. They can't believe Dugin is dead, killed in that awful fire, and with his poor daddy gone only two years. Just when it seemed Dugin might be filling his poor dead brother's—"

"Are you saying Dugin's father was *the* Jeremiah Kincaid?" Elizabeth interrupted. As a investigative reporter focusing on the movers and shakers of the Western states, she made it her business to know a little something about most of the prominent power brokers in the region, a group to which Jeremiah Kincaid had definitely belonged.

"Yes, *the* Jeremiah Kincaid." Lily Mae arched her eyebrows, mimicking Elizabeth's emphasis. "Rancher, rich man and, if I do say so myself, a bit of a rogue."

Elizabeth's mind was whirling. About the time of Jeremiah Kincaid's death two years ago, there had been a scandal involving a ranchers' association using its influence with a Montana congressman to steal grazing rights on land owned by one of this area's Indian tribes. Jeremiah Kincaid had headed that association before his death. The tribe had ultimately held on to their grazing rights, and their victory had been used as a precedent by other Native Americans facing similar situations.

So Whitehorn was home to the famous Kincaid ranching empire, Elizabeth mused to herself. Maybe this story assignment in the outer reaches of nowhere wouldn't be so deadly dull, after all. She smiled in encouragement at Lily Mae. "I guess I didn't realize the Kincaids were from around here."

"Their spread's not far out of town, up near the reservation. Jeremiah's granddaddy was one of the first to settle this area. He made a pile of money on cattle, invested it wisely, and the family's been raking in the dough ever since." Lily Mae sniffed. "My family settled here over a hundred years ago, too. But we're still waiting to make our fortune, and I—"

"Refresh my memory." Elizabeth broke in before the woman could get sidetracked. "How was it that the father, Jeremiah Kincaid, died?"

"He drowned after falling in the shower and hitting his head, poor man." Lily Mae chuckled, her merry expression at odds with talk of death. "Frankly, I always expected him to die a little more spectacularly. A mysterious hunting accident, maybe." Her voice dropped. "You know, something along the lines of a bullet in the back."

Though Elizabeth had already figured out that Lily Mae was a first-class gossip and speculator, she was still intrigued. "You really think Kincaid had that many enemies?"

"Glory be, the Cheyenne up on the reservation have been feuding with him for just forever. And for that matter, there were a lot of fathers, husbands and brothers who didn't weep at Jeremiah's funeral, either."

"Why is that?"

"Why do you think?" Lily Mae returned, chuckling suggestively.

Elizabeth laughed, too, which drew a glance from the man at the next table. The arrival of her dinner forestalled any other reply to Lily Mae's statement, as did the growing suspicion that the man nearby was listening to every word they were saying. Elizabeth toyed with the idea of inviting him to pull up a chair. He probably hadn't wanted to sit with Lily Mae because she was such a chattering magpie. But he shouldn't be eavesdropping now. It was unbelievably rude. To underline that opinion, Elizabeth gave him a cool, disapproving look. He met her gaze blithely for a moment, then looked down at the plate the waitress was placing in front of him, pretending to be absorbed in his meal.

Lily Mae ordered brownie cheesecake, sighing as she patted one ample hip. "I don't usually indulge in sweets, but Melissa's desserts are the very best."

"Melissa?" Elizabeth echoed, spearing a tender portion of salmon.

"Melissa Avery North owns the restaurant." Lily Mae nodded toward the attractive woman who was threading her way from the kitchen to the front register, laughing and pausing to speak to her customers as she went. "She's a dear girl, married just about a year and a half to that handsome Wyatt North. As you can see, they're expecting their first baby in a few months. Melissa grew up around here, left town as a teenager to live in California with her mother. Her mother..." Lily Mae put a hand to her chest in a dramatic gesture. "What a saint Melissa's mother was, raising her children all alone after her no-good husband disappeared."

"Oh?" Elizabeth murmured politely. Though she was eager to turn the conversation back to the wealthy Kincaids and away from the usual trials and tribulations that occupy most of the energy and time of any small-town gossip, she was very aware of Mr. Big Ears at the next table.

"It was such a shock when Charlie Avery's remains turned up out on the reservation."

Lily Mae's pronouncement sunk in and Elizabeth blinked. She forgot about the man who was probably listening. "Whose remains?"

"Charlie Avery's, Melissa's father," Lily Mae explained, looking as if Elizabeth should know these people. "They found him—or at least his bones—a few years ago, out on the reservation." She paused to shake her head. "And to think that for twenty-eight years I figured Charlie had skipped out of town with the little tart he was supposed to be seeing. He was dead all along, buried up there all this time."

"Are there any ideas about what might have happened to him?"

"A massive blow to the head." Lily Mae appeared to relish the information.

"Any suspects?"

"For goodness' sakes, no. They don't have a clue. They tried to convict one of the area ranchers of the murder, but couldn't. I wasn't surprised. Ethan Walker might be a loner, but I knew he was no murderer. My first husband always said—"

"When did you say all this happened?" Elizabeth cut in smoothly, hoping to forestall a pointless digression.

"Like I said, they found poor Charlie over two years ago, and then it took them some time to identify him. Ethan Walker was found innocent of his murder late last summer. The sheriff's department doesn't have any idea where to turn next, or they would have arrested someone else by now. I have to wonder what that does to poor Melissa, not knowing what happened to her father."

"Well, after all, it is a thirty-year-old murder," Elizabeth murmured, sympathizing with the sheriff.

"The more-recent murders are more important, I guess."

"*Recent* murders?" Elizabeth's fingers fairly itched to reach for the notepad in her purse. She didn't dare, however. While Lily Mae knew she was a reporter, the sight of her taking notes might stem the flow of information.

Lily Mae shook her head. "It seems like every time I turn around, there's someone else dead."

"People you know?"

"Not entirely. I knew Charlie and Dugin Kincaid, but of course they weren't murdered, or weren't supposed to be murdered, anyway."

"Do some people think they were?"

Lily Mae leaned forward, lowering her voice. "There is some talk, but I wouldn't want to spread any rumors, you know."

"Of course not," Elizabeth agreed, suppressing a smile. "Are those the only suspicious *recent* deaths?"

"Well...a woman died when a car exploded out on Route 191. She's never been identified, and that happened over a year and a half ago, as well."

"So the police are trying to identify the body of a woman killed in a car explosion?" My, but the local police were busy, Elizabeth thought.

"That's right." Lily Mae accepted her cheesecake from the waitress and sliced into it with gusto. "She was hitchhiking, I believe. She got in the car with a private investigator who was trying to figure out what had really happened to Charlie Avery." Lily swallowed, her features becoming transfixed with bliss. "You must try some of this," she said, pushing her plate forward.

Elizabeth shook her head, leaning closer. "You said there had been murders, plural."

"Around the time that poor Charlie's bones were found, a body showed up out at the Kincaid ranch—right after Dugin and Mary Jo Kincaid's wedding ceremony."

"Another unidentified body?" *This was becoming stranger and stranger.*

"I think they know who the man was, but no one has a clue what he was doing at that wedding. And poor Mary Jo." Lily Mae sank back in her seat, momentarily ignoring the dessert. "To lose her husband in such a tragic way."

"Her husband?" The body count was leaving Elizabeth hopelessly confused, but definitely intrigued. She thought small towns with this many dead bodies could only be found on network television.

"Dugin Kincaid," Lily Mae said, a frown drawing her plucked eyebrows together. "Like I told you, he was injured in this awful fire in a barn out at the Kincaid ranch. They got him to the hospital, and everyone said he was going to make it. Then boom! He's dead. Isn't Dugin's death the reason you're in town?"

Elizabeth could only wish that that was her assignment. After telling the woman she was an investigative reporter who usually wrote about corruption, greed and scandal in high places, she felt a bit silly admitting why she was really in Whitehorn. She swallowed the last delicious bite of her grilled salmon and vegetables, then murmured, "Actually, I'm here to do a follow-up piece on a little girl who was abandoned here in Whitehorn when she was a baby."

"You must mean little Jennifer McCallum!" With the same sort of enthusiasm she had displayed for cheesecake and unexplained death, Lily Mae launched into raptures about the abandoned baby girl who had become the darling of the entire town. A search for the parents had proved fruitless, and a local couple had adopted her. Lily Mae said the couple, Jessica and Sterling McCallum, were extremely well-thought-of and perfect parents. Sighing, she said, "Jennifer is a lucky little girl. Such a dear. When I think of her just being left at the Kincaids'—"

"The Kincaids'?" Elizabeth asked. She supposed that information was in the folder of clippings about Jennifer that the paper's research department had given her this morning. On the airplane coming down, she had barely glanced through them. All she really knew was that she was scheduled to interview the adoptive parents tomorrow morning. She didn't want this assignment and had spent most of the flight trying to dream up excuses to head back to Denver as soon as the plane landed.

"Jennifer was left on the doorstep of the Kincaid ranch house," Lily Mae said. "Found by Mary Jo herself, not long before she and poor, poor Dugin were married." Lily Mae scraped the last of the cheesecake from her plate, sighing. "There was lots of talk that the baby was Dugin's. I never believed it, of course. Dugin would never risk getting his daddy all riled up by fathering a bastard child. Now, in his prime, Jeremiah might have—"

Again Elizabeth cut in, sensing a pointless sidebar in the making. "What is it about Jennifer that's so special?"

"There's just something about her sweet little face," Lily Mae murmured with a gentle smile. "You know how adorable children can be, and Jennifer is more adorable than most."

Truthfully, Elizabeth knew very little about children, adorable or otherwise. Which made it even more ludicrous that her editor had sent her up here to do this fluffy, human-interest update on this particular child. He said the newspaper's publisher had followed Jennifer's story right after she'd been found and now wanted a big feature for the weekly magazine section. Elizabeth had been assigned to look up a number of abandoned children and see the different paths their lives had taken.

Elizabeth was replacing the reporter who usually did these kinds of stories because her editor was trying to punish her. If he weren't her friend and mentor as much as her boss, she wouldn't have come. But he had given her no choice. She either got out of Denver and came up here to do this piece of journalistic trifle or she cleaned out her desk. She winced, thinking about the scene that had happened between them before she'd left. She still felt raw from the encounter, a little adrift, too, like she had lost her best friend.

"Something wrong?" Lily Mae asked.

Elizabeth dragged her mind back to the present. "Not at all. I'm just tired."

"Well, I guess you are, coming all this way and—" Glancing down at her watch, the older woman let out a little squeal. "Heavens! I'm late for my favorite show on television. Now where's my check?"

Elizabeth's fingers closed over the bill the waitress had delivered only moments before. "Please let me get this. I've really enjoyed our talk."

Coughing erupted from the man at the table beside them. Elizabeth darted a hard look in his direction. He picked up a glass of water, not even glancing her way.

Lily Mae fussed a bit about Elizabeth buying her dinner, but in the end acquiesced. Hurriedly, she wrote out her telephone number on a corner torn from the check. "Just in case you need anything while you're here in town."

After waving goodbye to the gregarious woman, Elizabeth whipped her notepad out of her purse and made some quick notes. She made it a point not to look at the man whose presence she had been unable to ignore throughout dinner. She had bigger things on her mind than some nosey so-and-so who had obviously snubbed a sweet, if rather talkative, older woman.

Unidentified bodies.
Unexplained murders.
Car bombs.
Abandoned babies.
The involvement of a wealthy, influential family.

The fodder for stories in this little corner of Montana might be richer than Elizabeth had even dreamed when she'd protested taking this assignment. This could turn into her brand of fun, after all.

Eager to check into her room at the boardinghouse where she was booked for the evening, she gathered her belongings and pulled on her blazer. The café, crowded before, was almost empty now. And unfortunately, the man at the next table stood at the same time as she. They paused for a moment or two, long enough for Elizabeth to form some distinct impressions.

Tall and lean, he had a swimmer's physique. Broad shoulders beneath a charcoal jacket. Narrow hips encased in fitted, dark jeans. He wore his clothes with easy aplomb. Over one arm, he draped a trenchcoat whose silk lining bespoke its price. Elizabeth required less than a heartbeat to realize he wasn't some rough-and-tumble cowboy dressed up for town. She had found many cowboys attractive in a brash, masculine way, and strangely enough, this man was just as distinctly, disturbingly male. His sex appeal was all smooth edges, with a hint of restrained power and a touch of shadowed mystery in the dark-eyed gaze that wouldn't latch onto hers.

Both of them moved forward at the same moment, almost colliding.

"After you," he said evenly, gesturing toward the front, where several people were lined up to pay their checks.

Nodding, Elizabeth turned on her heel. She felt oddly off balance. Though noticing people and forming quick judgments about them was part of what she did, she rarely felt such a strong pull of attraction. She didn't like the sensation.

At the cash register, she was very aware of the man standing nearby as she paid her bills and complimented Melissa North on the cuisine. She planned to come back and talk to Melissa about her father's mysterious death, and decided it wouldn't do any harm to lay the groundwork with pleasantries now.

The pretty woman smiled her thanks and asked, "Are you staying in Whitehorn overnight?"

"Maybe longer than that. I need directions to the Amity Boardinghouse."

Armed with simple around-the-block instructions, Elizabeth hurried out the door, resisting the urge to glance back at the tall, attractive stranger.

Jonas Bishop watched the honey blond reporter leave with relief. He deliberately allowed a couple with a fussing child to pay their check ahead of him, hoping she would be gone by the time he came out of the restaurant.

All during dinner, he had fought the urge to leave. But he ate here at least twice a week. He liked to keep to a routine, to do little to call attention to himself. So he had decided to just eat his meal as usual. He could hardly help hearing most of what that gossip had told the reporter, but he knew he could have exercised a little more restraint in the number of glances he had sent the latter. She had caught him and become irritated. But it would seem that a woman with her peaches-and-cream skin and wide brown eyes would be used to glances from men.

Who would have guessed that the reporter whose tough exposés he had been reading for years in the Denver newspaper would have the delicate features of the porcelain doll that had once sat on his mother's dresser? She tried to disguise those looks, Jonas guessed. With her simply cut cap of shining hair. With her no-nonsense clothes and jewelry. But she indulged her femininity in other ways, he thought, remembering the scent of perfume he had caught when she brushed past him on the way to the register.

And there wasn't much she could do about her low, sexy laugh or the sensual curve of her lips.

He set that thought firmly aside as he paid his check and made small talk with Melissa. She was pleasant, although a bit rushed. Since her marriage, she didn't spend as much time at the restaurant as she used to. Jonas wasn't surprised when she locked the door behind him and pulled the blinds.

He felt loneliness pinch his gut.

Quickly, he grasped the emotion and shut it down. Loneliness was just one of the feelings he didn't allow himself.

Hesitating for a moment on the sidewalk, he noted that the temperature had dropped a good ten degrees while he had been inside. He shrugged into the trenchcoat he had brought along. The wind was whipping down from the mountains to the west of town, carrying moisture with it. It was early May, definitely not too late for a snowstorm. But Jonas suspected it would only rain. A glance at the clouds streaming across the sky told him the precipitation would come soon.

He set off down the sidewalk. Even though home was nearly two miles away, he always walked to dinner when the weather was decent. The exercise cleared his head. Because it was cold and raw for so much of the year, many of the folks who lived in town liked to be outdoors when it wasn't. So he fit right in. And fitting in was very important.

When he reached the shadows created by a burned-out street lamp just past the restaurant, he heard the *click-click* of a car trying to start on a dead battery. He turned around. A late-model white sedan was parked back along Center Avenue. And in the glow of a working streetlight, he saw the tall, slender reporter from Denver get out of the car and go around to the trunk.

Walk away.

He turned to follow the urging of his head, but got no farther than the corner. It wasn't late, only nine o'clock or so, but this street was largely deserted. The county courthouse was locked and silent across the way. The library beside the Hip Hop was shut, as well. Aside from the restaurant, the businesses at this end of town closed at six. But if the reporter really needed help, she could bang on the door of the café. Melissa and her staff were probably still inside. And the police station was only a block and a half back up the street.

But you're standing right here.

That insistent voice was the only remaining trace of the well-bred Texas boy he had once been. And it was a powerful force, instilled by his father's iron will and his mother's gentle but inflexible demands for well-mannered propriety. Jonas decided it was too bad their influence hadn't come to his aid at other moments in his life. Maybe he wouldn't be standing here now. Maybe turning around and going back to aid a pretty damsel in distress wouldn't be such a big, damned deal.

Sighing, he turned, imagining his mother's approving smile.

The reporter was now walking toward him, carrying what looked like a briefcase and a small overnight bag. She stopped as he stepped out of the shadows. Slowly, she set down her bag and thrust a hand in the pocket of her blazer.

"It sounded like you've got a dead battery," he said.

She eyed him with distinct wariness. "No joke."

He gave her what he hoped was a pleasant smile. "I could call the garage for you. There's a pay phone at the other corner."

"No, thank you," she replied.

"You sure? I know exactly who to call. You could wait in the Hip Hop and get out of this wind."

She glanced quickly at the café, where the lights inside immediately snapped off. Jonas saw her hesitate.

"Melissa and her staff park in an alleyway out back," he said. "She can't have left. I'll go get her."

The reporter paused a second longer, then thrust her chin upward a notch. "She told me the Amity Boardinghouse was just around this corner and down the block. They're expecting me at any minute. I can walk. I'll call a garage to take care of the car in the morning. You can just go on to your car."

"I'm walking, too."

She fell back a step, those shapely lips of hers forming a silent *O*.

"Listen," he said finally. "I'm already walking that way to get home. I can either walk with you and help carry this stuff, or I can go on ahead."

"I can handle my stuff."

He shrugged. "Fine with me."

At that moment, a fine, cold rain joined the cool breeze.

"Well, this is just great," the reporter muttered.

Without further comment, Jonas shucked off his trenchcoat, held it out to her and picked up her overnight bag. "If it makes you feel any better, there are houses down this way, and it's quiet enough in this town that if you screamed, you'd get some help." He took a few steps forward.

She didn't budge. "That's not much comfort and I refuse to take your coat."

He dropped the garment over her outstretched arm and kept walking around the corner. "I can promise you I'm not on any Most Wanted lists."

A moment later, she fell into step beside him, his coat draped over her shoulders, her purse and briefcase, which on closer inspection was a laptop computer, clutched at one side. Down this way, the street lamps were farther apart, but old trees branched over the sidewalk, partially shielding them from the rain.

"See that?" Jonas asked, pointing toward a lighted sign visible at the end of the block. "That's the boarding-house. So you really don't have far to walk with me."

After they had gone a few steps farther, she said stiffly, "I'm sorry. I'm not usually so skittish. But you can't be too careful these days, and as you *overheard* Mrs. Wheeler tell me at dinner, there have been some strange events around here, including some unexplained deaths."

He grinned at her emphasis. "I want to point out that my auditory powers would have to be severely impaired if I couldn't *overhear* Lily Mae Wheeler. She always manages to make herself heard."

"She seems harmless enough."

"She's a malicious gossip."

"Doesn't every small town have one or two?"

"That doesn't make it right."

"If you're a minister or something, you could preach a sermon on it."

"I'm not a minister."

Her chuckle was dry. "I didn't think so."

He drew to a stop. "Just don't believe everything that woman told you, all right? Whitehorn is really a pleasant, peaceful town."

"Oh," she murmured, walking again. "So you're saying Lily Mae lied to me."

"No."

"Then was there a mysterious dead man at the Kincaids' big wedding?"

"Yes, but that was over two years ago."

"And didn't a car blow up outside of town and kill a woman they haven't identified?"

"Yes, but you have to understand—"

"And what about that man who had been buried over twenty years ago out at some Cheyenne reservation?"

"Who knows what happened to him?"

She drew to a halt in front of the iron fence that surrounded the boardinghouse. Light from the front porch touched her delicate features with a golden glow. "Yes," she whispered. "Who knows? And who knows what's going on behind each and every one of these closed doors on this street?"

Jonas set her bag at her feet. After a long pause, he said softly, "You're very good."

"Pardon me?"

"I watched you with Lily Mae tonight. Granted, she didn't need much encouragement, but you kept her right on track. And just now, the way you fired those questions at me. Very nice." He nudged open the iron gate with the toe of his boot. "Tell me, *Ms. Elizabeth Monroe,* is that the technique you used when you annihilated Senator McCoin after you discovered his drug problems?"

She was silent a moment. "You heard me introduce myself to Lily Mae."

"Yes, and I've read your work. You're very thorough. You cut straight to the bone."

"Were the people of Wyoming supposed to approve of a senator with a drug problem?"

"Of course not."

"Then I did everyone a favor."

"And you did it with relish, didn't you?"

Her eyes narrowed. "What does that mean?"

"Nothing," he replied, shrugging. "Reporters who relish their work sell papers, don't they?"

She didn't reply.

Jonas took a step backward. "I hope Whitehorn turns out to have nothing to interest you, Ms. Monroe. I happen to like this town. I wouldn't want you to rip it to shreds with your usual zeal." He turned, flipping up the collar of his jacket as he stepped into a rain growing heavier by the moment.

"Wait," Elizabeth called, moving forward as well. Sarcasm drenched her tone. "I never got your name. I'd want to spell it correctly in any article I might write, you know."

He paused in the center of the street. "Jonas," he said, and then disappeared into the misty rain.

Elizabeth caught her breath, rubbed a hand across her eyes. Where had he gone? She moved out from under the trees, her fingers probing for the small canister of Mace she had placed in her jacket pocket before getting out of her car. He was nowhere to be seen. Even the sound of his footsteps had been swallowed up by the rain.

Shivering, she gathered her belongings and hurried up to the front porch of the boardinghouse. She rang the doorbell, glancing over her shoulder in apprehension. Only when she drew the trenchcoat tighter around her shoulders and smelled the mingled scents of expensive aftershave and tobacco did she realize she still wore his coat.

While he was off in the cold rain without it.

As the door to the boardinghouse swung open, Elizabeth could only wonder why the thought of this man shivering in the rain disturbed her so profoundly.

TWO

Jonas sneezed and cursed himself for giving in to his up-bringing and letting that bewitching reporter have his coat. As if in agreement, the Siamese cat sitting on his bed meowed.

"Shut up, Poe," he muttered, passing a towel over his hair once again. The gentle rain had become a downpour during the last mile of his walk home. Even a long, hot shower hadn't completely chased the chill from his body. He sneezed again, and a cold, wet nose pushed against his leg. He looked down into the adoring eyes of his faithful black Lab.

"That's right, Raven, old girl. That's the way a good pet treats her master. You could give Poe some lessons."

The cat merely meowed once more. Raven hid behind an open door.

Chuckling, Jonas pulled on sweatpants and a thick terry-cloth robe. He left the room and mounted the stairs to the third-floor study of his restored Victorian-era home. Raven padded after him.

"What's the matter?" he asked the dog. "Are you scared to stay down there alone with Poe? I know, I know. You spent the evening alone with him and that's quite enough, right?"

Jonas kept up a running stream of conversation with his pet while he lit the logs already stacked in the room's small fireplace. Carrying wood up here was a bitch, but on nights when the cold and damp of the outside threatened to intrude, the glow of the fire helped.

Only tonight it wasn't the weather that was creeping around his carefully locked doors.

The computer in the corner called to him, but he resisted the urge. Instead, he poured himself a few swallows of brandy, lit his pipe and sat down in his battered, leather easy chair in front of the fire. Raven settled at his feet. Soon Poe leapt to his usual place on the arm of the chair. Jonas wondered if this was the way someone would one day find them—the skeletal remains of three lonely souls. Just as with that poor bastard they had found up on the reservation, people would scramble around, trying to figure out what might have happened.

Elizabeth Monroe would find out.

"Damn her," he said into the fire. But he was really damning himself. He should have steered clear. Though his scandal was an old one that had happened far from here, he had probably riled her, so that she would go poking around, trying to come up with something about him. Maybe no one still cared. Perhaps his missteps would now seem trivial. He wanted to believe so, but it wasn't a theory he was willing to test.

He had started to feel too safe, he decided. Nearly nine years in this town had spoiled him. He had started to believe nothing of the big city and its bright, intrusive lights could encroach upon him here. Denver wasn't L.A., but it was a far cry from Whitehorn. And no matter what city she lived in, Elizabeth Monroe would be a good reporter.

He had seen from her stories that she was a tough nut, taking on a variety of troublemakers, uncovering any slimy creature that dared try to hide. Corrupt politicians. Unscrupulous businessmen. Wealthy slumlords. She didn't seem to mind tackling any of them. And Jonas had no problem with those types. It was just stories like the one about Senator McCoin that got to him. The man had had a problem. Wouldn't the threat of an exposé have been enough to get him out of Congress and into rehab? Did it have to be headline news for days on end, spread out where it drilled the man and his family right between the eyes every time they walked out of their home?

Jonas knew every journalist in the country would argue with him. He didn't care. He knew what it felt like to be in that glare of publicity. Trapped like a bug under a drinking glass. Every time the glass moved, you tried to escape. But it always came crashing down. He knew that so well. He should have remembered it tonight. Instead, he had walked straight to her.

Come into my house, said the spider to the fly.

Groaning, he set his brandy and pipe aside and crossed to the window at the end of the room. The third floor was smaller than the two below and commanded a nice view of the town, rather like the room at the top of a lighthouse. He stood now, surveying the area, wondering, as he often did, about the people who might have stood here before him.

Jonas imagined this had once been a servant's room. From records in the town library, he had learned that the house had been built by a wealthy man who had made a fortune putting a railroad through the area in the late 1800s. This massive, sturdy home had been built for the comfort of the man's wife, who had lived here only one year before the cold and snowy winter drove her back East. The man, however, had remained in Whitehorn until his death. Who had tended him? Jonas wondered. A stoic gentleman's gentleman? Or perhaps a lovely maid? Maybe she and the railroad man had been in love. Maybe he used to come to her in this room at night.

Perhaps here he had caressed her skin.

Perhaps here she had let down her curling, honey blond hair.

Perhaps here he had looked into her warm, brown eyes.
Eyes like Elizabeth Monroe's.

Memories of her subtle perfume and husky chuckle filled his head.

"Oh, Lord, don't let me dwell on her," Jonas prayed, resting his forehead against the cool window. Why was he torturing himself this way? Why think these thoughts about a woman who was even further off-limits than all the other women in the world?

A reporter.

God above, she was the last thing he needed.

He stood at the window until the logs in the fire burned to ashes. He stood and looked at the town, at the houses where couples slept together in their beds, where children dreamed innocent dreams.

His town.

Where everyone knew him.

But no one knew who he was.

In the dining room of the Amity Boardinghouse, Elizabeth took a long, satisfying sip of coffee and gazed out at the sunshine that had replaced last night's rain. It was only a little past eight, but she had been up for hours. A local garage had already picked up her keys, replaced her defective battery and delivered the sedan to the street outside. Elizabeth had already fed a page worth of notes and theories into her laptop computer.

Her mind had never shut down long enough last night to allow her to sleep deeply. But instead of feeling tired, she was pumped up. Over and over again, she had gone through all that Lily Mae Wheeler had told her. Of course, she had to check out the validity of the woman's stories, but judging by the mysterious Jonas's reactions last night, there was indeed some truth in the tales. She didn't see how anyone could dispute that there had been some odd events in this little town during the last couple of years. Were they all unrelated? Undoubtedly the sheriff's office was working on a connection. Elizabeth planned to talk with them soon. But not too soon. Perhaps she could bring a fresh perspective to the puzzle, could piece it all together before they did.

She wanted to. Not only because solving puzzles was what she loved. But because that man named Jonas had told her not to.

Now why was anything that man said important to her?

"More coffee, Miss Monroe?"

Elizabeth jumped, rattling her cup in its saucer. An apple-cheeked young woman of Native American heritage stood beside the table, coffeepot in hand. Elizabeth hadn't heard her come into the empty dining area. People in this place came and went with unsettling silence, she decided, thinking of Jonas Bishop's quick disappearance last night.

"I didn't mean to startle you, ma'am."

Elizabeth took a deep breath. "That's okay."

Smiling, the woman poured some coffee and glanced at the sunshine-filled window. "It's a nice morning for daydreaming, isn't it?"

Having been raised to believe that daydreaming was a sinful waste of time, Elizabeth had no opinion on the merits of when to do it. Habit had taught her to save her daydreams for times when she was assured of not being caught in the act. "I guess," she said, because the young woman seemed to expect a reply.

The woman's smile wavered. She started for the door, murmuring, "Your breakfast will be ready in a minute."

"Wait, please." Elizabeth summoned a smile of her own. After all, it wasn't this woman's fault that daydreams and other such frivolities had been forbidden in the household of Reverend Monroe.

The woman turned back to Elizabeth. "Yes, ma'am?"

"Your name's Lucy, right?"

"Yes, ma'am."

"Please don't call me ma'am," Elizabeth said. "It always makes me feel so ancient. It was bad enough that I found a gray hair yesterday morning. Please don't make it any worse.''

An easy smile curved Lucy's mouth.

"Have you always lived in Whitehorn?'' Elizabeth asked her.

"Laughing Horse Reservation.''

"That's north of here, right?''

"Yes.''

"But I guess you know a lot of people here in town.''

"Quite a few.''

"How about a man named Jonas?''

A frown knit Lucy's brow.

"Tall, dark, handsome. Probably in his early forties,'' Elizabeth offered. "He dresses very well, I think.''

"Jonas Bishop,'' Lucy answered quickly.

"Who is he?''

Lucy shrugged. Explaining that she didn't remember when he had moved to town, she pointed in the direction that Jonas had appeared to be heading last night. His house, she said, was a big old place at the edge of town on Mountain Pass. It had a stone fence around the yard.

"A stone fence? Isn't that kind of odd?'' Elizabeth asked, trying to visualize such a place.

"It's always been there.''

"Really? And what does Jonas Bishop do?''

Wariness stole into Lucy's features. "I think he writes.''

"Writes what?''

"I don't know.''

Elizabeth wasn't sure she believed her.

"He's quiet and keeps to himself,'' Lucy added.

"Which is exactly the way most serial killers are described by their neighbors,'' Elizabeth said with a slight laugh.

Lucy didn't crack another smile. Clearly, Elizabeth had pushed a little too hard for her small-town sensibilities. Murmuring, "I'll get your breakfast,'' the waitress retreated almost soundlessly into the kitchen, as silently as Jonas Bishop had retreated last night.

"Must be some special shoes," Elizabeth mused aloud, trying to remember what sort of footwear Jonas Bishop had been wearing.

Then she quickly brought her thoughts of the man to a halt. He was sexy and disturbing. But so what? She had other, more important matters to ponder.

First, she had to get through this interview with little Jennifer and her adoptive parents. Elizabeth started to groan, but smothered the sound as Lucy appeared with her breakfast. She downed an omelet, half a grapefruit and flaky homemade bread while flipping through the folder of information she had been given concerning Jennifer.

It wasn't that Elizabeth didn't think the plight of a small, abandoned child wasn't important. And she believed any newspaper should publish a portion of good news. But good news wasn't where she excelled. That was the argument she had tried to use when her editor, Ted Cornish, had said he was sending her to Whitehorn.

Ted was a big man, a former linebacker who at age fifty-eight still had a hard belly and a neck like a bull. A brilliant newsman himself, he had recognized Elizabeth's talent when she was a nineteen-year-old pulling stories from the wire services and writing obituaries. He was tough talking, hard-nosed, and Elizabeth loved him in ways she had never been able to love the quiet, pious and remote man who had raised her. Through the years, Ted had prodded and encouraged her, rejoicing in her triumphs and holding her feet to the fire when she screwed up.

Recently, they had clashed over a series of stories Elizabeth was doing on state lawmakers who had voted themselves a hefty pay raise. She had detailed the extravagant life-styles and private fortunes of these men and women. The stories had raised a ruckus with both taxpayers and political honchos. The reaction made Elizabeth want to dig even deeper, certain she would uncover dark, illegal secrets. Ted had asked her to leave the story be.

"You did a good piece of work," he had told her just last week. "But unless you've got something concrete you're digging for now, let's move on."

"Why should I?" Elizabeth had demanded. "I'm on to something that's selling papers."

Ted settled back behind his big, old scarred desk. "Is selling papers what you do now, Elizabeth? I thought you were a journalist."

She flushed. "I think what I revealed about those greedy bastards was important."

"So do I. And you were very thorough. Do you still have some questions about them?"

"I'm sure I can find something—"

"*Find* something?" Ted snapped, abruptly sitting forward. "Are you digging because you really smell a rat or just for the sake of digging?"

She drew herself up, incensed. "I don't manufacture news, Ted. I leave that to the tabloids."

"There's a fine line between us and them, you know."

"That's crap. There's a world of difference between what I write and what those rags print."

"I hope so. But if you lose your perspective—"

"I won't."

"Really?" Ted asked. "I'm not so sure. Right now, you're talking about continuing to pursue a story that's done, that you've covered. Why, I don't know. If I let you keep this witch-hunt in operation, you're not going to have a single person in government who will talk to you."

"That's their problem."

"That'll be your problem someday when you're on to a big, *important* story and you can't find a source to help you."

Elizabeth's stomach clenched, whether from anger or because she feared he was right, she wasn't sure.

"You need to make some changes," Ted said. "In your work and your life."

"What are you saying?"

"That all you do is work. You have no personal life. You've lost touch with anything and everything that doesn't have to do with a *story*." He wiggled his fingers as if to bracket the last word in quotation marks. "You've lost the human touch, Elizabeth. Furthermore, I think you get a charge out of destroying people."

Now she was sure it was anger that fired her belly. "I get a charge out of exposing wrongs. I'm a good reporter, Ted. You know I'm—"

He stopped her with an upraised hand. "You're a great *writer,* Elizabeth. But until you recover your sense of balance, I can't call you a really good reporter."

She had stormed away, fury coursing through her. And in her spare time, she had continued to pursue the story he'd told her to let alone. To her disgust, all that her digging had turned up was dust. Some of it drifted Ted's way.

And that's why she was sitting in Whitehorn, Montana, preparing to interview a three-year-old.

As she recalled her conversation with Ted, Elizabeth was struck by the similarities between what Ted had told her and what Jonas Bishop had said last night.

Jonas.

The man's deep, smooth voice twisted through Elizabeth's mind again. And again she snapped that door shut. She would much rather think about Ted, even about their disagreement.

What was it Ted had told her? That she needed to get out of town. To that end, he had sent her up here. And after that she was to take a vacation, somewhere far away from the city, someplace where there was no chance any of the people who were furious with her might run into her.

She needed to *reassess,* Ted had said again yesterday morning. Not just her career. But her life choices.

Baloney, she thought now, swallowing a last sip of coffee.

But an hour later, holding little Jennifer McCallum on her lap, it was difficult not to have a moment's regret for some of her choices. Jennifer looked up at her with wide blue eyes framed by impossibly long, thick lashes, smiled, and the hard-nosed reporter melted.

"I can see why you fell in love with her. She's beautiful," Elizabeth murmured to Jennifer's mother, Jessica McCallum.

"We think so," Jessica replied, beaming first at Jennifer, then at the tall, muscular man who sat beside her on a long, comfortably cushioned sofa.

Sterling McCallum was a police detective, a dark-haired man with military bearing and hard features. But his eyes softened in adoration when he looked at his pretty, sable-haired wife and the little girl perched on Elizabeth's lap.

Envy tugged at Elizabeth for a moment. These two people were so obviously in love—with each other and with Jennifer. This kind of family bond was something Elizabeth had never known, would probably never know.

She recovered herself quickly and got down to business. The McCallums didn't want to discuss Jennifer's abandonment in front of her, something Elizabeth could understand. So while Jessica settled the little girl in another room to play, Elizabeth went over the facts with Detective McCallum.

Jennifer had been found at the Kincaid ranch. Sterling McCallum had been the officer in charge of trying to find Jennifer's parents. He'd become involved with Jessica, a social worker, when she was assigned to Jennifer's case. They had married, and when months passed and no parents were found for Jennifer, they had adopted her.

"You make a beautiful family," Elizabeth said, scribbling down notes. "Jennifer is a lucky little girl."

As Jessica reentered the room from the hall, she said, "We're the lucky ones. She brings us a lot of joy."

Elizabeth focused on Sterling. "Are you afraid her parents might show up and try to claim her?"

He and Jessica exchanged a long look, giving Elizabeth the impression that this was a question they had considered.

Sterling spoke with deliberation, as if choosing his words carefully. "It would seem to me that her parents would have a lot of explaining to do if either of them showed up now. Jessica and I have shown her more love than whoever left her on the Kincaid doorstep. We're her parents. We would challenge her biological parents' rights."

"And yet you might lose," Elizabeth said quietly. "The courts still seem to favor biology over other considerations in many cases."

Jessica sat down beside her husband again. Beneath her sweetly serene exterior, Elizabeth glimpsed a core of iron. "Sterling and I will take on that problem if and when it comes up."

"And if her parents do show up, but you retain custody, what will you tell Jennifer?"

"Let's put it this way," Sterling said, eyes narrowing. "I won't lie to our daughter."

Elizabeth met his gaze straight on. "That's a good policy, Detective McCallum." He had no way of knowing she was speaking from personal experience. Glancing down at her notes again, she frowned. "I have to tell you I'm a bit surprised you consented to this interview, given that there is a chance Jennifer's parents might see this, realize where she is and come forward."

Once more the McCallums exchanged a long look. Jessica spoke first, measuring her words carefully. "We think Jennifer's birth mother knows where she is."

Before Elizabeth could formulate a question, Sterling added, "When Jennifer was in the hospital, just after she had been found out at the Kincaids', a woman called, saying she was from the *Whitehorn Journal,* our local newspaper. At the time, there was no female on staff there. I felt that the woman was really Jennifer's mother, calling to check up on her. She may have even followed what happened to her. In a town this small, it wouldn't be hard to do. Everyone knows everyone else's business.''

Jessica laughed softly. "When we adopted Jennifer, the newspaper printed a picture and a big 'Congratulations' right on the front page.''

Elizabeth asked, "So you think Jennifer's mother was a local woman?''

"Maybe.'' Sterling rubbed a hand across his jaw. "But when Jennifer was found, I checked every hospital, every clinic and midwife in the area, even up on the reservation. There were no births unaccounted for, no reports of pregnant women who suddenly turned up without a child. My gut tells me her birth mother was just passing through and left her baby on the nicest doorstep she passed, which just happened to be the Kincaids'.''

"And then perhaps hung around long enough to make sure the baby was in a good home," Elizabeth theorized. "But wouldn't a strange woman in town arouse a lot of curiosity?''

Sterling shook his head. "Not if she just blended in with the rest of the Yellowstone Park tourists.''

"Whatever the case," Jessica said, "I've always had the feeling that if she were going to come forward, it would have happened before now.''

Thoughtfully tapping her pen against her notepad, Elizabeth settled back in her chair. "Tell me this, what's the most important thing you'd like this story to say about your daughter?''

Jessica slipped her hand into her husband's, lacing her fingers through his. "We'd like everyone to see how well adoption can work. People shouldn't be afraid to open their hearts and homes to a child. And on the other hand, if someone is in an unworkable situation with a child they can't care for, they should know there are people willing and eager to be good parents. No child need ever just be thrown away, like Jennifer was."

The emotion in the woman's voice touched Elizabeth. She grinned at the McCallums. "I have a feeling your home and your hearts are open to more children."

The two exchanged a warm look. Jessica flushed. "We're working on that."

But before anything else could be said, their daughter called out in the next room. Jessica scurried to see what she needed.

Smiling, Elizabeth flipped her notebook closed. "I think I can definitely write a happy ending to Jennifer's story, even if her birth is still a bit of a mystery."

Sterling shrugged. "Some mysteries are just never solved. That's a fact of police work I've had to accept."

In this remark, Elizabeth saw the opening she had been waiting for. "I understand the sheriff's department has been pretty busy lately."

The detective's big hands flexed against his neatly pressed uniform pants. "What do you mean?"

With deliberate casualness, Elizabeth ran through some of the things she had learned last night from Lily Mae.

He cleared his throat. "How long did you say you've been in town?"

"Got in last night."

"Umm," was all he said, pointedly not commenting on anything she had mentioned.

Elizabeth was considering how to address the subject again when there was a knock on the front door, followed by heavy footsteps in the front hall. McCallum got to his feet.

"Judd," Jessica said. "Come on in."

"Thanks," a deep voice replied. "I came to pick up Sterling. The state boys just sent back a report on the Kincaid arson case."

At the word *arson,* Elizabeth stood and turned toward the hall.

"Judd," McCallum said quickly as Jessica preceded a tall, black-haired officer into the room. "This is Elizabeth Monroe, a *reporter* from Denver." Elizabeth didn't miss the note of warning in his voice.

Frowning slightly, the other man paused near the doorway, his long dark hair brushing the collar of his uniform shirt as he nodded. "Miss Monroe."

"This is Sheriff Judd Hensley," Jessica said, completing the introductions.

McCallum turned to Elizabeth. "If we're through here, the sheriff and I need to get to the office."

"We're using some pictures your local newspaper ran awhile back," Elizabeth said. "So that's all. Thank you for your time, Detective. I know you're *very* busy."

McCallum's eyebrow cocked at her emphasis, but he said nothing more. He kissed his wife, then left with Sheriff Hensley.

Elizabeth turned back to Jessica with a wide smile. "I've always thought it took a special woman to be married to a law-enforcement officer."

"You're right." Jessica gestured for Elizabeth to take her seat again and offered more coffee from the pot on the table between them.

Declining the refill, Elizabeth kept her tone light as she said, "Your husband and the sheriff certainly fit the stereotype of the hardened lawmen of the West."

"You think so?" Jessica chuckled. "I suppose they do look tough."

"And aren't they?"

"Tough, yes, but with hearts that are as soft as—" She broke off, eyeing Elizabeth uneasily, as if just remembering she was talking with a reporter. "They're good at their jobs," she amended. "Whitehorn's lucky to have a top-notch sheriff's department. Why, just last night, Wolf Boy Rawlings..." Again Jessica paused and bit her lip. "What I meant to say was that *Rafe* Rawlings tracked down a notorious robber."

Elizabeth made a point of tucking the pad in her purse and selecting a cookie from the plate beside the coffeepot. Quite casually, she said, "Is 'Wolf Boy' Officer Rawlings' Indian name?"

"No," Jessica answered, looking nervous.

Snuggling back in the chair, Elizabeth smiled and changed the subject, commenting on how much she loved the color Jessica had chosen to paint this room.

But when she left an hour later, she knew quite a bit about Rafe "Wolf Boy" Rawlings's strange past. She had gleaned some other interesting tidbits about Whitehorn, including that Jonas Bishop had moved to town more than eight years ago.

The first thing Jonas had noticed when he'd visited Whitehorn was the quiet. During his initial year here, there had been days when the silence pressed in like a smothering cloud. Even now, especially on long, lonely winter nights, it sometimes got to him. But when he worked, the peaceful lack of distractions was welcome.

So it was startling to be jarred from his deep concentration by Raven's raucous barking in the front yard. The dog was so gentle and so well-acquainted with the few people who stopped by, she usually confined her barking to the squirrels or birds she sometimes chased.

But this wasn't that kind of bark.

Peering out the window, Jonas's hands fisted in anger. Moments later, he barreled out his front door and down the broken stone walk, demanding, "What in the hell are you doing?"

On the other side of the black iron gate where Raven was raising such a fuss, Elizabeth Monroe was pressed back against her car. "What am I doing?" she demanded. "What about this vicious creature?"

Jonas took hold of Raven's collar and dragged her back from the gate. "Hush, girl. It's okay." Dropping to his knee, he patted and reassured her. "It's okay, girl. The mean old reporter isn't going to bother us."

"I wouldn't think this *It's A Wonderful Life*, Bedford Falls town of yours would require an attack dog, Mr. *Bishop*."

Jonas glared as Elizabeth used his last name. "She's just protective of her territory, and she doesn't know you." To demonstrate his point, the "vicious" creature directed a sloppy, doggy kiss across Jonas's cheek.

"What a big baby," Elizabeth muttered.

"She is that."

"But what about her companion?"

Following the direction Elizabeth pointed, Jonas found Poe sitting atop one of the stone pillars that flanked the gate. The cat was regarding the entire ruckus with typical feline disdain.

"He's the real guard around the place," Jonas said. "Poe probably alerted Raven that you were here."

"Poe and Raven?" Elizabeth repeated. "That's a little strange. Even for you."

"What do you mean?" Jonas asked, suddenly suspicious. She spoke as if she knew something about him.

Darting an anxious look up at the cat, Elizabeth took a step toward the gate. She was wearing a navy blue skirt today. Simple and straight, it ended just above her knee, revealing legs as long and well-shaped as Jonas had imagined last night. Just as her conservative white blouse accented, rather than disguised, her slender but unmistakably feminine build.

She said, "You disappeared like a piece of fog last night. Before I went to sleep, I halfway convinced myself that you were a figment of my imagination."

The image of her lying in bed, thinking of him, presented an all-too-appealing picture to Jonas's own imagination. He straightened. Anger was the best weapon against attraction. He employed it now.

"What are doing here?" he said tersely. "Snooping around?"

Elizabeth's shoulders straightened. "Why would I do that?"

"You tell me."

"But you're the one who's accusing me of snooping."

"You're here, aren't you?"

"Is that a crime?"

"We're naturally wary of strangers around here."

"You sound as if you're a native of Whitehorn, Mr. Bishop. Are you?"

"What difference does that make? I live here now. You don't. That makes you a stranger and makes me wonder what you're doing out here at my home. And since snooping is part of your job description . . ."

She gave him a long, considering glance. "Forgive me if I sound like a typical reporter, Mr. Bishop, but you act like a man who has something to hide."

Jonas bit the side of his mouth to keep from protesting too quickly. Damn, but this was one vexing woman.

She stepped right up to the gate, close enough that Jonas could appreciate the sparkling gleam in her warm brown eyes and the rich shine of her honeyed hair.

"What's going on in there?" she asked with the husky chuckle that had taunted the edges of his memory last night. "What are you hiding, Mr. Bishop?"

"Stop calling me that." The command escaped before he could stop it.

"Why?"

He blew out an exasperated breath. "That's one of your standard replies, isn't it? Who, what, when, where and why."

"I just do what comes naturally."

"Then return the favor. Answer a question for me."

"Only if I can ask the same of you."

"All right," he retorted. "Tell me why you're here."

Her grin flashed as she held up the coat that was draped over her arm, a coat Jonas hadn't noticed in his perusal of her other, more attractive apparel. "You left this last night."

"I know."

"I was sorry you had to go off in the rain without it."

"No sorrier than me."

"Do you want me to just leave the coat here on the gate, or are you going to open it?"

He hesitated only a moment. To continue talking with her through a barred gate would only serve to heighten her suspicions. "It's unlocked," he said, summoning a smile.

She sent a surprised glance toward the latch. "So it is."

"Come on in."

As the gate creaked open, Poe leapt nimbly from the fence to the ground and disappeared into the bushes. Raven growled low in her throat as Elizabeth approached, but Jonas grasped her collar again and spoke in soothing tones.

Elizabeth handed him his coat and extended a hand to the dog. With little hesitation, Raven sniffed her fingers and quickly gave them a friendly lick. "She's a pretty dog."

"Thanks," Jonas said. "Thanks for the coat, too. It was nice of you to bring it out." He took a step toward the gate, intending to escort Elizabeth out of the yard.

"Not so fast."

He half turned at the command, cocking his eyebrow in Elizabeth's direction. "Excuse me?"

"You promised me the answer to a question."

Jonas folded his arms. "All right."

She stepped close enough for him to see the faint, purplish shadows beneath her eyes, close enough for him to catch the remembered scent of her perfume. Her gaze never wavered from his. The question was just as straightforward. "What's a man like you doing in this town?"

A man like him.

What did she know?

"I don't know what you mean," he murmured when the silence between them had gone on too long. "A man like what?"

"You're not a native."

"How can you be so sure?"

"For one thing, I asked around."

"So?"

"So," she repeated. "You can answer my questions any time you want."

"I like mountains."

She blinked. "What?"

"That's the reason I live here." He gestured toward the ragged peaks that ranged to the west. "I happen to think this is some of the most beautiful country in the world. That's why I live here."

Of course she didn't buy it. If anything, the speculative gleam in her eye sharpened. Jonas had begun to wish his dog was a little more vicious. Or that he had stayed up in his office until she left.

Chuckling, she leaned down to pat Raven once more. "All right. I guess I'll just have to put you on the list of mysteries in this town."

"A list?"

"There's too much smoke for me to believe there isn't a fire somewhere."

And she was drawn to the heat. Moth to the flame. *Hell.*

Jonas could think of one more cliché that applied. It had to do with holding your friends close, but your enemies even closer. The best thing he could do for himself was help her, show her there wasn't a story and then get her out of town.

"Miss Monroe—"

"Elizabeth, please, *Jonas.*" Her smile flashed.

Trying to ignore the effect that smile had on him, Jonas gestured toward the house. "Why don't you come in? Let's talk over these mysteries a bit more."

Three

"Big house for one person," Elizabeth said as she followed Jonas through his front doorway.

He turned, one of his slim, dark eyebrows arching. "How do you know I live alone?" He swung the massive oak door closed, the sound punctuating his comment.

Elizabeth was startled. It had never occurred to her that someone might live here with him. Neither Lucy nor Jessica had mentioned a wife or children or a roommate of either sex. Of course, they might not know.

"So you *don't* live alone?"

He grinned. "Except for Poe and Raven."

"Then it's a big house for just the three of you."

"I'll show you around."

With little of the hesitation she might have expected from a man with something to hide, he took her through the first floor. The animals, who had followed them inside, went from room to room with them as Jonas told her what he knew of the history of the house. It had been used as a private school for a time after the original owner's death, but had eventually been taken over for back taxes and had stood empty until he'd found it and fell in love.

He was proud of it, Elizabeth decided, listening as he described the days of labor involved in removing the debris of decades of abandonment. He had lavished time and attention on his home.

High of ceiling and broad in scope, the rooms featured lovingly restored hardwood floors. Dark woodwork was buffed to a high sheen. Most of the walls were painted creamy white and featured art that suited the bygone era the house represented. Besides the big foyer, there was a front parlor with a smaller room set behind pocket doors at its rear. They passed through a dining room, a butler's pantry and yet another parlor. There was also a huge library featuring floor-to-ceiling shelves stocked with a wide array of books, popular titles as well as classics.

All the furnishings were exquisite antiques. Jonas said he had thoroughly researched the era and commissioned a firm in New York to find the right pieces. He pointed out some empty corners he was still trying to fill.

The cheerful kitchen was the only room not restored to its original state. There, modern appliances gleamed amid terra-cotta-tiled counters and new white cabinets. At one end, two easy chairs were drawn up in front of a fireplace. A pipe and an open book indicated that Jonas might spend some time here. Raven dropped onto the half-moon rug by the hearth, seemingly at home.

The rest of the first floor looked untouched, empty. Like a museum, Elizabeth thought.

Or a carefully crafted front.

But for what?

"So what do you think of my home?" Jonas asked as he poured her a glass of bottled water at one of the kitchen counters.

"You mean there's no tour of the rest of it?"

"I'm still working on the rest." He smiled easily and held the icy glass out for her.

Smiles transformed his features, Elizabeth decided. They lifted the mystery from his dark eyes. And deepened his formidable appeal.

Telling herself not to notice, she took the glass, her fingers brushing against his. His gaze flicked to hers, lingering for the briefest of moments. Then he turned away to pour himself a drink.

Elizabeth took a hasty gulp of the water and attempted not to notice the way his faded jeans cupped his taut rear. Or how the worn seams of his denim shirt stretched over his shoulders. He was a supremely fit specimen of manhood.

Manhood.

The word brought a tingle of color to her cheeks. And when she looked at his face, he was regarding her with a quizzical expression. She fought the tide of warm heat that threatened to suffuse her face by wheeling away, heading for the bank of windows in the wall next to the fireplace.

Outside was a tidy backyard bounded by a stone fence much like the one out front. A neat garage of recent construction was off to the left. Parked in front was a late model Jeep. Mr. Jonas Bishop was obviously a very rich man. She could only wonder at the source of that wealth.

"You have a beautiful home," she said with complete sincerity as she turned back to him. "But you have to pardon me if I still question why you'd choose to live in Whitehorn."

He perched on one of the bar stools drawn up to the kitchen's central island. "Why not here?"

"Because it's small and limited."

"Big cities are only a plane ride away."

"So do you travel much?"

He shrugged. "I prefer home."

"And what do you do here?"

"Do?"

"To occupy yourself."

"I write a little."

"That's what everyone told me."

One eyebrow lifted again. "Everyone?"

"The people I asked in town. They couldn't tell me what you write."

His expression grew stony, but he didn't look away. "That's because I only dabble in a few little mysteries. Nothing serious. It's for fun, mostly."

She started to ask another question, then caught herself, remembering the way he had sneered about her "firing" questions at him last night. There were definitely better ways to find out what she wanted to know. Charm always worked best.

But when she smiled at him, there was an odd but definite zing in the air between them. If she smiled, he smiled back. And it was easy to lose track of her thoughts that way. Hastily, she gulped the rest of the water down as she stared out the window again.

"I wanted to hear your list," Jonas said, after several tense moments passed.

She looked up. "My list?"

"Of Whitehorn, Montana, mysteries."

She seized the subject gratefully. "This little town of yours is a mighty strange place."

"Surely we're not the only small town beset by some form of violence in this day and age. A few deaths—"

"A *few?*"

He acknowledged her question with an upraised hand. "All right, all right, so there's a bit more going on than you might expect from a town this size. But it's all happened over the course of a few years."

"Odd things have happened in this town before this present crop."

"If you mean the man who died out on the reservation—"

"And what about 'Wolf Boy' Rawlings?" Elizabeth interrupted.

Jonas looked surprised. "Who told you about him? I lived in town for three years before I heard his story."

"Jessica McCallum mentioned it. It's not every town that has a boy who was supposedly cared for by wolves until he was found out in the woods."

"It's just a legend. One that I imagine Rafe Rawlings would like to see put to rest. How would you feel about being called 'Wolf Boy'?"

"I'm sure it wasn't easy growing up," she mused. "But it's interesting that little Jennifer wasn't the only baby abandoned here."

"Children are given away every day, everywhere."

"But abandoned in the forest or on a doorstep? Surely you have to admit that's not something that happens every day."

"Don't tell me you're trying to connect the events."

Elizabeth crossed the room to set her empty glass on the counter near the sink. "Of course, I can't see any obvious connection between Rawlings and Jennifer, but I might use it as a sidebar in the story I'm writing about her."

"Is Rawlings agreeable to that?"

The sharpness of Jonas's tone made Elizabeth turn. "I don't really need his permission."

"But wouldn't that be the charitable thing to do?"

They exchanged a long, level glance.

Then Jonas looked away, shaking his head. "I should have known better than to try to introduce charity to a *journalistic* endeavor." There was a sneer in his voice.

Elizabeth ignored it and changed the subject rather than get into a debate on professional ethics. "Jessica McCallum told me a lot of things about the town today. Do you know a man named Homer Gilmore?"

"Homer is someone everyone knows about, but few people really know. He's an eccentric, a hermit of sorts."

A lot like you, Elizabeth thought, though she bit back the words. "I understand Homer disappeared last year."

"They found him. He's getting on in years. He probably just lost his way up in the mountains."

"He thinks aliens tried to kidnap him."

Jonas slipped off his perch. "Since when is the *Denver Free Press* interested in alien-kidnap stories? Isn't that a little lowbrow for your normal readership?"

"We're not interested in that, per se," Elizabeth protested. "It's just that, combined with everything else that's going on—"

"There's nothing going on."

"Do you call arson nothing?" She quickly explained the suspicions that Dugin Kincaid's barn had been deliberately set on fire. "And now he's dead, too."

"Okay, that's a mystery. It's strange. But all you've really got is a bunch of admittedly unusual but unrelated events."

"The editor of your local weekly newspaper isn't convinced they're unrelated."

Groaning, Jonas passed a hand through his hair. "Don't tell me you went in and stirred up sweet old Mr. Greenbaum at the *Whitehorn Journal?*"

"That sweet old man has been a newspaperman his entire life. And even though he's spent most of that time printing notices of stock sales and pictures of county-fair winners, he's pretty darn sharp."

"What'd you do? Feed him some cock-and-bull theory that links the space-alien visit with Jennifer's appearance?" Jonas snapped his fingers. "That's it. She's really from outer space, the first wave of colonization from a dying planet well beyond the reach of our most powerful telescopes. You'd better check the wire services right away. There might be a rash of abandoned babies all over the country, even the globe. All sweet and cute, they'll probably mesmerize the world the same way Jennifer captivates most people who meet her."

Elizabeth pursed her lips. "You're very insulting. Did you know that?"

"No, *you're* insulting."

"What's that supposed to mean?"

"Only that I think your entire interest in all of this crap is to entertain your readers at the expense of this town."

She clenched her hands at her sides. Ted had also falsely accused her of becoming an entertainer rather than a journalist. "That's not true," she said, her voice thick with fury.

"You clearly have little regard for small-town life or the people who lead it. All you've done is question me about why I'd want to live here."

"Well, it is strange."

"Last time I checked, most Americans are free to live just about anywhere they please."

"But why would a rich man choose this place?"

He stepped toward her, his dark eyes glittering down into hers. "I told you why I chose it. I love the country. I like the town. It's a refreshing change from big-city smog and traffic. The state of my finances has little to do with it. Why should anyone require any other explanation?"

"Because I think you're lying."

Letting loose with an explicit, four-letter curse, Jonas sucked in his breath. "You know what I really don't understand? What gives you the right to even start asking questions about me? I'm a private citizen."

"Last time I checked, America had freedom of speech," she retorted, mimicking his earlier statement. "Can't I ask you anything I want?"

"Yes, you can ask."

"But you won't answer."

He started to say something, but Elizabeth saw him bite back the comment. He took another deep breath. His voice was even as he said, "I don't want to argue with you. But whether you think I belong here or not, this is my home. I like these people. They're accepting—"

"And you need to be accepted?"

A muscle began to twitch just above his right eye. "Is there any way you could *not* turn everything I say into another question?"

"If you have nothing to hide, what does it matter?"

"It matters because you irritate the hell out of me!"

The words exploded out of him, betraying a depth of fury Elizabeth hadn't really expected. It drove her back a step. But she quickly squared her shoulders and started to go around him toward the door. "Excuse me. I think it's time I—"

"Elizabeth."

Her name rolled easily off his tongue. His hand closed on her elbow. She looked back at him.

"Elizabeth," he repeated. And she realized he said her name the way it was supposed to be said, with each syllable distinct from the other, not all rolled together, the way most people pronounced it. For the first time in her life she was glad she wasn't called Liz or Beth or Libby, or any of the other shortened forms of her name she had wished for as a child. Maybe that was one advantage in growing up amid the formality of the Reverend and Mrs. Monroe's home. She now had this nice, long, proper name for this man to say in a voice that was deep and crisp, with just the hint of a drawl at the end of his words.

"Elizabeth, I'm sorry," he said now. "I didn't mean to lose my cool."

"The press is obviously your hot button."

Again he started to speak, but changed his mind. A slight smile touched his mouth. "I'm afraid to say anything. No matter what it is, you'll somehow find a way to turn it back on me."

His words painted a distinctly unflattering picture of her, reminded her of what Ted had said about her work becoming her life. Ted thought she was uninterested in anyone or anything that didn't have to do with a story. And though she didn't agree with that assessment, the echo of Ted's words coming from Jonas Bishop was disconcerting. For most of her life, Elizabeth had felt oddly disconnected from most other people. She had always believed that distance lent her objectivity she could apply to her work. But if her intensity made people afraid to talk to her, what did that leave her? Lonely?

Telling herself not to be foolish, she tried to shake off a sudden, deep sense of sadness. "I'm just curious," she told Jonas. "It's not just my job. It's who I am. If I weren't curious, I wouldn't have this job."

"I bet you were a trial to your parents."

Familiar pain bloomed in her chest, forced its way into her voice. "You don't know the half of it."

The fingers that still gripped her elbow squeezed lightly. A touch of human comfort. Somewhat impersonal. It shouldn't cause the response that ricocheted through her.

Elizabeth fought against a languorous, sinking feeling, even as she turned back toward Jonas. "Who are you?" she whispered, though the question was halfhearted.

He lifted his hand to her shoulder, his fingers just skimming the ends of her hair. His gaze seemed to search her face. "I told you who I was."

"Just a wealthy guy who writes little mysteries on the side?" Try as she might, Elizabeth couldn't keep her gaze off his mouth, couldn't help wondering how he might taste, how he would feel.

"Elizabeth?" he murmured, his voice husky.

She felt like a kid riding the first few rounds of the Scrambler at the amusement park. The speed was just beginning to accelerate, the circle within the circle just beginning to spin. She was just a little bit dizzy.

And she wanted off.

She stepped back, pulling her gaze from his face.

He moved away just as quickly.

"I have to go," she said.

"I'll show you out," he replied.

They didn't look at each other or say goodbye.

A minute later she was in her car, headed back to the Amity Boardinghouse. Halfway there, she stopped to roll down the window and gulp in several lungfuls of fresh Montana air. Only then did the spinning really stop.

In the doorway of Jonas's office, Poe waited, his slanted gaze supremely censorious.

"I know, I know," Jonas told him. "That was stupid."

The cat meowed his agreement.

Dropping into the chair in front of his computer, Jonas tried in vain to return to the work that had consumed him before Elizabeth's intrusion. The words could have been written in Chinese for all the sense they made.

He felt raw. Like he used to back home on the first day of football practice in the summer. Bruised and burning, every muscle screaming.

He hadn't wanted anyone in a long, long time. That part of his life was sealed away, relegated to the glamorous, empty memories of his previous existence. He had made his choices long ago.

Then along came Elizabeth.

How stupid to be aching for her even when he knew she could bring a lot of unwelcome attention to the town and to him. If she started writing about alien kidnappings and "wolf boys," God only knew what sleazy tabloid artists would crawl out of the woodwork.

Briefly, Jonas pressed the heels of his hands against his eyes. Then he faced the computer again. But his mind began straying once more. And not just to Elizabeth's sweetly tempting lips and infuriating curiosity.

He thought of unidentified bodies.

Unexplained deaths.

Alien abductions.

Using the same skills he called upon to work out his "little" mysteries, he took it all apart, piece by piece, and tried fitting it back together. He wound up with one pretty strange picture.

And a lot of questions.

"Damn her to hell," he muttered. "There *is* something damn weird going on around here."

He could only hope Elizabeth would soon tire of trying to figure it out and leave him and the town in peace.

After all, a man was free to wish in America. Even for the impossible.

Elizabeth's second morning in Montana dawned much like the first, just as the night had passed in the same flurry of tossing and turning as the previous one. Finally, she had gotten up and made some headway on the story on Jennifer.

Concentrating wasn't easy. Her head was a jumble of ideas and theories. Overlaying them all was the memory of Jonas Bishop's body bending close to hers. A moment more and her lips would have lifted, met his. And then she would have been lost. Out of control.

In the shower, she lectured herself. Elizabeth Monroe didn't lose her grip. She was tightly focused at all times. She had learned that lesson early in life. The few times she had strayed from that principle, she had regretted it sorely. She regretted it even now.

"I'm just adrift up here," she told herself as she dressed. She was also running out of clothes. Today's black slacks and red blouse were her last clean pieces. The rest would have to go to the laundry if she expected to remain in Whitehorn for several more days.

She was clipping on her customary gold earrings when the phone jangled on the beside table. It was Ted.

Elizabeth sank down on the edge of the bed, overwhelmed by how happy she was to hear her editor's familiar voice, even if she was still resentful over what had transpired between them the day before yesterday. She knew her emotions showed in her voice.

"Are you okay?" he asked, sounding worried.

"Of course."

"You got the story on the little girl?"

"I want to finish up a couple of things this afternoon before I fax it in."

"I need it by three. The pictures from the local paper came in yesterday afternoon. They're good."

"I know."

He paused. "Are you still angry?"

"Somewhat."

"Oh, Elizabeth, you know you need to do some thinking. You need a vacation. Have you decided where you're going?"

She twisted the phone cord around one finger, then said, "I think I'll stay here for a while."

This pause stretched even longer. "Why?"

"It turned out to be an interesting place."

"Well, that's good," he replied, though he sounded uncertain.

She took the final plunge. "I think there's a story up here, Ted."

This time the silence went on so long that she asked, "You still there?"

"Elizabeth . . ." he began in warning.

"Just listen, all right?"

As quickly as possible, she gave him everything. Dead bodies. The Kincaids. Unearthed bones. Exploding cars. Arson. Aliens.

When she was finished, the phone line popped and crackled in her ear. "Ted?"

"You've lost it," he said. "You're seeing ghouls behind every tree and dreaming up stories where there aren't any. And I'm damned sick of it."

"But Ted—"

His voice began to rise. "I sent you up to a nice little town, expecting a nice little piece on a sweet little child. And you're giving me aliens? *Aliens?*"

Elizabeth held the phone away from her ear, still trying to get a word in edgewise. Ted wouldn't let her speak.

"I want the story I sent you up there to do," he said tightly. "I want it today. Then I don't want to see you or hear from you for at least two weeks. I want you to get a grip on what has become an overactive imagination."

"Ted, damn it—"

"An inquisitive mind is one thing. That's a reporter's asset. But when you let your imagination get out of control . . . well, that's a reporter's worst enemy."

"Ted, these are facts. I haven't made any of this stuff up."

"I don't care if you see the aliens yourself or if bodies start popping up out of the ground at your feet. I don't want to hear about it from you!"

The phone popped one last time. The line went dead.

Elizabeth sat, lips pursed, wondering why everyone seemed to go ballistic when she mentioned the aliens.

She tried to call Ted back, but his secretary said he wasn't available. Not to her, anyway.

That's when Elizabeth got mad. Ted had trained her. If anyone should believe she knew a story when she smelled one, it should be him. But he had acted as crazed as Jonas Bishop.

She was going to show both of them.

Four

The sky was deeply, limitlessly blue. Blue as only a Montana sky could be as Jonas strolled down Whitehorn's Center Avenue. His mood matched the perfect weather. Last night he had forced Elizabeth Monroe and her list of town mysteries to the back of his mind, and completed another chapter of his current book. Today, after reading through the pages and making some revisions, he was so pleased with himself he'd decided to take a walk to the Hip Hop Café for a late lunch.

Elizabeth's white rental sedan wasn't parked at the Amity Boardinghouse when he passed. She might be out pursuing some of her elusive story ideas, but Jonas hoped she had given up and left town. Grinning at that prospect, he began to whistle as he approached the restaurant.

His hand was reaching for the door when it flew open. He stepped back in time to avoid a collision with Police Officer Rafe "Wolf Boy" Rawlings. The young policeman's face was set in angry lines. At his heels was his equally distraught-looking wife, Raeanne.

"Excuse us," she said to Jonas as she brushed past him. She hurried down the sidewalk and caught her husband's arm. He stopped and faced her while she spoke quietly.

Jonas couldn't hear what Raeanne said, but evidently it was enough to soothe Rafe. They talked for a moment more, then hugged—one of those tight, hard, what-would-I-do-without-you sort of hugs that Jonas had only observed, written about or long ago framed with a camera.

The sort of hug he would probably never experience first-hand.

He realized he was staring at the young officer and his attorney wife. Not that they noticed his rudeness. They were completely immersed in one another, as a couple married only a little more than a year should be. No doubt their hug was the culmination of some newlywed spat.

Irritated by the well of yearning in his chest, Jonas stepped inside the Hip Hop and immediately looked into Elizabeth's brown eyes.

She was seated at a table for four by the window. Her blond hair was mussed, as if she had recently thrust a hand through it. Her cheeks were flushed, as well. And for half a heartbeat as he stared at her, Jonas was rocked back to yesterday, when he had touched her hair and swayed toward her. A man could lose his footing just looking at her.

But Jonas hung on to his composure. He noticed a half eaten salad pushed to one side and a laptop computer in front of her on the table, where there were two coffee cups in addition to her own. There was also a buzz in the air and some speculative glances coming her way from the other diners in the half-empty restaurant.

Jonas looked out the window. Rafe and Raeanne were crossing the street, holding hands. Suddenly, he knew they hadn't had a newlywed spat; they had run into Elizabeth.

Forgetting caution, he crossed to her table and in a low voice demanded, "You just had to do it, didn't you?"

A line appeared between her eyebrows. "Do what?"

"Try to sensationalize his past."

"Whose past?"

Jonas sat down across from her, trying as always not to draw undue attention to himself. "I'm talking about Rafe Rawlings."

Elizabeth straightened. "How did you know I talked to him?"

"He almost mowed me down outside. I recognized the ambushed-by-the-press terror in his eyes."

Her defensive expression dissolved to one of interest. "And how would you recognize that sort of terror, Mr. Bishop? What side of the press have you been on?"

Jonas drew back, intending to get up and leave. But at that moment, the Hip Hop's proprietor, Melissa Avery North, appeared beside the table to ask if Jonas would be joining Elizabeth for lunch.

"Elizabeth?" Jonas echoed, glancing from one woman to the other. The two seemed awfully chummy.

"Melissa's been telling me all about Whitehorn's history," Elizabeth said, her expression decidedly smug. "She's given me some wonderful background for a story."

The pretty and very obviously pregnant woman grinned. "A nice series about the town can't do the tourist business any harm."

Jonas didn't think Elizabeth's and Melissa's ideas about a "nice" series would have anything in common. "Some folks would just as soon do without the tourists."

"Not me. I'm a businesswoman." Cheerily, Melissa picked up the coffee cups that had been left at the table. "Rafe and Raeanne sure didn't stay long. I must have been in the back when they left."

"They said they had a lot to do," Elizabeth explained smoothly. Jonas had to grit his teeth to keep from telling Melissa what he imagined had really happened between the Rawlingses and Elizabeth.

With a last smile, Melissa moved away and sent a waitress over to take Jonas's order.

He still wanted to bolt, but knew that would cause comment among the people around them whom he recognized. He was used to blending in, so he stayed where he was, ordered a sandwich and tried not to glare at the woman across the table. Perhaps he could put this time to good use in convincing Elizabeth to leave Whitehorn.

She seemed to know how irritated he was. With false sweetness, she said, "Go ahead. Let me have it."

He kept his expression and his voice calm and even. "You know how I feel about the sort of story you're going to do. I won't bore you with a repetition of my arguments."

"What I don't know is why you care so much."

"I told you yesterday—"

"I know what you said." She made an airy, dismissive gesture with one hand. "But I think your aversion to the press is motivated by something more personal than a desire to preserve the privacy of this town. In fact, I think I could add you to the list of mysteries in Whitehorn. I'm just wondering how you fit in with the rest."

She was his worst nightmare come to life. As the waitress deposited a glass of lemonade in front of him, Jonas eased back in his chair, considering how best to convince her there wasn't a viable story in this town—or about him.

Keeping his tone mild, he said, "You have an overactive imagination."

She made no reply.

Sensing a sore spot, Jonas pressed on. "It makes me wonder about all those stories of yours that I've read over the past few years."

Elizabeth's eyes narrowed. "Wonder about what?"

"About the way you pursued them."

"The night you walked me home, you said I relished my work."

"But this edge of desperation doesn't show in the writing."

"I don't know what you mean by that," she replied in a tight voice.

"Your writing is always so sharp, cool and factual, even when you're annihilating someone. Quite frankly, I had you pictured as a cold bitch."

"And now you've changed your mind?"

"Yes. You're much more...passionate." That wasn't the adjective Jonas had intended to use; it slipped out. But it fit. She had an obvious passion for her work. Undoubtedly that fire would be applied to every aspect of her life. When she cared about something. When she loved...

The thought made him sigh. Miss Elizabeth Monroe, with her honey hair and melting eyes, would be an ardent lover. As if he were framing a scene for a movie, Jonas pictured this woman in his bed, her slender curves wrapped around his body, a smile like morning sunshine touching her lips and warming him, making him feel as he hadn't felt in so long, in forever.

He wrenched his thoughts back to reality. A blush nearly as red as her blouse deepened on Elizabeth's cheeks. Had his thoughts been that clear? Her gaze avoided his as she said, "It takes a lot of *passion*..." She glanced at him and then quickly away again, before continuing. "It takes *determination* to pursue a story."

"You don't like dead ends, do you?"

"Who does?"

He sighed and sipped his drink. "And isn't it tempting to slant the facts?"

She went very still. "Slant?"

He leaned forward. "You know...play up certain parts of the story, the most interesting parts, the parts you feel so passionately about."

"I only write the truth."

"So you write only to inform?"

She hesitated for a moment. "I believe it would be more accurate to say I write to inform and to enlighten."

"Umm."

Elizabeth frowned, but his turkey submarine sandwich arrived before she could make a reply to his intentionally evasive murmur. She sat rigidly in her chair, fingers drumming ever so slightly on the bright yellow tablecloth, while Jonas made small talk with the friendly waitress, who obligingly fetched ketchup from another table for his french fries.

When the woman was gone, Elizabeth glared at him. "What exactly are you trying to say to me about my work?"

"It's not up to me to say anything." Jonas concentrated on his lunch, struggling not to smile as Elizabeth fidgeted and stewed across from him. When he finally allowed her to catch his eye again, he feigned surprise. "I'm sorry. Have I made you angry about something?"

"Of course not." She downed the last of her coffee, grimacing a bit, then flipped off her computer and closed it with a firm little click.

"You leaving?" Jonas asked, with as much lack of interest as he could muster.

"I have a story I need to fax to my editor."

"First installment of your series?"

"The story I was sent up here to do. I hope it's just the first."

"I guess the paper is salivating over your suspicions."

She hesitated again, for several moments this time. Jonas thought she looked uncomfortable. She glanced away when she said, "I don't know if 'salivating' is the proper term."

"Umm."

His murmur snapped her gaze to back to him. "Now what did that mean?"

"Nothing."

"Yes it did," she insisted. "And if you want to say something about my work or the way I approach it, I wish you'd just come out with it. I don't like playing games."

"Don't you?"

"Oh, please." She picked up the check for her lunch and began rooting around in her purse.

Jonas continued, "Weren't you playing games with Melissa when you pumped her for information by letting her think you were going to do a pleasant little story on the charms of our town?''

"I never told her exactly what the story would be about."

"Were you just waiting for the right time to ask her about her father's remains turning up on the reservation after almost thirty years?"

She looked up from her purse, her gaze defiant. "I probably would have asked her about it, yes."

"After you softened her up, right?"

Not answering, she closed her purse.

"I bet you lured Rafe Rawlings here by a similar subterfuge, didn't you? When you had him at ease, you moved the conversation around to the old 'Wolf Boy' gossip."

"I didn't lure him anywhere," Elizabeth protested. "He simply came in with his wife while I was sitting here finishing my story on Jennifer. I noticed his name on his uniform. The restaurant was crowded, so I invited them to join me. While we were talking, I asked Officer Rawlings a perfectly legitimate question about himself. You're the one who told me the charitable thing would be to talk to him about his past before I included it in any story."

"But he doesn't want to be part of a story, does he?"

She evaded the question. "Speculation about his past is a matter of public record. I found several stories about it in the archives at the *Whitehorn Journal* this morning. I also discovered that he's a brave, respected member of the police force, a highly regarded citizen."

"But no one would remember that," Jonas retorted, fighting to keep his voice at a reasonable level. "All they'd remember from the article is that when he was a baby he was found in the woods, that people thought wild animals had kept him alive and that for most of his life, he's been taunted with the name Wolf Boy. That's what the headline would say, that's how the story would be slanted and that's what would sell your newspapers."

"I'm not trying to sell newspapers," Elizabeth replied.

"That's right!" Jonas snapped his fingers and, with pretended remorse, said, "I'm so sorry. I forgot that you have a nobler motive. What you try to do is *enlighten* your readers."

Real fury blazed in her eyes. "That's right."

"And just what would be enlightening about Rafe's story?"

"People are always interested in the unusual backgrounds of others."

"And that sells newspapers. And gets ratings on tabloid TV shows. And sometimes in the crossfire of it all, people get hurt. People who might not want their private business spelled out in the papers. People like Rafe."

"And people like you?" Elizabeth added.

Jonas said nothing. He just stared at her. Long and hard. With contempt.

Her chair scraped across the tiled floor as she stood. Grasping her purse in one hand and the computer in the other, she walked away without another word or a backward glance.

Jonas cursed himself. Far from making her realize there was no story of real interest here, all he had done was make her angry and probably more suspicious of him than before. Why the hell hadn't he stayed home where he belonged? It wasn't safe for him to walk the streets with this woman in town.

He darted a look around the restaurant. He'd felt as if he was shouting at her, but evidently, they had kept their conversation at a level that hadn't drawn much attention from the few remaining diners. He managed a smile for a woman two tables down who looked vaguely familiar. Then he returned to his sandwich, which was now about as tasty as dirt. He wasn't leaving until he was damn sure

Elizabeth Monroe was gone. He wanted no further contact with her.

His back was to the door and the front of the restaurant, but he could hear the low murmur of voices and feminine laughter. The bells on the door jangled, and he glanced over his shoulder, hoping for a glimpse of Elizabeth's departure. But she was leaning against the counter near the cash register, talking with Melissa, who had glanced up to greet a well-dressed blonde, Mary Jo Kincaid.

Jeremiah Kincaid's daughter-in-law. Dugin Kincaid's widow.

Jonas heard Melissa introduce Mary Jo to Elizabeth and turned back to his sandwich with a hastily stifled groan. He could practically hear the ideas spinning in Elizabeth's brain. And for once he couldn't blame her.

Mary Jo, with her stylishly coiffed blond hair, her trim figure and well-made-up face, had struck him as something of a mystery ever since he'd become aware of her three years ago. She had come to Whitehorn as the children's librarian. Jonas had met her at the library when he was doing some research for a book. But she had scarcely settled into the job before she married Dugin Kincaid in a lavish wedding. That wedding had been the topic of conversation everywhere Jonas had gone for months, particularly here in the Hip Hop Café, where most of the town's gossip was digested along with the food. But it wasn't Mary Jo's dress or the Kincaid's big-wheel guest list or the reception buffet that had been at the center of all the talk.

It was the dead body that showed up at the wedding. The body of a man no one in town knew, whose presence at the wedding had never been explained.

And then there was Mary Jo's husband, Dugin, killed after his barn was deliberately torched.

Jonas knew that if Elizabeth latched on to Mary Jo, she would never abandon the notion of poking around here in town. Looking toward the front of the restaurant again, he saw Melissa push through a door to the back, while Elizabeth engaged Mary Jo in conversation. He turned sideways in his chair, pretending to study the day's dessert specials written on a blackboard on the restaurant's far wall. He still couldn't hear what Mary Jo and Elizabeth were saying. Mary Jo took a lace-edged handkerchief from her purse and dabbed at the corners of her eyes as she shook her head.

"I'm very sorry, but no," Mary Jo said, loud enough for Jonas to hear. Then Melissa reappeared and handed her a pastry box. Mary Jo gave her some money and exited, waving off Melissa's offer of change.

Elizabeth stared at the door, frowning, until she turned and looked right at Jonas. And her frown deepened.

Embarrassed at having been caught watching her, he picked up his check and got to his feet. Pointedly ignoring her, he strode to the cash register.

The woman customer Jonas had smiled at earlier was making her way to the front as well, but instead of approaching the cash register, she stopped at the counter. While Jonas withdrew some money from his billfold, he heard her ask Melissa about catering a party for a group of teenagers.

"So you do catering, too," Elizabeth commented.

"She did my wedding reception this winter," the customer replied. "It was really special."

Melissa laughed. "That's because the Gilmore-Hunter union was special."

"Gilmore?"

Elizabeth's voice made Jonas glance her way. Her back was to him, but he could sense her sharpened interest.

"Are you related to Homer Gilmore?" she pressed.

Smiling, the woman nodded. "He's my father."

Melissa performed the introductions. The customer was Moriah Gilmore Hunter, whom Jonas knew was a recently returned native of Whitehorn. She had married Dr. Kane Hunter, a physician of Native American heritage, whom Jonas had seen when he'd had a bout with the flu last year. Kane and Moriah were childhood sweethearts who'd had a daughter born out of wedlock after Moriah left town as a teenager. But they were together as a family now. As one might expect, their union after all these years had caused quite a stir around town. Moriah's father, Homer Gilmore, was the old eccentric who claimed to have been kidnapped by aliens last year.

"I'd like to talk to your father," Elizabeth said to Moriah, her tone as innocent as could be.

To her credit, Moriah seemed wary. "Why?"

"I hear he went through quite an ordeal when he was lost in the mountains."

Moriah looked away. "Yes, well, he's..."

Jonas watched Elizabeth put her hand out to the woman. "I hope he's okay," she murmured. She sounded so sincere that Jonas wasn't surprised when Moriah's expression softened. In a few minutes, she would probably be taking Elizabeth to meet Homer.

It was none of Jonas's business. He should just put his check and his money on the counter and leave Elizabeth and the trouble she could cause him. If she went ahead with the story, he could always get out of town for a while and come back when the dust had settled. She would probably never learn anything about his past. For what connection would Jonas Bishop of Montana have with the man he had been nine years ago?

But then he thought about poor old Homer. The man was an independent old cuss, a rugged individual of the sort one might expect to inhabit a part of the country where there was still some wilderness to be found. Jonas had always liked the way most Whitehorn residents just accepted Homer as he was. Even the old guy's stories of an alien abduction last year had been repeated with kindly smiles. But if Elizabeth got hold of Homer, she would grill him good. In the story, he'd be an object of ridicule, a crazy old coot.

Jonas decided he just couldn't let that happen. No matter what risk was involved in further debate with Elizabeth Monroe, he couldn't stand idly by. Stepping forward, he took hold of her elbow, murmuring her name.

Though she had been aware of Jonas standing at the register behind her, Elizabeth jumped at the sound of his deep voice, at his touch. Glancing up, she saw that his charming smile was in place, but his dark eyes were just as cold as they'd been when she left him at the table. She started to pull her arm from his grasp, but his fingers applied a light but firm pressure.

"I see you ladies are helping Elizabeth with her story," he said to Moriah and Melissa.

"And I'm keeping you waiting. I'm so sorry." Melissa moved toward the cash register.

Releasing Elizabeth, Jonas held out his check and money. "This should cover mine and Miss Monroe's lunch."

"No," Elizabeth protested.

He held up a hand. "I insist. It's not every day that a big-time reporter comes to town and promises to make Whitehorn famous."

Elizabeth frowned. "I don't know if famous—"

"Infamous is more correct, of course," he said, his smooth and gracious smile still in place.

"Infamous?" Moriah Hunter pushed a strand of red hair over an ear, her wariness returning.

Elizabeth turned to reassure her, but Jonas spoke first. "Miss Monroe told me over lunch how much she's looking forward to this series she's doing on Whitehorn. The place reminds her of one of those TV towns."

Melissa's brow had knit. "What sort of TV town?"

"You know," Jonas replied. "A small town with hidden secrets. Secrets like abandoned babies. Unsolved murders." He slyly angled a glance at Moriah. "Strange disappearances."

"Like *Peyton Place*," Moriah murmured.

"No," Elizabeth protested, glaring openly at Jonas. "I never said that—"

"No, no, you're right," Jonas agreed, cutting in. "You said it was more like another TV show. One that was on just a few years back. It had a big cult following. I can't remember the title now, but the whole town had these weird characters, like a woman who talked to a log. People died in mysterious ways—"

"'Twin Peaks' was the name of the town and the show," Melissa said, frowning at Elizabeth.

Moriah shivered. "That program gave me the creeps."

Jonas leaned nonchalantly against the counter, ignoring the warning Elizabeth tried to telegraph his way. "Do you remember how everyone in that town congregated at the local diner to talk over the strange goings-on?" He glanced around the restaurant. "Sort of like everyone comes to the Hip Hop."

Elizabeth formulated a protest that died on her lips. Jonas's clever seeds of suspicion had already taken root with their two companions.

"There was so much evil in that town," Moriah murmured. "That's not like Whitehorn."

"I never said it was." Elizabeth forced herself not to look at Jonas. She knew if she did, she would lose her temper in a big, big way.

"Why did you want to talk to my father?" Moriah asked.

"And why did you ask Rafe Rawlings to sit down with you?" Melissa added. "I thought it was strange that he and Raeanne left so quickly." Her mouth thinned in an angry line. "Are you trying to make something of his past?"

Elizabeth flushed. "I'm just trying to do a story."

Melissa turned to the cash register. Her voice was cool. "I don't think we want the sort of story you're planning."

"No, we don't," Moriah agreed.

Jonas said, "You'll have to forgive me, Miss Monroe. I'm afraid I've interfered in your story, haven't I?"

Fury as cold as his eyes swept through her, producing only a sputtering answer.

He merely gave her a mocking salute, smiled at the other two women and left.

Moriah and Melissa were regarding Elizabeth with hostile glares. She was used to hostility. When she was digging for dirt with which to build a story, she had to expect to get a little muddy herself.

Digging for dirt? The words echoed in her brain. Was that what she had been doing with these two nice women? For a moment, she heard Ted telling her she had lost her objectivity. She remembered the contempt in Jonas's eyes. But they were wrong. There was a story here, an intriguing mystery.

But that was cold comfort as she faced Melissa and Moriah's anger. Why was it that everyone she met these days seemed to look at her the same way?

"Mr. Bishop has it all wrong," she told them. "My intention wasn't really to bad-mouth your town."

"Then what are you trying to do?" Moriah demanded.

"It just seems to me that some odd things have happened around here in the past few years."

Melissa's fingers flashed over the keys of the cash register, punctuating her words. "What happens here is no one's concern but ours."

Moriah's chin lifted, as if in challenge. "I'm sure the local authorities don't need your help, Miss Monroe."

Recognizing that anything else she said might do more harm than good, Elizabeth murmured, "I'm sorry." She was genuinely sorry to have upset these women, but her fury at Jonas Bishop didn't abate as she swept out the door.

On the sidewalk, she looked in the direction he had walked the night they'd met. He was nowhere to be seen. But a pivot to her right revealed his lean, blue-jeans-clad frame climbing the broad steps of the nearby library.

"Hold it right there," she called out, sprinting toward him.

Not only Jonas, but everyone else on the block—several shoppers, some businesspeople and a couple of cowboys—looked her way. Elizabeth didn't care. She was intent on Jonas.

He stopped on the top step, hands on his hips, frowning as she came to a halt on the sidewalk below him.

"You've got some nerve," she shouted up at him.

Glancing up and down the street, he came down to meet her, demanding in a low voice, "Must you make a scene?"

"What about the scene you just made?"

"I didn't want you taking advantage of them."

"I wasn't taking advantage of anyone." A lift of his eyebrow brought color to her face. "All right, all right," she admitted, "Maybe I was taking advantage of their friendliness to get a little information. But it was none of your business."

With a muttered curse, Jonas took hold of her elbow and drew her to the side of the steps. "Haven't we debated your journalistic ethics—or lack of—enough?"

She jerked away from him. "I don't want a debate, either. I just want you to stay out of my way."

"Leave town and that won't be a problem."

"I'm not leaving town until I'm good and ready."

"Not until you've stirred up a hornet's nest of trouble, you mean."

Elizabeth took a step closer. She had faced tougher obstacles than this man in pursuit of a story. And Jonas couldn't really do anything to stop her from investigating anything she wanted. If she were smart, she'd just leave him be and go about her business. But something about this man got under her skin.

Eyes narrowing, she studied the lean angles of his face. Who was he? she wondered, as she had since they'd met. What was a man like him doing in Whitehorn, Montana? He just didn't fit the fabric of the town. Almost without thinking, she verbalized her next thought. "What are you so afraid of me finding out about you?"

"I'm not afraid of a damn thing." He turned on his heel.

But Elizabeth wasn't letting him get away. She grabbed his arm. "You are afraid. Or else you wouldn't be making such a big deal out of all this."

He stiffened, but didn't turn. Shaking off her hand, he started up to the library door again.

Elizabeth took the steps two at a time and blocked his way at the top. "I'll make you a deal. If you'll give me your story, explain who you are, I'll forget about the rest of the weird stuff in this town."

Sidestepping her without a comment, he pulled open the library door.

She followed him inside a short, tiled vestibule, through another set of doors into a large, two-story room paneled in dark wood. Vaguely, Elizabeth noted the mingled scents of lemon wax and old books. She was aware of muffled voices and quiet activity across the room, but she was single-minded in her pursuit of Jonas, who was headed for the shelves of books to the right.

"Would you please stop?" she demanded in a stage whisper.

Jonas drew to a halt. His broad shoulders slumped before he turned toward her. When she started to speak, he held a finger to his lips and drew her back toward the doors. "In case you haven't noticed, this is a library."

"Where you were going to try and hide from me," she replied in equally hushed tones.

"I'm not hiding. I just don't want to talk to you anymore. Not ever. So goodbye. Okay?"

"But I said I'd make a deal with you. Tell me your story, and I'll forget about my series on the town."

He focused on some point above her shoulder. A muscle twitched in his jaw. "I have no story."

Her voice rose. "Baloney. I can smell the mystery on you."

"You're mistaken." He looked her right in the eyes. Elizabeth almost faltered. He seemed somehow . . . dangerous.

Which is nonsense, she told herself, pressing on. "Come on, Jonas. Tell me about yourself and I'll forget about Charlie Avery's murder still being unsolved after nearly thirty years."

"There's nothing to tell about me."

"I'll forget about that car explosion that killed the woman outside of town."

"Elizabeth . . ." he said in warning.

"I'll forget the 'Wolf Boy' story. And I won't push Homer Gilmore for his tales about the aliens in the mountains. I'll be satisfied to find out what you're hiding."

He sent a nervous look over his shoulder. "Would you hush?"

Some demon of perversity made Elizabeth deliberately raise her voice. "What's wrong? Afraid someone else will start wondering about you? Better be careful or you'll replace Dugin Kincaid's death as the mystery of the moment around town."

The silence that followed that last statement was profound, even for the hushed interior of a library. Elizabeth looked to her left across the room. At the far end, a group of women arrayed in colorful spring suits and dresses, with teacups and cookies in hand, were staring at her and Jonas with their mouths open. Mary Jo Kincaid was at the center of the group. At her side, in a vivid chartreuse dress, was the town gossip, Lily Mae Wheeler.

"Oh, it's you," the woman exclaimed, hurrying toward them, her expression one of avid interest.

Before Elizabeth could react, Jonas thrust his arm around her waist and pulled her close to his side. Against her ear, he muttered, "Play along with me or I may be forced to hurt you."

She had only a moment to take that in before Lily Mae bore down on them, wide-eyed. "Is everything all right?"

Jonas looked as contrite as a small boy. "We're so sorry. We were having a discussion and became so caught up in it that we forgot where we were." He waved toward the other women and smiled. "Please pardon our rudeness, ladies. We didn't mean to interrupt."

Lily Mae seemed uncertain as she looked at Elizabeth. "Then there's nothing wrong?"

"Of course not," Elizabeth lied, though she had no idea why he thought this little charade was necessary.

Jonas's arm tightened around her. He cocked his head so that his jaw just brushed the side of her hair. His arm felt solid and strong against her back. He smelled like tobacco and the outdoors. Like a man, Elizabeth thought, reacting to his nearness despite herself.

Lily Mae's interested regard turned to blatant speculation. "It looks like you two have become friends."

"Yes... *friends.*" Jonas's voice deepened just slightly on the word, conveying a meaning that Lily Mae would be the last person to miss.

She giggled like a delighted child. "Come join us for tea. We're just making final plans for the annual book sale we hold during Pioneer Days. I'm sure you'd have some good ideas."

Elizabeth was formulating her excuse when Jonas answered, "I'm afraid I've got to run. But *darling*—" He turned to her with a smile slicker than any politician's she had ever met "—I bet you'd like to stay."

She yearned to use her computer to punch him in the gut, but forced herself to mimic his sugary tone. "I'm sorry, *honey*, but I have a story I need to fax to my editor."

"Then I'll see you later, *sweetheart*," Jonas said.

Then he kissed her. Hard. On her mouth. For Lily Mae's benefit.

But it made Elizabeth's head swim all the same.

He left her standing there, dazed.

As he pushed through the doors, Lily Mae whispered, "Oh, my."

Those two simple words summed up exactly what Elizabeth was feeling.

Oh, my.

The warm, clear day faded to a cool night, with a wind blowing down from the mountains that sent clouds across the face of the moon. Jonas, who found he couldn't work and therefore avoided his study on the third floor, built a blaze in the kitchen fireplace. With his faithful pets nearby, he sat and smoked and brooded.

And remembered the softness of Elizabeth's lips beneath his.

"I'm a fool," he said.

From where Poe was curled in front of the fire, his blue cat's eyes glinted in agreement. But Raven laid a cold but comforting nose against Jonas's hand. He stroked her shining black coat. "It's nice to have one forgiving soul in the house." Poe yawned and stretched, unwilling as always to court Jonas's favor by letting him off easy. That was a role he left entirely to the dog.

"So you think I shouldn't have kissed her?" Jonas asked the cat.

As if the question was moot, Poe merely licked a paw.

"You're right, of course. I shouldn't have."

He hadn't meant to kiss Elizabeth. That whole ruse about the two of them being *friends* had been a mistake, a hasty but unwise improvisation. But when he'd looked up and seen that busybody, Lily Mae, barreling across the library, he'd thought he had to diffuse the situation.

Jonas was certain everyone at the library-committee tea party had heard part of what Elizabeth had said about him being a mystery. Some of those women, and others in town, would agree with her. But most of the citizens of Whitehorn seemed to have accepted him at face value and left him alone to live his life, much as they had Homer Gilmore. He didn't want that to change. Respect for individuality and privacy was what had drawn him here more than eight years ago. He didn't want anyone asking questions he wouldn't answer. So today, all he could think to do was give those ladies something concrete to speculate about. Like him being involved with the pretty but nosy reporter from Denver.

He had grabbed Elizabeth, pretended to be captivated by her, kissed her to set fire to Lily Mae's wagging tongue.

Only maybe he wasn't pretending.

And maybe Lily Mae wasn't the only reason he had kissed her.

"Damn."

Setting aside his pipe, Jonas took his brandy snifter from the table by the chair. But he didn't drink. He sat, swirling the deep amber liquid in the glass, inhaling the rich aroma and wishing he could turn the clock back several hours. If he had that power, he would have worked all day instead of going out to lunch and running headfirst into trouble. Most of all, he wouldn't have tried to duck into the library like some cowardly fugitive. Although that's what he was. A fugitive.

On the run from the past.

Funny, but he had almost convinced himself he wasn't really running. He had settled here. Had come to think of it as home. Yet somewhere deep down he had known he couldn't stay forever. With all the celebrities and power brokers from his former life who were running from the West Coast and trying to buy the wide-open spaces for themselves, even little Whitehorn, Montana, would have become too crowded for his comfort. But he had imagined that would be years from now. He had thought he still had time before the shadows caught up with him.

A log fell in the fire, and Jonas studied the cloud of sparks, trying to give this matter a positive spin. Maybe he did have time. Maybe Elizabeth would back off. And even if she didn't, his worst fears might not be realized. He might still be able to live here unrecognized, separated from the past he had come here to forget.

But if he stayed, he knew he would always be looking over his shoulder, waiting for another Elizabeth to show up.

Sighing, he took a big gulp of brandy, then asked the animals, "So where do you want to move?"

Raven cocked her head to the side. Poe paused in mid-bath.

Amazed to have both of their attention, Jonas continued, "India, maybe? Or perhaps Ireland? A newly independent Soviet state? I think no matter what you say, it's going to have to be somewhere out of the good old U.S.A."

Springing to full alertness with a grace peculiar to his species, the cat padded to the doorway that led to the front hall. Raven retreated behind Jonas's chair, but growled deep in her throat.

"Gee, I didn't expect you to be this upset."

When Poe didn't pause for a withering look, Jonas set down his brandy, listening. But all he heard was the crackle and hiss of the fire, the hum of the refrigerator, the faint *tick-tock* of the antique clock on the mantle. "What is it, guys? What do you hear?"

Poe slunk into the darkness of the hall, and in a curious show of courage, Raven followed.

"This better not be just another of those rats you love to torment," Jonas warned, trailing them.

He was midway to the front door when the pounding began. Jonas frowned, slipped into the shadows under the stairs. No one ever came here at night.

As if on cue, there was a shout. Elizabeth. "I know you're there, so open up, Jonas. I want to talk to you. Now."

The headache that had been nagging at his temples all evening was upgraded to a full-fledged throb. He considered leaving her out on the porch.

"I'll stay here all night if I have to," she warned.

And he was sure she would. "Damnation." He stalked down the hall, threw on the outside lights and flung open the door. "What do you want?"

She stepped back, to the edge of the porch. The wind, which had grown fiercer since nightfall, whipped her hair around her head. She blinked in the light, her face pale. But Jonas could see that her hands were clenched at her sides.

"Well?" he said.

"You're not going to scare me away," she told him.

"What does that mean?"

"The phone call."

"What phone call?"

"The one I got not twenty minutes ago."

He thrust a hand through his hair and blew out a frustrated breath. "What would that phone call have to do with me?"

"It was you calling. You told me to get out of town or else."

"Or else?"

She groaned. "Would you stop answering everything I say with a question?"

"I would if I knew what in the hell you were talking about."

"I got a phone call that sounded electronically altered or something. But I heard the message all right. The caller said I was too nosy for my own good, and I should get out of town and quit asking so many questions." She paused, taking a deep breath. "Or else."

Jonas stared at her, wanting to believe she was lying or hallucinating. But something told him she wasn't. There were many different levels on which he didn't trust this reporter, *any* reporter. But he knew she had received a phone call tonight. The truth was there in her eyes. And somewhere, just beneath the bravado, there was fear. He suspected that wasn't an emotion Elizabeth allowed herself to experience often.

He held out his hand, hoping to reassure her. "It wasn't me, Elizabeth. I didn't call you."

She blinked. He watched the muscles work in her throat as she swallowed. "I believe you," she said finally.

They stared at each other for one long, silent moment. Then she looked over her shoulder. Into the inky blackness of the Montana night.

Somewhere behind them in the hall, Raven growled. Something scuttled in the shrubbery beside the porch.

Jonas pulled Elizabeth inside his house, into his arms.

Where she was safe.

Where he was in danger. From her.

Five

Elizabeth didn't know why she was so cold. The fire was warm. The room felt cozy, though it was lit only by the fireplace and two dim lamps. She had on a jacket and had tossed an afghan over her knees, but she couldn't stop shivering. Crossing her arms at her midriff, she sat forward, seeking more of the fire's warmth.

Why didn't Jonas come inside?

After settling her here, he had taken the dog to investigate the rustling they had heard in the bushes out front. At first Elizabeth had been glad to be left alone. She needed time to compose herself. It wasn't every day that she threw herself into a man's arms as she'd done when Jonas hauled her inside. Not every day? She almost laughed out loud. She had never done that in her life. And she didn't want to think about how nice it had felt to be held by Jonas. How warm and comforting. How safe.

But he was gone now. He'd been gone for a long time.

Shivering again, she directed a nervous look toward the darkened hallway just beyond the open door to the right. Dear God, why had that phone call unnerved her so? This wasn't the first time she had been warned off a story with threats. She'd been in worse danger, as well—much worse. Maybe the difference was that she wasn't in Denver. She wasn't surrounded by familiar people and places. The few times she had been frightened before, Ted had been only a phone call away. But Ted had cut her loose.

A lump rose in her throat as she considered how alone she was. Ted wouldn't hesitate to help her if she were really in trouble, but after the conversation they'd had this morning, she would have to be in the midst of a crisis before she would call him. She was alone in this town. Alone with a man whom she was certain was hiding something.

And where was he?

The house was very quiet. Elizabeth could hear the wind sighing through the trees outside. She could hear ... something more. Glancing at the curtains drawn across the broad window to her left, she went very still, straining to catch that miniscule sound once more. There it was. *Scrape, scrape.*

"Elizabeth?"

Jumping, but suppressing the cry that rose in her throat, she jerked around. Jonas stood in the doorway, his dog and cat positioned at his sides.

"I'm sorry," he said.

"I heard something outside." She held up a hand for quiet, listening until she heard it again.

Jonas crossed in front of the fire. "There's a tree limb that needs to be cut just to the side of this window."

"Oh." Elizabeth sagged back against the leather cushions, feeling foolishly relieved.

"You warm enough?"

She suddenly realized how she must look, huddling beneath this afghan like some eighteenth-century woman with the vapors. This wasn't her normal mode of operation. She should have been outside with him instead of hiding here in the house. Throwing off the cover, she stood. "What'd you find outside?"

With a chuckle, Jonas bent to stroke the Siamese cat, which was rubbing its face against his blue jeans. "I think Poe escaped when I opened the front door. He was in the bushes when Raven and I went outside to check. That's probably what we heard. We looked around just in case, but didn't find anything unusual." The dog flopped on the rug by the fire, accepted a stroke or two and promptly closed her eyes.

Elizabeth nodded. "The cat sounds like a reasonable explanation for the noise." She paused, then added, "I guess."

He straightened, scowling. "What else do you think it could be?"

"Probably nothing. I just got spooked, that's all."

"You don't think you were followed over here, do you?"

"I didn't see a single car on the road."

"Just a quiet night in Whitehorn."

"Yes," she agreed. But she shivered once more when she thought of the voice on the phone.

"What is it?"

"I wish I could have recorded that call. The voice was eerie. And sort of familiar."

"I thought you said it was electronically altered."

"That's how it sounded. Like one of those voices they distort when someone's identity is being protected on television."

"Then how could it be familiar?"

"Just . . ." She rubbed a hand across her forehead, trying to recall exactly what she had recognized in the voice. "It was the diction, maybe. I remember thinking how very properly this person spoke."

"And that made you think of me?"

She wanted to laugh. His one, clipped, distinctly spoken question illustrated why she might be forgiven for thinking the voice on the phone belonged to him. From the very beginning, she had noticed how he spoke, how he pronounced the syllables of her name, never slurring, with only that hint of a drawl to give any indication of a regional accent. A hint that had not led her to any conclusions yet.

Jonas was shaking his head. "I think you just immediately assumed the caller was me."

"But I really didn't. Even though your diction is superb."

He looked puzzled. "But if you didn't think it was me, why charge over here and accuse me?"

Hesitating beneath his intense regard, she moved close to the fire again. She didn't want to admit she had run to his house because she didn't want to be alone. It had certainly crossed her mind that the caller might have been Jonas, but her accusations had been halfhearted. That call just wasn't his style. Or was it? She bit her lip, wondering how she had arrived at that judgment. She didn't know him well enough to recognize his style.

"Elizabeth?" he prompted.

She glanced at him over her shoulder, considered confessing just how frightened the phone call had left her, then thought better of it. The way she'd clung to him earlier made her seem weak enough. "You're right," she fibbed. "I did immediately assume it was you who called."

"But it wasn't."

"I know."

"And why do you believe that?"

The softly spoken question made her turn to face him. She studied him for a moment. As always, he struck her as an impressively masculine figure. Tall and lean. Dark. With a face whose lines hinted at suffering. This was a man with a past she would like to unravel. Only she didn't believe her discoveries would be much of a surprise. She doubted that whatever he was hiding would prove he was anything other than decent at heart. It was just a hunch she had. And despite having met him only the day before yesterday, she was following her instinct.

"You didn't call," she told him. "You wouldn't do that."

He didn't press her for a deeper explanation of her trust. Instead, he got a brandy snifter from the dim recesses of the kitchen, splashed a sip or two from the bottle beside his chair and held out the glass to her.

"All right," he said, taking up his own snifter. "Since we both know I didn't call, we're left with a mystery."

She grinned at him over the rim of the glass. "A mystery? In this town?"

He tossed back a swallow of brandy. "I hate admitting you're right, but..."

"I take it you've deduced that something weird might be going on around here."

"Let's say I'm intrigued by a series of odd but probably unrelated events."

She wasn't impressed by that admission. "That's exactly what you said yesterday. That's not progress."

"If you want me to believe any of this is tied together, then give me some proof. After you left the other day, I tried piecing the events together and came up empty."

"Yes...proof." Elizabeth finished her brandy and sighed. "Proof of a connection is what I don't have yet. But I have to be on to something, or else why would I get the phone call?"

"Maybe you just pissed a lot of people off today."

"You mean Melissa North and Moriah Hunter?"

"And the Rawlings, too."

"None of them are the type to make threatening phone calls."

Jonas agreed. "Who else did you see today?"

"I was all over town. I went to the newspaper. Mr. Greenbaum said he'd heard I was asking a lot of questions. I also talked to Sheriff Hensley, and his wife, too. She was in his office with their little girl."

"She's the forensic anthropologist who identified Charlie Avery's remains, isn't she?"

Elizabeth set her snifter on the table between the two chairs. "Her name's Tracy. Since she identified those remains and remarried her ex-husband, she's been working strictly as a consultant to the FBI. She's also writing a book with her father. She told me he's a historian with a special interest in the pioneers and folklore of this area of the country."

"Sounds like you got plenty of information from her."

"Oh, the sheriff and Mrs. Hensley were eager to talk about most everything except who might have killed Charlie Avery nearly thirty years ago."

"The D.A. tried to convict some local rancher."

"Tried and failed," Elizabeth pointed out. "And now the sheriff and his wife don't want to talk to me about it."

"But I hardly think either of them would call you up anonymously and try to scare you out of town. If Judd Hensley wanted you gone, he'd tell you outright."

"And wouldn't that make a nice little story—tampering with freedom of the press."

Jonas swore and drained his glass.

"What?" Elizabeth asked, puzzled by his reaction.

"Do you see everything in terms of a story?"

The question stung. Ted had asked her the same thing. Maybe it was time she paused to listen to everything people were saying to her. Avoiding Jonas's gaze, she sat down in the chair she had vacated earlier and took a deep breath. "I'm sorry," she offered at last. "Of course everything isn't a story. It's just that my work is so important to me."

"Maybe too important?"

His challenging tone made her glance up, then down to the fingers she had laced together in her lap. "Maybe," she admitted.

"Take it from me, that's not a very healthy way to live."

"I know, I know," she said wearily. "But journalism is all I've cared about since I was sixteen."

"That's young to decide what you're going to do with your life."

"But when you're sure..."

"Yes," Jonas concurred. "When you're sure."

The pensive note in his voice drew Elizabeth's gaze back to him. He was half turned away from her, his eyes focused on the fire. Something in the set of his jaw, the line of his mouth, was so sad. She watched him for a moment. The light from the flames played across his features, burnished him in gold. Standing there, unmoving, he looked like a statue. The very picture of a lonely man.

Elizabeth was reluctant to say anything, lest it be construed as a probing, reporter's question. But quite apart from any role he might play in any story, he intrigued her on a much deeper level. So she screwed up her courage and dared a personal question. "How about you? Did you always want to write fiction?"

He looked as if his thoughts had been miles and miles away. "Pardon me?"

She repeated her question. "You sounded as if you understood when I said I always wanted to be a reporter."

"I do understand," he said slowly. "I did know at a pretty young age that I wanted to be creative."

"A creative writer?"

"Just creative." His smile was evasive as his words. "I just wanted something more than Texas dust—"

"Texas?" Elizabeth exclaimed, straightening up. "That's where you get that little drawl you have at the end of your words."

He looked dismayed. "Did I say Texas?"

She couldn't resist a triumphant smile. "You slipped."

"But I don't have a drawl."

"Oh, you've almost lost it," she assured him. "Most people probably wouldn't pick up on it, if you're worried about giving yourself away."

"You wouldn't have guessed if I hadn't said the state."

"I'd have gotten it eventually. I lived with a fellow reporter who was born and raised in Abilene." She pronounced the city's name with the broad twang she had learned from her roommate.

"Did he sound like me?"

"*She* hadn't worked quite so hard to lose her accent," Elizabeth replied. "Not like you."

"It wasn't that difficult."

"Why? Weren't you a native Texan?"

He merely smiled, which didn't surprise her.

But Elizabeth used his slipup to press on. "I bet you grew up someplace small."

"I bet you did, too."

That surprised her. "You're right. In a little wide place in the road in eastern Colorado."

"Over near Kansas?"

"Almost on the border. What gave me away as a small-town girl?"

"You seem to have an understanding, if not a respect, for small towns."

"I couldn't wait to get out of there."

He leaned one shoulder against the edge of the mantel. "Was it so horrible?"

"Suffocating. I was so bored the summer I turned sixteen that I went down and volunteered at the local weekly newspaper. The smell of newsprint hooked me the first day. Within a year, I was stringing for the *Free Press*." She paused. "You know what stringing is, don't you?"

"You covered local events for them, right?"

"And I loved it. After high school, I packed my bags and headed for Denver."

"And your parents just let you go?"

Elizabeth's chest tightened the way it always did when she thought of the people she had called mother and father. "I didn't give them a vote on my future," she answered shortly.

He didn't ask for details, but she caught the speculation in his gaze and forced herself to shake off the old, ugly memories. "It looks like we have a few things in common," she continued. "Small towns—"

"I didn't say that's where I grew up."

"But I'm certain all the same," she replied with cocky assurance. "And you set your sights on a goal at a young age, just like I did. I'll bet you were shaking Texas dirt off your boots when you were just a kid. Don't you think knowing what you want makes your life easier in some respects?"

"Being so goal-directed can be a misery, too."

"Especially if you don't achieve your goals."

He gave a nod of agreement.

Elizabeth used that as another opening. "Is that what's wrong with you, Jonas? Haven't you achieved your goals?"

His look at her was long and level. "Who said anything's wrong with me?"

"You don't seem happy."

That made him laugh, but there was little mirth in the sound. "If I may say so, and I think I will, neither do you."

She pursed her lips, then muttered, "Touché."

They remained as they were, each studying the other, until she ended the stalemate. Dragging a hand through her wind-tousled hair, she sagged back in the chair. "You know something? I don't want to get into it with you again."

Jonas set his snifter on the mantel. "Backing down from a challenge? That's unusual for you."

"I guess I'm tired."

"You want me to take you back to the boarding-house?"

"I'm not afraid to drive myself," Elizabeth replied, but made no move to stir from her chair. "I just wish I had a clue who made that call."

"Well, who else did you see today?"

"All those ladies at the library." She began ticking off names with her fingers. "Mary Jo Kincaid, Lily Mae Wheeler—"

Jonas groaned, cutting her off. "The library broadens the field of suspects tenfold."

"It's difficult for me to imagine anyone at that tea party threatening me."

He rubbed a hand along his jaw. "But I imagine at least half of those women told someone about us interrupting their meeting. By now you're probably a household name around town."

"Thanks to you."

"Me? You're the one who chased me in there and started yelling in the middle of the library."

"And you're the one who kissed me."

Her words brought the memory to vivid life for Jonas. Not that it had been dormant. He'd been thinking of that kiss before she'd showed up on his doorstep. He'd thought of it when he'd pulled her into his arms. He'd been trying to force it out of his head as they had talked here in front of the fire. She was so lovely, so vibrantly alive. She made him realize how cold and dead his life was. Not reaching out to her had required a supreme effort. But he'd succeeded. Until now.

Now that she had brought this afternoon's brief, but potent kiss into the open, he couldn't avoid the thoughts at all. He kept feeling her lips, kept experiencing that strange jolt that had pumped through him. After not kissing, not holding anyone for so long, maybe his reaction wasn't unusual. And maybe his reaction was so strong because she was who she was. Elizabeth.

"Why did you kiss me?" she asked, in exactly the blunt fashion he might have expected from her.

He latched on to the first explanation that came to mind. "I decided to give Lily Mae a thrill."

"I'm sure she enjoyed it."

"And did you?" The moment the question was out, Jonas would have given his true identity to take it back.

Elizabeth's eyes widened. In a nervous motion, she ran her hands down her denim-clad thighs.

"I'm sorry," Jonas said quickly, forestalling any comment from her. "That was a dumb question. The kiss was dumb, too. Impulsive and dumb. I apologize."

She hesitated, then managed a weak smile. "I guess Lily Mae and the others really have spread it all over town by now. The elusive Mr. Bishop and the big-city reporter."

"Your car parked out front will add fuel to the blaze."

"If anyone sees it."

"Someone will. Someone always sees everything in a small town."

"Makes me wonder why a man like you would choose this town as his home. You stick out here, you know. You're not a cowboy."

"Not everyone in town is."

"But most of them fit in." She paused, cocking her head to the side as she looked at him. A shining tendril of blond hair fell across her cheek. She hooked it behind her ear and knit her brow as if she were concentrating. "I'm trying to decide just where you would fit in. New York, I think. Or Seattle, maybe. I hear it's a happening place these days."

All Jonas could think was that he'd like to put his hands through her hair, pull her face close to his and kiss away the concerned little line between her eyebrows. If she weren't who she was, he thought he might do just that.

"Or how about L.A.?" she suggested.

The mention of that city blew some of the romantic cobwebs from his brain. "Elizabeth, I live here, okay?"

But she wasn't ready to drop it. "What it is they say? To avoid being found, hide in plain sight." She stood, holding up a hand to stop the next protest he began. "Okay, okay, I'm not saying another word."

"Good."

"I should go."

He should want her out of here, but he didn't. *God help him, he was being foolish.* Clearing his throat, he said, "You think you'll be okay at the boardinghouse?"

Again she looked at him, her brown-eyed gaze searching his face. He wondered what she was looking for, what she saw, what she might guess of the direction of his thoughts. There was an odd tension in the air between them. It was so real, he thought he might be able to touch it.

He watched Elizabeth bite one corner of her mouth and hesitate. When she spoke, her voice was soft, tentative. "What's the alternative to the boardinghouse?"

Jonas's mouth went dry. He didn't know what to say or do. Was this an invitation? God, how the old crowd would laugh at him. Aeons ago, he would have assumed she was asking to spend the night with him. It would have required no thought at all to accept, to reach out, take her hand, draw her close....

But aeons *had* passed. He wasn't the man he had been. And having her here was impossible. Getting close to anyone was something he had sworn not to do. So he looked away and said, "There are some motels just outside of town, near I-90. You could move—"

"Yes, well, that won't..." Color bloomed in Elizabeth's cheeks as she turned toward the doorway. "That won't be necessary."

Feeling as awkward as she looked, Jonas followed her into the hall. "I could drive out with you, make sure you were okay—"

"I'll be fine where I am," she mumbled.

He took hold of her arm. "Elizabeth, please . . ."

She pulled away and headed for the door. Even in the dim light, Jonas could see how straight her shoulders were, how her hands were fisted at her sides. He realized he didn't want her to leave this way. Not angry or hurt. He didn't want her to leave at all.

He caught up to her just as she touched the doorknob. He settled his hands on her shoulders, and she went very still. But she didn't resist. He moved closer and pressed his face to her hair, breathing in the delicate, feminine fragrance he had first noticed the night they'd met. An expensive scent. He knew because once upon a time he had made it his business to know about the finest of material possessions.

Releasing her breath in a long sigh, she leaned back against him. She lifted a hand to where his rested on her shoulder. She turned her head, and her mouth was temptingly close. But Jonas hesitated to claim it. Could she hear his heart drumming? Did she sense how long it had been since he had felt this way? She was so near. So soft. Her body so slender against his own. His own body was reacting exactly as it should. Tensing. Hardening. After his years of working to shut these reactions down, nature was taking over without missing a beat.

"You could stay," he whispered. "You could stay here with me tonight, Elizabeth."

Instead of replying, she turned in his arms, caught his lips with her own.

And the kiss went wild right from the start. Fast. Furious. Absorbing. Kissing Elizabeth was like a leap down a mountainside, something Jonas had done many times. He knew the sensations. The way the plunge took his breath. Scared the hell out of him. Made him want to keep going, on and on, down an endless trail of slick, white speed. Once he had lived for thrills like this.

But had anything he'd done ever felt this good, this free?

And was this ride worth the risk?

The answers to those questions seemed unimportant as Elizabeth's mouth opened beneath his, as her arms twined around him. He pressed her back against the door, lifted his hands to her soft, honey hair. One of her legs snaked between his own, pressed upward just slightly, just enough to increase the pressure in the one part of his anatomy that didn't need the encouragement. Suddenly Jonas understood how a prisoner felt when the gates swung open to let him out.

"Stay," he murmured, reluctantly breaking the kiss.

"This is crazy." Eyes closed, she turned her face to the side.

Taking her chin in his hand, he made her look at him. "This has been inevitable since the minute we saw each other."

"I don't believe in inevitabilities. Everyone has a free will, a choice."

"Then let's choose this." Once more he kissed her. Deeply. Then softly. Then furiously again.

She kept pace. Meeting each caress with an abandon that matched his own growing arousal. His hands went to her waist, then up to her breasts. Through her thin cotton sweater and bra, he felt her nipples harden. His fingers circled and stroked, while her breath grew ragged. She moaned when he kissed her neck, murmured his name when he pushed her tweed jacket off one shoulder.

But as quickly as the slide into passion had begun, she stopped it. She went suddenly still in his arms, protesting, resisting when just seconds before she had been responding.

Caught off-balance, Jonas stepped back. "What's wrong?"

"This." Not looking at him, she straightened her jacket and shoved a hand through her hair. Once more, she turned her back to him. "This is nuts. I can't do it." She reached for the doorknob.

But Jonas closed his hand over hers. "What are you doing?"

"I have to go."

"After this?"

"We're acting like fools. We don't even know each other."

"So?"

She twisted round to face him, eyes flashing. "So that's not how I am."

"It's not how I am, either."

"Yeah, right," she muttered. "You seemed pretty practiced to me."

"Practiced? Dear God, Elizabeth, if you knew how long..." Jonas bit off the words and stepped back, sighing. What did it matter how long it had been since he'd been with a woman? What mattered was that she had come to her senses. Just in time, too. For in the heat of the moment, he had forgotten how dangerous she was. He had forgotten everything but the thrill. His gut clenched as he realized how easily he had lost control.

With her hands folded in front of her like a child awaiting punishment, Elizabeth said, "I'm sorry, Jonas."

He nodded, trying not to be curt. "So am I."

"I know I started this," she said. "I gave you the wrong signals. I don't know why I—"

"It doesn't matter."

"Yes, it does. I'm not like this. I've never been like this—"

"Just hush." He took hold of her hand and pressed it between his own. "Just hush and go home. I'm not blaming you for any of this."

"But I feel so ashamed—"

"Go, Elizabeth. Now."

Something in his voice or his expression must have convinced her. She left without another word, went out the door and across the porch, disappearing into the darkness beyond the reach of the lights. Jonas followed her down the walkway, saw her get safely into her car and drive away.

Then he stood there, once more behind his own prison gate, until her taillights faded from view.

At the boardinghouse, Elizabeth turned the lock on her door and made a quick survey of the room. It was just as she had left it. One lamp burned beside the polished brass bed. The lilac-sprigged comforter was rumpled where she had been stretched out when the phone rang. The nightshirt she had been wearing was draped over a chair. A half eaten apple rested on the bedside table. Nothing was changed. Except for her. She didn't feel anything like the woman who had dashed out of here just hours before.

With her back pressed to the door, she replayed those final moments with Jonas. When he'd asked if she felt safe coming back here, why had she asked if there was an alternative? What in God's name had she been expecting?

Exactly what I got.

That answer made her grow warm all over. Because it was true. Standing there in Jonas Bishop's kitchen, in front of his warm and cozy fire, she hadn't wanted to leave. She had wanted to step into his arms. She had wanted to know if the afternoon's hard, fast kiss could be improved upon.

So now she knew. She really, really knew.

It would be easy to stand here, reliving the kisses, the touches and the sighs, to speculate on what might have come next. But the whole incident was too mortifying to continue to contemplate. It wasn't like her to have done any of those things.

For thirty-three years, she had lived her life by a certain code, a rigid set of rules. She was a methodical person, an investigative reporter capable of sifting through hundreds of facts to arrive at a logical conclusion. Though she might think quickly on her feet, her actions were always prompted by shrewd judgment. That orderly nature applied to more than her work. She had been raised to think things through, to be sensible, responsible. She wasn't the sort of woman who fell into quick couplings with strange men. Her parents had been very careful to squash her urge to be reckless. She was definitely not impulsive.

Or was she?

Elizabeth closed her eyes and considered her actions over the past few days.

She had used the town gossip's word to jump on the possibility of a story.

She had chased Jonas down the street today, made a scene in the library.

She had raced over to his place after tonight's phone call.

She had thrown herself into his arms.

She had very nearly made love with him, right there in his hall, up against his front door.

And those impulsive acts were only what she had done since arriving in Whitehorn. What about back in Denver? That story she had been working on before Ted lowered the boom on her—what was that if not pure impulse? If she were honest, she'd have to admit she'd been jumping from one thing to another for quite some time.

So maybe Ted had been right to send her away. Maybe she was coming apart at the seams, losing her touch. Maybe she did need to get a life.

Shoulders drooping, Elizabeth kicked off her shoes and headed for the bathroom. As she hung her tweed jacket on a hook beside the door, she was suddenly homesick. But not for her half furnished apartment. This room was more homey than that. No, what she longed for was her tiny, cluttered cubicle at the newspaper office.

"But that's what's wrong with you," she told her reflection in the bathroom mirror. "You don't have a life apart from that paper."

It was true. Her few friends were all co-workers. There hadn't been a man in her life since a disastrous affair with a source for a story several years ago. There was no balance in her life. Certainly no excitement.

Until tonight.

The memory of kissing Jonas ran through her head like a coming-attraction trailer for a movie.

Groaning, she pushed those thoughts aside, scrubbed her face, brushed her teeth and gave herself a lecture. Instead of throwing herself at an impossible, unsuitable man, she should go on a cruise, lie in the sun and drink margaritas. When she got back to Denver, she would be tanned, relaxed, ready to make a new beginning. She could let herself be fixed up with all the brothers, friends of friends, nephews, cousins and next-door neighbors that everyone was always trying to foist onto her. She could break out of this rut she was in.

The first thing she needed to do was forget this story. She knew she would always believe there was a mystery to be solved here in Whitehorn, but she wasn't the one who would do it. She would tear up her notes, expunge her computer files and leave town in the morning. Filled with determination, she flipped off the bathroom light, marched into the bedroom toward the desk, where she had left her things when she'd come in after dinner. She had been too tired to work...

So why was the computer on?

Elizabeth stared at the glowing blue screen, which she hadn't noticed when she came in a few minutes ago. She hadn't switched it on tonight. She turned slowly, looking into every corner of the room. Nothing was different from the way she had left it, except for the computer. And she couldn't have left it this way. She distinctly remembered just setting it here on the desk. After she had gotten undressed, she had picked up her notepad . . .

Her notepad. It wasn't on the bed where she'd left it.

She knew it had been there. She'd been flipping through the notes she had taken today when the phone had rung. Out of habit, she had written down what the caller had said. Then she had dressed in a hurry, grabbed her car keys and headed downstairs. She hadn't had the notepad with her. She knew because she had almost come back for it, but then reconsidered, anxious to get over to Jonas's house.

And now the notepad was gone.

Quickly, telling herself it had to be here, she looked under and around the bed, in her purse and throughout the rest of the room. The search was futile. She shivered, going cold at the realization that someone had been in this room while she was gone.

After retracing her steps to the desk, Elizabeth shivered again, as if touched by a cold breeze. Then she realized there *was* a cold breeze. The curtains at the side window were belling outward. Not really blowing in the wind, just moving ever so slightly. She pushed them aside and found the window open about half a foot. But she hadn't opened the window. It had been closed when she'd drawn these curtains earlier.

She stared at the gently moving white fabric for a long moment. She tried to believe that she might have opened that window and forgotten it. But she knew she hadn't, the same way she knew she hadn't turned on the computer or lost her notepad. Because for all the impulsiveness that had seized her recently, she was still orderly, methodical and organized.

Backing away from the window, Elizabeth reached for the phone and punched in the extension of the couple who owned the boardinghouse.

"I'm sorry," she said, when a sleepy voice answered. "I know it's late, but I wanted to tell you that I'm calling the police. Someone's been in my room."

Later, as she waited downstairs, Elizabeth was struck by several thoughts.

One, that she wouldn't be leaving in the morning, after all.

Two, that she couldn't wait to tell Jonas.

And three, that staying in Whitehorn and seeing Jonas again held infinitely more appeal than any cruise or any romance with anyone's brother, cousin or nephew.

Elizabeth thought how disappointed the Reverend and Mrs. Monroe would be to find out what a wide and wild impulsive streak had survived their very careful raising of her. Then she grinned. Perhaps it served them right.

Six

Jonas gave Elizabeth a puzzled look. "Tell me why anyone would steal your notes and hightail it out a window."

"You're the mystery writer. You tell me."

Because he had no ready answer, he concentrated on filling her mug with coffee. They were in his kitchen, standing at the island in the center of the room. Morning sunshine streamed through the windows over the sink. In the bright, flaw-revealing light, Elizabeth looked fresh and pretty, with a careless, girl-next-door beauty. Jonas had known women who paid extravagant sums to spas and surgeons to achieve her natural glow. But no chemical peel, nip-and-tuck job or cosmetics could duplicate her sparkling eyes, clear skin or honeyed-silk hair. Looking at her now, Jonas kept remembering how soft her skin had been, how the tendrils of her hair had filtered through his fingers last night....

"Jonas?"

He realized Elizabeth had said something to him. "Sorry," he murmured, setting down the thermal coffee carafe. "My brain doesn't always function this early in the morning."

She picked up her mug. "I would have called if your number were listed."

"No problem. Although I am a little surprised to see you." Astounded was a more correct term. After the way they had parted last night, Elizabeth was the last person he had expected to see at eight-thirty this morning. "I was barely up when you rang the doorbell."

"Yes, I can see...." She darted a look at him, colored slightly and turned away, gulping her coffee.

Jonas glanced down, too, and realized he hadn't yet bothered to button his shirt. He'd just gotten out of the shower when the doorbell rang. Thinking it was a delivery service with a package he had been expecting from his literary agent, he rubbed a hasty towel through his hair, pulled on some jeans and this shirt and hurried downstairs, with Poe and Raven at his heels. But instead of a man with a box of books, Elizabeth had been on the porch, holding a bag of doughnuts and announcing that someone had broken into her room at the boardinghouse.

Shutting the door in her face would have been the safest route for Jonas to take. But what had he done? Welcomed her in, of course.

He had sent the animals out for their morning romp in the yard, made coffee, and now he and Elizabeth stood, avoiding looking at each other. Like him, she was undoubtedly trying not to remember what had occurred between them last night, trying to ignore the zing of attraction in the air. Which might be easier if he were fully dressed. With a furtive glance at her averted profile, Jonas buttoned his shirt.

Perching on one of the stools drawn up to the island, he brought the conversation back to the disappearance of her notepad. "Tell me again what the police said."

She sniffed. "The police keep suggesting that *I* turned on the computer, lost my notes and left the window open."

Jonas paused, wondering if they were right.

Elizabeth set her mug down with a little bang, splashing coffee on the counter. "Don't you dare look at me that way. My notes are gone and the last place I had them was in that room. And besides that, the police can't explain the broken trellis."

"What broken trellis?"

"The one on the side of the boardinghouse," she re-torted. "Beneath the window I found open, there's a roof. It covers an addition that juts out to the side of the house. Down the side of that addition is a trellis that's been half pulled off the wall."

"So?"

"So the owners say it wasn't that way yesterday after-noon."

"Are they sure?"

She glared at him. "You sound just like the police."

"Policemen and mystery writers are paid skeptics."

"Well, the owners *insist* the trellis was just fine when they were working in their flower garden late yesterday afternoon. So there."

"Again, I repeat, so what?"

"Don't you see? Someone got into my room and crawled out over the roof and down the trellis. Maybe they were in the room when I came home, heard me fitting my key in the lock and had to leave in a hurry."

Jonas frowned. What she hypothesized could have happened, although he thought it sounded like an incred-ibly inept burglar. "Why wouldn't whoever was in the room just take the computer?"

"Maybe they planned to, and it was too awkward to handle while climbing across a roof."

"Then why turn it on at all?"

"I don't know," she said impatiently. "But that's how I found it."

"Hmm." He rubbed his chin, trying to picture the sce-nario she was suggesting. There were pieces that just didn't fit.

But Elizabeth seemed to have it all figured out. "Who-ever called me obviously saw me leave and broke into the room."

"But how would they know you'd leave after they called?"

She frowned. "That is kind of strange, isn't it?"

"And how'd they get into the house? Up the trellis and over the roof? How would they know which window was yours?"

"That wouldn't be too hard, since I'm the only current guest of the Amity Boardinghouse. But as for getting in, Max Perkins, the man who owns the house, went out for a run about nine, which is just about the time I got over here to your house. He says he left a side door open."

"He runs every night," Jonas remarked.

"How do you know?"

"I've seen him lots of times over the past few years since he and his wife bought the boardinghouse. He runs in the morning, too, the same as I do sometimes. He's training for a marathon, and we've talked on occasion."

Eyes growing wide, Elizabeth picked up her mug again. "Probably most people in town have seen him."

"And what does that prove?"

"That anyone wanting into the house might suspect there'd be a door open."

With a short laugh, Jonas said, "Your overactive imagination is showing on that one, my dear."

"Okay, okay." Taking a seat on the stool beside his, she settled one arm on the counter and stared off into the distance. "Let's forget that for a moment. But let's remember that a side door *was* unlocked. Mr. Perkins says he leaves it open every night and never had a reason to worry about it before this."

"What about Mrs. Perkins? Where was she while he was running?"

"In the kitchen at the back of the house, making some phone calls."

Jonas snapped his fingers. "Wait a minute. Any call to you was routed through her, right?"

"I already know what you're thinking," Elizabeth said. "She doesn't remember if it was a man or a woman who called for me last night. She thinks it might have been a man, but she's not sure."

"If you're the only guest, how could she *not* remember?"

"She's in charge of some booth for that Pioneer Days festival the town is planning. She told the detective who stopped by this morning that she probably made or received two-dozen phone calls last night, and she honestly can't be sure about who called me." Glumly, she took a sip of coffee. "I wish I'd asked her about it right after the call came in."

"The voice was probably disguised, anyway."

Nodding, Elizabeth opened the bag she had brought with her and selected a chocolate-iced doughnut. "Of course the voice was disguised. Whoever called doesn't want me to know who they are. Because they hold the key to the whole weird chain of events in this town."

He pulled out a doughnut as well. "You're assuming a lot of things. What did the police say about your phone call?"

Elizabeth polished off the pastry in a few bites, then unceremoniously licked icing off her fingers, looking disgruntled. "Police Detective Clint Calloway admits that call must have been upsetting for a *little lady like me*—those are his words, not mine—but he doubts the call has anything to do with my missing notes or my computer being on or the window being open. Aside from that trellis, he doesn't think there's reason to believe anyone was in my room other than me."

"It doesn't sound as if the two of you hit it off too well."

"I think he's a big, chauvinistic he-man with an excess of machismo. Calloway is under the delusion that this is still the wild, wild West, where women are delicate but simple-minded flowers who must be humored and protected."

Her outraged expression made Jonas laugh, though he felt compelled to defend Calloway. "Despite the trappings of civilization, it is still a hard land."

"But it's also the twentieth century. Someone ought to let Calloway in on that secret."

"At least you didn't have to deal with Officer Rawlings. After yesterday, he might not have been as kind as Calloway."

"Oh, he came by this morning, as well."

"So at least your call warranted two officers."

"I think Rafe came on his own. And he was actually very nice. I apologized to him for yesterday."

Jonas was surprised, especially since she had insisted she'd done nothing wrong where her dealings with Rawlings were concerned. "What'd Rafe say?"

"That he was sorry for getting angry yesterday, and that the mystery of his past was something he was still trying to deal with."

"Sounds like a good guy."

"And unlike Calloway and others in the town—" she shot Jonas a look "—I think Rafe Rawlings believes there's something weird afoot around here."

"Did he say that?"

"Not to me." Fidgeting slightly, she reached for another doughnut.

He regarded her with suspicion. "What'd you do, eavesdrop?"

"Well…" She tore the pastry in two, downed half of it, then looked up at him with a sheepish grin. "The two of them were talking out by their cars, and I just happened to be standing behind an arbor in the side garden—"

"And what did you just *happen* to hear?"

"Rafe was wondering why anyone would go to all this trouble to try and scare me away if there weren't something strange going on."

Jonas had to admit that question was weighing on his mind as well, though he couldn't imagine the answer.

"I'm going to get to the bottom of the mystery."

The quiet determination in Elizabeth's voice made him uneasy. "Wouldn't it be safer to just let it go, let the police deal with it?"

"I'm not afraid."

"You were last night."

She lifted her chin. "No, I wasn't."

He looked straight into her steady, brown eyes for several moments. "Why is it so hard to admit being frightened?"

"Because I'm not."

"No one would blame you for being uneasy after getting a weird phone call and having some stranger go through your room."

"I've been in scarier situations."

"Like what?"

"Like having a knife to my throat."

He did a double take. "What?"

She calmly reached for a third doughnut. "You heard me."

He regarded her in silence for a moment, not sure how to respond to her matter-of-fact revelation. "What happened?"

"I was doing a story on prison conditions about six years ago. I had an interview with a guy who was a prison activist—"

"A convict?"

"Twenty to life for murder."

"How'd you find this guy?"

She paused. "He was highly recommended and had been behaving like a model prisoner, had gotten a law degree, was working on his own appeal and doing some writing about ways to improve the system. We'd had several interviews in one of the conference rooms at the prison, and then one day..." She stopped and took a deep breath, her offhand facade slipping. "One day..."

Jonas reached out, touching her arm. "You don't have to tell me, Elizabeth. I know it has to be a disturbing memory."

"But I've told it a hundred times," she protested, straightening her shoulders. "The guy had made a crude knife. He pulled it out and managed to get it to my throat before the guard who was with us could react. He used me as a hostage, a bargaining chip to get out." She glanced down, her dark lashes shielding her eyes from Jonas's view.

He had a hard knot in his gut. A knife had been pressed to her slender, white neck, pressed to the throat he had kissed last night. He didn't like imagining what might have happened. "Did he get away?" he demanded hoarsely.

Elizabeth's gaze met his again, her eyes more black than brown as she shook her head. "A sniper took him out."

"While he was holding you?"

She nodded.

Shocked, Jonas combed his fingers through his damp hair, while his other hand tightened on Elizabeth's arm.

"You know what's the worst part?" she said slowly, as if measuring her words. "It was the way he used me. I trusted him, and he used me. Afterward, I was so stunned. I never saw his betrayal coming, and I should have."

Jonas wondered who else might have betrayed her. And there had been others. He knew that by the world-weary tone of her voice.

"Oh, darn," she muttered. "Would you look at this?" Slipping her arm from his grip, she opened her hand. She had flattened her doughnut, icing and all, in her fist, while she so calmly talked about near-death and betrayal.

"So you've told this story a hundred times?" he said.

She looked away. "Okay, so maybe it still bothers me a little."

Not commenting on her flagrant understatement, he retrieved a paper towel from the rack across the kitchen. Wordlessly, he stood by the island and watched her wipe the gooey mess from her palm.

"Do you see why I'm not scared now?" she asked. "What's a phone call or a burglary compared to that?"

Jonas just looked at her, not believing her bravado. He had no idea why she thought she had to put up such a front, but he wasn't going to debate the issue. "Since you're not backing down on what's going on here in town, I guess I'm going to have to help you."

She stiffened. "You don't have to. No."

"But if that's not what you want, why'd you come back here this morning?"

Instead of replying, she took another paper towel and used it to mop up the coffee she had splashed on the counter.

Jonas knew he shouldn't press her on the subject of last night. His life would be simpler if the kisses they'd shared faded to a dim memory. But something inside him, some gremlin of self-destruction, wouldn't let the matter go. "Why come here again, Elizabeth? It's not like we parted as friends."

That made her look up. "I told you I was sorry. I don't know why—"

"Yes, you do know," he retorted, suddenly impatient with her evasions. "When what went on between us last night happened because you wanted it to."

"That's not true. I just—"

He held up a hand to stop her protest. "Don't bother lying. You may be good at playing games in order to trick a source on a story, but your acting skills don't extend to the more intimate, interpersonal level. I know why we ended up the way we did last night. Because I wanted you, and you wanted me. That's all there is to it."

She slid off the stool, angrily reaching for the car keys she had flung on the counter. "You and I are strangers. You don't know me or what I want or what I think. One kiss—"

"Which was mind-blowing."

She glared at him, though her cheeks flushed scarlet. "One kiss does not make you an expert on any interpersonal interaction with me."

Tucking his hands in his back pockets, Jonas just looked at her and grinned. "First of all, there were several kisses, not just one—"

"That doesn't matter—"

"And second, there's not much room for deception in the kind of kissing you and I were doing." He paused, let his voice deepen. "You know what kind of kissing I mean. All hot and...wet. Remember?"

He could see that she did. Her eyes closed, and the muscles in her jaw clenched and unclenched before she looked at him again. She injected her voice with heavy sarcasm. "I suppose you can tell so much about a person from just a few kisses because you've had so much practice."

He let his grin spread into a wide smile. "Yeah. I have." *It wasn't really a lie. He'd done plenty of kissing up until nine years ago.*

With a sound of disgust, she turned on her heel. Jonas almost laughed out loud. He kind of enjoyed getting her so riled up. He struggled to keep his laughter under control as he asked, "Have you?"

She jerked around. "Have I what?"

"Done much kissing."

She blinked in surprise. "That's none of your business."

He shrugged. "Last night I kind of felt like you hadn't."

"*What?*"

He retreated a step in the face of her indignation. "It's not that I'm criticizing or complaining, of course."

"You've got a lot of damn nerve." She stalked away, toward the hall.

But Jonas followed, laughing. "Elizabeth, good God, I'm teasing you. Haven't you ever been teased?"

She wheeled to face him. "I don't think you're funny."

"What do they do to you reporters, anyway—make sure you trade in your sense of humor before they'll give you a byline?"

"Since you hate the press anyway, why do you care? And since you disapprove of so many things about me, including my profession, why did you kiss me in the first place?"

"Maybe I never met a reporter like you before."

"Maybe never one as determined as I am."

"Never one I wanted to make love with. At least as much as I want to make love to you."

Her mouth half-opened before her gaze fell beneath his. In the ensuing silence, she nervously jangled her keys.

Figuring he might as well go for broke, Jonas murmured, "What about you, Elizabeth? What do you want?"

She took a long time replying. "I intended to leave Whitehorn today."

"Because of what happened between us last night?"

Her hair swung forward on her cheeks as she nodded. "But then someone got in my room, and beyond that... Well..."

"Yeah?"

She looked at him again. "Beyond that, I just wanted to see you again. Sometime between last night and just now I realized that I really, really wanted to see you again."

"Because you want my help on this story?"

"No."

"Because you think I'm part of the mystery in town?"

A smile began to curve one edge of her mouth. "I'm not ruling out any possibilities, but that's not really why I wanted to see you."

Jonas thought he might explode if he didn't touch her soon, so he reached out and took her hand. Her fingers entwined quite naturally around his. "Tell me why."

"Because you're right," she whispered, stepping closer. "Because I liked what happened between us last night."

"Liked it?"

"Very much."

"And you want it to happen again?"

She hesitated only a moment. "I think so."

He kissed her then. Softly. Without last night's explosive power. Oddly enough, however, he found this kiss just as arousing. He suspected she felt the same way. When he pulled back, she stayed in his arms, and he could feel her heart racing, keeping time with his own.

"I still think this is crazy," she whispered against his chest.

"So do I." He caught her hand and brought it up to his lips. "But I can't seem to help myself."

He felt the quiver that ran through her body, so it was a shock when she stepped away and said, "I've got to go."

"Go?" he repeated.

"I've got an appointment with Lily Mae Wheeler."

Now it was his turn to be astonished.

"Don't look at me that way," she said defensively. "I realize she's a gossip, but she knows a little bit about everyone and everything in town."

He shook his head. "You shouldn't trust her."

"I won't. I'll just listen and maybe pick up a few things that we can use."

"*We* can use?"

"Aren't you going to help me figure out what's going on?"

"I'll help you, yes, though I'm still not completely convinced there's anything going on. Your caller and your prowler could be nothing more than an overzealous citizen who doesn't appreciate busybody reporters sticking their noses into things."

"Sounds like someone I know."

He gave her a slow grin. "As you said before, don't rule out any possibilities."

"I haven't," she retorted. "Maybe we can meet for dinner and I'll fill you in on what I come up with today."

Jonas thought of all the hours that stretched between now and dinnertime. Hours in which he could get his head on straight about this woman. It was too much time, he decided. Time enough for doubts to creep in. Instead, he suggested they meet after lunch and take a drive up to Laughing Horse Reservation. "Get yourself some hiking boots, and we'll go to the place where Charlie Avery's remains were found and maybe stop off where Homer met up with those aliens of his."

Instead of responding to his teasing tone, she hesitated. "Jonas, are you sure you want to help me? I mean, even if someone's just trying to scare me off because they're thinking I might be bad PR for the tourist trade, they went so far as breaking and entering last night."

"I've been in much scarier situations," he said, echoing her earlier words.

She lifted an eyebrow. "Like a knife to the throat?"

"Knives are not the only weapon with a thin, deadly edge."

Eyes narrowing, she cocked her head to the side. But instead of the questions she might have asked the day before yesterday, she held her counsel. They agreed to meet in front of the library downtown at one-thirty.

Then she left. Almost as quickly as last night.

Jonas went up to his study to work. But all he could hear was Elizabeth's laughter. All he could see was her smile.

The only words that came and went in his head were, *You're a fool.*

This whole reckless association was doomed. Maybe if they could keep it purely physical, he would burn her out of his system. But quick, easy sex wasn't Elizabeth's style, even though she was strongly attracted to him. Hell, it wasn't his style, either. Not anymore. He had left the world of short, intense liaisons behind in L.A. But any deeper relationship with Elizabeth would require an honesty he couldn't imagine.

Giving up on work, he succumbed to a masochistic urge that hadn't beckoned in years. He took a brass key from his desk and used it to open the bottom drawer of a filing cabinet tucked away in a corner. Inside were several fat files of press clippings bound with rubber bands.

His climb.

His fall.

His shame.

Other reporters had chronicled the story Elizabeth was itching to know. And what would she say if she saw these? What would she think if she read those words others had chosen to apply to him?

Ruthless.

Decadent.

Murderer.

If she read these, would she trust him? Would she understand? Would she take the time to hear the whole truth? The press had once tried and convicted him. Just because she had awakened a part of him that had been dead for so long, was that any reason to think she would look beyond the sensational and the tragic and see what had really happened on a long-ago spring night when his way of life was shattered?

He tortured himself by reading the vilest of the articles that had been written about him. He brooded over each word. He told himself he couldn't take a chance on Elizabeth finding out who he really was.

But at one-thirty, he pulled his black Jeep into a parking space at the Whitehorn library. His sensible side, cultivated since coming to Whitehorn, was telling him to make an excuse not to spend the afternoon with Elizabeth. The wilder part of him, tamed for so long, had some half formed notions about exploring something more personal than the site where Charlie Avery's remains had been found.

He sat, the two sides of him at war, until Elizabeth came running down the library steps.

In her trim blue jeans and plain white shirt, with hiking boots in one hand, a camera in the other, and her eyes brightened by the prospect of adventure, she looked so alive, so vibrant. And Jonas knew there wasn't an excuse, a risk or a consequence that could make him stay away from her. His wild side won.

He figured he was doomed. Or damned. Maybe both. And he just didn't care. For the first time in nine years, there was something more important than playing it safe.

Elizabeth sat quietly as Jonas headed west out of Whitehorn, toward the rugged mountains that rose against the blue sky of a perfect May afternoon. Not far beyond the city limits, he turned the Jeep north, on a road that wove in and out among the foothills and ran parallel to the snow-capped peaks. It wasn't the most direct route to their destination, he explained, but he thought she would enjoy the drive.

Glad that Jonas seemed as disinclined to talk as she, Elizabeth concentrated on the passing scenery. Stands of aspen and cottonwood were dressed in midspring green. Cattle grazed on verdant fields in the distance. Ranches flashed by, marked by gates emblazoned with names like

The Spinning Top or The Rusty C. Some half an hour out of town, a low stone wall appeared on their left.

"This is the Kincaid spread," Jonas said. He slowed the Jeep so that Elizabeth could survey the ornate iron gate and the elaborate flower beds that flanked the entrance. The house, which Elizabeth had on good authority from Lily Mae was a mansion, couldn't be glimpsed from the road.

Twisting around to take a long look at the place, Elizabeth found Jonas watching her. He quickly turned his attention back to the road, but she was left with an unsettled feeling. He looked so...uncertain.

Which was exactly how she felt. This morning, when she had admitted out loud and then demonstrated just how attractive she found him, she'd had immediate regrets. A few kisses might tell him a lot about her, but he remained an enigma, a man of mystery.

For the fifth or sixth time since this morning, she ran through the facts she had accumulated about him. He was wealthy, intelligent and sophisticated. He had came from a small town in Texas, wrote mysteries not found in the library or known to anyone else she had talked with, and he had lived here for almost nine years. That was it. Unless, of course, she added that he had a sexy intensity that was almost frightening in its powerful effect on her. There wasn't much to go on.

Her lack of knowledge about him had made her call the newspaper office in Denver just before noon. Elizabeth had spoken with Dawn, a full-time researcher who regularly used computer networks and everything else at her disposal to track down needles in haystacks.

Dawn hadn't wanted to talk to Elizabeth. She'd said everyone on staff was under strict orders from Ted not to give Elizabeth any assistance if she called in. Though Elizabeth had wheedled and cajoled Dawn to see if she could run down any information on a Jonas Bishop, the woman had been steadfast in her refusal. Elizabeth had given her all the pertinent details she knew about him, but Dawn had finally just hung up.

Elizabeth was planning to call her back on Monday morning. Unless, of course, she managed to find out what she wanted this weekend.

This weekend? Was she actually thinking of spending the entire weekend with him?

She risked a glance at Jonas's profile, only to meet his gaze again. She looked away, battling a grin and feeling like a kid playing peekaboo. Only she wasn't a kid. She was a woman driving off into unfamiliar, remote territory with a man she had known for only three days. Though she suspected Jonas was only dangerous in the most sensual aspect of the word, Elizabeth had made a point of telling Lily Mae where the two of them were headed for the afternoon. Which meant, of course, that everyone would soon know. So if Elizabeth turned up missing...

"Which is silly," she said aloud, to her own consternation.

"What's silly?" Jonas asked.

"Nothing."

But he didn't accept that. "Something Lily Mae told you?"

Elizabeth seized that excuse. "You're right. She was telling me about this local woman who's a psychic."

"Winona Cobbs?"

"You know her?"

"I know of her. She's kind of an eccentric figure around town, like Homer Gilmore."

"Lily Mae says this psychic had a vision that helped the authorities identify Charlie Avery's remains. The psychic saw a woman with two faces, two men fighting and a rock hitting."

"Hitting Charlie?"

"She had the vision before they found his skull, and they determined he'd been struck on the head."

"But they identified him through his dental records, not some psychic's visions."

"Yes, but the psychic seemed to be on the right track."

With a disbelieving grunt, Jonas said, "Maybe her vision was what they used to try and convict that rancher of Charlie's murder. I heard there wasn't much more evidence other than a long-ago feud between the two men."

Elizabeth reached into her purse and brought out a newly purchased notepad on which she had taken notes after talking to Lily Mae and going through some more back issues of the local newspaper. "There were hairs found with Charlie's skeleton that indicated a woman might have been involved in his murder."

"A crime of passion?" Jonas suggested with a wicked grin.

"Maybe." She flipped through her pages of notes. "Someone named Lexine Baxter was mentioned in court when they were talking about motives that rancher might have had to kill Charlie. Lily Mae told me that Charlie and this Lexine, who was only a teenager at the time, were lovers."

"Where was she when he disappeared?"

"As near as Lily Mae can remember, Lexine disappeared about that time, too. A distant relative filed a missing persons report, but nothing came of it. A lot of folks thought she and Charlie ran off together. Until his remains were found, of course."

Jonas raised an eyebrow. "Seems to me that Lexine is the person the police should be talking to about Charlie Avery's death."

"Apparently the trail on her is cold. She was traced to a city out East where she dropped out of sight a few years back."

"How do you know?"

She smiled and lapsed into sleazy-detective-film lingo, à la Humphrey Bogart. "I got the info on the qt from Rawlings, sweetheart."

"My, my," Jonas drawled, "you really were busy this morning. You and Rafe must be becoming good friends."

"He's definitely more receptive than any other lawman I've run into around here." Turning a few more pages of her notepad, Elizabeth frowned. "Something else occurred to me today while I was going through some records at the library."

"What's that?"

"Rafe was found in the woods as a baby right around the time that Charlie and this Lexine person vanished."

Jonas shot her a quick, startled glance. "Rafe wasn't found anywhere near Charlie's body, was he?"

"Quite a distance, from what he explained today."

"So he talked to you about it?"

"Yeah." Elizabeth stared down at her notes, but what she kept seeing was the bleak look in Rafe Rawlings's eyes when he had talked about wanting to solve the mystery of his birth. He'd said he'd had a good home growing up with his adoptive family, and he had a solid, loving marriage now. But he had questions that no one seemed able to help him answer. Elizabeth empathized with him; she understood what it was like to have a hole in your past.

"So is Rafe going to be one of the stories in your series on the town?"

"No."

Jonas looked surprised. "How come?"

"I just..." Elizabeth didn't want to tell Jonas that Rafe had gotten to her. She wasn't sure how to explain why she was leaving him out of any proposed series of stories without explaining her own background, something she had never shared with anyone since leaving home. She had tried for so long to be tough and unemotional when it came to her work. Obviously, she hadn't been altogether successful at that, but she didn't want to get into subject matter that was too personal.

She shrugged, deliberately downplaying her decision. "I decided Rafe's story wasn't important stacked up against all the unsolved murders there are around town."

"Nothing like dead bodies to up the circulation figures."

Elizabeth could have argued with him. Three days ago she would have been all too eager to challenge him to a First Amendment debate. But now she was strangely reluctant.

Why did she care what this stranger thought? The answer had to do with smoldering sexuality, arousing kisses and an appealing aura of mystery. But nothing in that answer did much to settle her nerves.

Before the silence between them could grow awkward, Jonas took a sharp left turn off the main highway onto a narrow county road. That soon disintegrated into a rutted dirt track.

Grabbing a handhold to keep from being jostled out of her seat, Elizabeth said, "Didn't the sign back on the highway say it was ten more miles, straight ahead, to the Laughing Horse Reservation?"

"I guess."

"And aren't we going to the reservation?"

He took his eyes off the road long enough to smile. "What's wrong? Feeling a little nervous about being in the middle of nowhere with me?"

That was exactly how she was feeling, but she hated that he knew it. She focused on the fast-narrowing trail in front of them. "When they make a movie about this, I hope they find someone with an off-center sense of humor to play you."

"And what's the requirement for the actress to be cast in your role?"

"Tolerance." At that moment the Jeep bumped into a particularly vicious pothole. Elizabeth bounced up and came down hard, wincing in pain.

"Maybe the actress could use a well-padded backside, as well," Jonas suggested with a laugh.

"It couldn't hurt." Elizabeth peered ahead to what seemed to be the end of the path. "Are we there yet?"

"This is just the beginning." Jonas applied the brakes. "From here we walk."

"You mean you can't drive to where the bones were found?"

"They were on sacred Cheyenne ground."

Dimly, Elizabeth remembered reading about that in some of the newspaper articles written about the bones' discovery and identification, but she didn't remember the significance. "Can we walk on sacred ground?"

"Of course we can. We're just not supposed to disturb the spirits."

"And how will we know if we're disturbing them?"

"Oh, we'll know," Jonas replied with a smile that did more to unnerve than reassure. Then he got out of the vehicle.

Glancing around at the dense spring growth of vegetation, at the newly leafed-out trees arching overhead, Elizabeth felt a tickle run up her spine. It was the feeling of being watched. She quickly scanned the area around the Jeep, but found no one looking at her but Jonas. Telling herself not to be silly, she changed into the heavy socks and hiking boots she had purchased in town. Jonas retrieved a lightweight backpack from behind his seat.

"I have just one question," Elizabeth said as he settled the pack in place. "Aside from the spirits, will any of the Cheyenne who are alive mind if we go up here?"

"That's why I'm taking us in the back way."

"And how did you discover this path?"

"Trial and error."

"Why were you looking?"

"First I was a little curious about those bones."

She shot him a triumphant smile. "Mmm-hmm, now the truth comes out. You've been intrigued by the things happening around here before I came along and started asking questions."

"Initially just curious about the bones," he insisted. "Then curiosity became research." Turning, he started down the path.

She hurried to catch up. "For one of your books?"

He hesitated only slightly before answering. "Sections of the latest book take place on a reservation."

"Sounds like a very different mystery novel." The rocky slope they were climbing forced her to fall behind him, but, hopeful of learning something more about him, she kept the conversation going. "Tell me about the story."

Drawing to a halt at the summit of the rise, he looked over his shoulder, his expression thoughtful.

"Oh, come on," she cajoled. "Tell me."

"It's about a murder, of course."

"Of an Indian?"

"Yes, a woman."

"How's she killed?"

"Someone takes her to sacred ground."

"And then what?"

Jonas put out his hand to help Elizabeth up beside him, then kept his fingers firmly clasped around hers. "Sure you want to know?"

"Of course."

"Okay." Again a disconcerting smile played about his lips. "Once the murderer has the victim where he wants her, he cuts out her heart."

Elizabeth gasped and jerked her hand away.

Chuckling, Jonas merely turned and continued down the path.

The path to sacred ground.

Seven

Several moments passed before Elizabeth recovered her poise. Fuming, she shouted at Jonas's fast-retreating back, "Very funny, Mr. Bishop."

"I was only telling you about the book, like you asked," he called in return.

"And childishly trying to rattle me."

He turned to face her, laughing. "Loosen up, Elizabeth. Have some fun, okay?"

"Your idea of fun leaves something to be desired."

"Oh, come on. Unless, of course, you really are rattled."

Muttering about juvenile males, she squared her shoulders. At the same time, she felt that funny tickle run up her spine again. She glanced behind them, but saw only the trees moving in the breeze.

"Aren't you coming?"

She started to tell Jonas about her uneasy feeling, then reconsidered. He would just think she was being a nervous female. With a toss of her head, she said, "I'm right on your heels."

It was slow going. They scrambled down a steep embankment, across a small stream and then over another rise. But after that, the path became smoother. At that point, Elizabeth caught up with Jonas, her earlier irritation nearly forgotten in her curiosity about their surroundings. "If this isn't the reservation, whose land are we on?"

"The Kincaids'."

"Aren't they the type to shoot trespassers?"

"They were, I guess, but the only Kincaid left is Mary Jo, and she's not the type to carry a gun."

"Is that so?"

Jonas pushed a low-hanging tree limb out of their way and asked, "Don't you agree?"

Elizabeth shrugged. "From everything I've heard that's happened to Mary Jo Kincaid since she came to Whitehorn, I suspect she's a stronger person than she appears."

"Or maybe just a naive, simple woman."

"I don't know," Elizabeth insisted. "First there's Baby Jennifer dumped on her doorstep just before the wedding. Lily Mae said there was talk that Jennifer was Mary Jo's husband's child."

"True."

"Then an uninvited guest turns up dead at the wedding reception."

"The police still don't know why he was there, do they?" Jonas rubbed his chin. "There's really too much unconnected stuff, isn't there? It makes you think there must be a pattern somewhere."

Elizabeth patted him on the back. "Now you're beginning to see it my way."

He groaned. "What a terrible thought."

Ignoring him, Elizabeth continued her recitation of the perils of Mary Jo Kincaid. "It wasn't too long after the wedding that Mary Jo's father-in-law died. And I understand her husband wasn't exactly the man to fill Jeremiah Kincaid's shoes."

"But then why would anyone want him dead?"

"That's the question, isn't it? The barn fire was arson, but the police say Dugin's fatality was due to a head injury. He died at the hospital."

"But not right away."

"No," Elizabeth agreed, and she repeated what Lily Mae had told her about Dugin's condition being stabilized before he died. Lily Mae thought the doctors were puzzled over his death.

Jonas didn't think much of that information. "Who knows where Lily Mae got that?"

"She volunteers at the hospital."

"She volunteers everywhere, just so she can pick up little germs of information. Considering all that woman purports to know about everything, one could surmise she's the connection among all the mysteries."

Halting abruptly, Elizabeth stared at Jonas, open-mouthed. He sucked in a breath. Then together, they both said, "No, she couldn't be."

Chuckling, Jonas turned back to the path and pointed off to the right. "There's Beartooth Creek. It separates the Kincaid ranch from the reservation."

Through a break in the cottonwood and other dense vegetation, Elizabeth glimpsed a creek much wider than the stream they had already crossed. To their left were open fields, grazing pastures where cattle could be seen in the distance.

Jonas pointed up the creek. "It's shallow enough to cross up there. Then we just have to climb up the other side and backtrack a bit to the place where the bones were found."

When they broke through the trees onto the creek bank, Elizabeth gasped. The 'climb up the other side' involved a limestone-and-shale cliff that soared at least a hundred feet above the creek.

"Don't worry," Jonas told her. "It's much more accessible up around the bend."

"Why are we doing this?" Elizabeth grumbled as they followed the curve of the creek.

"You wanted to see where the bones were, didn't you? Scene of the crime and all that jazz."

"Yes, but—"

"And besides," he interjected before she could protest, "could there be a more beautiful place in all the world?"

He had a point. There was a majesty to this land that Elizabeth had never experienced before. Unspoiled. Graceful. Unexpected. She could apply dozens of adjectives to the beauty that surrounded them. Tipping her head back and breathing in the clear, cool air, she began to relax. Overhead, a mother bird squawked at her young. Around her were the rich smells of soil and trees. And at her side was Jonas, striding along with athletic ease, the sun glinting off his coal black hair, smiling at her in his teasing, disconcerting way.

Elizabeth realized it was the first time in a long, long while that she had just enjoyed a moment for itself alone. Maybe she was beginning to understand why a man like Jonas would make his home in a place where this sort of natural high could be found just up the road from a comfortable home.

After they had walked a bit more, she asked, "This book you wrote—did it require any research other than finding this sacred ground for the setting?"

"I spent some time with the tribal police. They were very helpful."

"So if you're friends, why are we hiking in the long way?"

"Because this is the way I first found the place." Taking her hand, he steered them toward the creek. "It's one of my favorite places in the world. I wanted you to see it the same way I did the first time."

His desire to share this with her was so unexpected she didn't know what to say.

But Jonas didn't seem to expect a reply. "Here's where we cross," he said, pausing at the edge of the water.

Getting to the other side was simply a matter of hopping from rock to rock. The climb up a ten-foot cliff was a little more daunting until Jonas showed her the hand-

and footholds nature had conveniently scored in the limestone. Though pebbles fell in abundance as they scrambled to the top, they made it with no problem. Elizabeth was slightly more dubious about the climb down.

"Don't worry," Jonas said, taking her hand again. "I'll help you."

A short hike took them back to where the cliff soared much higher above the creek. The place were the bones had been found was a quiet meadow bounded by dense woods and the cliff. The elevation offered an exceptional view of foothills, mountains and ranch land. And Jonas was right, there was something about it that reached out and grabbed you. Elizabeth thought it went deeper than the sheer natural beauty of the place.

After taking some pictures, she set her camera down and joined Jonas at the edge of the cliff. "I understand why they call it sacred."

Pleasure softened the angular lines of his face. "So you feel it, too? Sort of a mystical presence in the air?"

She stood still for a moment, listening to the rustle of trees moving in the breeze. "It's something like that."

"Like magic and music," Jonas said, seeming to read her mind. In a move that felt quite natural, he looped an arm around her shoulders and pointed off to the southeast. "I believe old Homer Gilmore got lost up in that forest near the mountains. We'll go up there if you want."

Elizabeth sighed. "Somewhere out in all this wilderness, someone left Rafe. I wonder why his mother or father were so desperate." She had become so intrigued with Rafe's story that her mind was whirling with ideas.

"Changing your mind about writing about him?"

"It's still tempting."

"But you'll resist?"

"I think so." She laughed as she said the words. "If my editor could hear that, he wouldn't believe it."

"I'm sure he doesn't want his star reporter to lose her edge."

"Frankly," she admitted with a rueful smile, "he'd like for me to get it back."

Jonas looked surprised. "What does that mean?"

From there it was easy to tell him about the lecture she had received from Ted and the reasons why she had been sent to Whitehorn. Jonas set down his backpack, and they perched on a large flat rock near the cliff's edge, both staring out at the view while Elizabeth explained that she now realized she had lost some of her perspective about her work. Listening intently, Jonas said very little.

Finally, Elizabeth hugged her legs to her chest and made a difficult admission. "I suppose this is the place where I say you were kind of right about me."

He pretended amazement. "Right? Me?"

"I'm being serious," she protested. "The first night we met you said that in my work I seemed to relish annihilating people. You said pretty much the same thing just yesterday. And I think you were right. Unfortunately."

To his credit, he didn't gloat. In thoughtful tones, he asked, "Doesn't it take that sort of zeal to be a journalist in the first place?"

"It takes zeal, yes, but not the desire to destroy people. And I certainly didn't start out that way."

"So you had the purest of intentions when you got into the business?"

"I just wanted to report the truth. And then maybe..." Sighing, she slipped off the rock. With her back to him, she added, "Maybe it all got too personal."

"How's that?"

She crossed her arms at her midriff, wondering why she was spilling her guts to him when that was exactly what she hadn't wanted to do. But she couldn't seem to stop herself. "There was this man," she began.

"A romance?"

"A source," she corrected, turning to face Jonas. "At least at first he was a source."

"And became much more."

"I thought I loved him."

Frowning, Jonas slid off the rock. The prospect of hearing Elizabeth's tales about a lost love wasn't very appealing.

But she didn't seem to notice his reluctance. She said that for six months she and this man had worked together. He gave her information about irregularities within a branch of the city government, and over the course of time they became deeply involved. When the story broke, followed by a storm of resignations and official investigations, he'd ended up with a huge promotion. Then he'd dropped her.

"Why?"

"Because he'd gotten what he wanted from me."

"He was obviously slime," Jonas said, his tone much rougher than he intended.

"Ambitious slime. And I fell for him." She laughed mirthlessly. "The crazy thing is that he was so surprised when I was hurt. He said he thought I understood the score, that we had a business arrangement. He didn't view what he had done as a betrayal."

"What did you do?"

Brown eyes troubled, she shook her head. "I didn't deal with it. My work, which had always been important, became everything. And I went after stories and people with all I had. I was just so...so *angry* that I wanted to take on the world." She turned her back to Jonas once more. "It wasn't a conscious choice, but I began seeing things in a much more negative light. So many people in my life had been untruthful to me, I just assumed everyone I met had a secret agenda."

Expelling a deep breath, he raked a hand through his hair. He could see that Elizabeth had been deeply hurt. But he was also unfortunate enough to understand something of the man who had used her. Because he had once been such a man. Ambitious above all else. With an agenda he'd been determined to fulfill at whatever cost. Funny thing was, that sort of ruthless drive was exactly what he had believed Elizabeth possessed in connection with her work. Now, if he could believe her, it would appear she wasn't really like that at all.

If he could just believe her.

The last time he'd believed in a woman she had sold their story to the highest-bidding tabloid.

He closed his eyes, told himself Elizabeth wasn't that woman. Moving to her side, he asked, "Why do you think you're realizing all of this now?"

Instead of looking at him, she kept her gaze fixed on the horizon. "Maybe it's this town."

"What about it?"

"The people—little Jennifer McCallum and her parents, Rafe and his wife, Melissa North and Moriah Gilmore, Lily Mae, even Mary Jo Kincaid and that infuriating chauvinist Detective Calloway—they all remind me of people I knew growing up, people I trusted."

"I thought your hometown suffocated you."

She shook her head. "I know that's what I told you, but it's not exactly true. It was home that was suffocating...my family..." She brushed the subject aside with a wave of her hand. "The point is that where I grew up, for all its small-town faults, was a town made up of people."

"Aren't all towns?"

"But those people were individuals to me, and these people here...well, they seem so nice, so genuine, much more than just names to go in a story." She lifted her gaze to meet his, her expression unreadable. "Like you're not just a name."

His pulse accelerated. *What did she know?*

"You're the first person I've wanted to trust in a long time, Jonas."

The simple, direct words made him ashamed of his suspicions. He touched her cheek, and he meant every word when he said, "I want to trust you, too."

"But that's not easy, is it?"

"No."

"Because you've been hurt?"

He nodded and could see her waiting, wanting him to explain. He wanted to, as well. But all his pain had been bottled up for so long, buried in the solitary existence that was all he thought he deserved. Even looking into Elizabeth's warm, trusting eyes, he couldn't let it out.

"You don't have to tell me now," she finally whispered. "Maybe sometime later."

"Maybe..."

She stepped into his arms and kissed him. She kissed him with all the openness he had denied her in not answering her questions. It was as if she were sealing her trust in him. Jonas felt a momentary flicker of guilt, then he just took what she offered.

Kisses like a gentle rain after a summer drought.

Touches like a balm to a lonely soul.

His arousal was quick and complete. Every sense was heightened and focused on Elizabeth. Her delicious scent. Her subtle curves, fitted so perfectly to his body. Her husky sighs. Her sweet taste. Her brown eyes that tilted at the corners as he drew away.

"I want you," he told her. "So much." It was no stretch to imagine taking her here beneath the sun and the sky on this special, hallowed ground. Here, he would lay her down, undress her slowly, kiss the sleek flesh he was certain she hid beneath her utilitarian clothes. And maybe if he took her here, she would truly be his, to trust.

Finally, someone to trust again. Finally, after all the dark days of having no one.

While he tried to crowd the thoughts of trust and betrayal from his mind, he kissed her again. He knew she could feel the desperation in the way he touched her, the way he said her name. But he sensed the same in her. Her fingers tugged his shirt free of his pants and then moved in slow, arousing movements up his back. When he fumbled at the buttons of her blouse, she pushed his hands away and unbuttoned it herself. Her bra was white, with a front closure that parted easily to reveal small, rosy-tipped breasts. Breasts that begged for his touch, pebbled against his palm.

Elizabeth arched against him, head thrown back, while he trailed kisses from her throat to the valley between her breasts. He moved his mouth over her nipple, bathed it with a circular stroke of his tongue. Once, then again and again. Hands threading through his hair, she held him closer, offered herself with an eagerness underscored by her low sounds of pleasure.

Finally, muttering her name, he claimed her mouth with his again. Her lips accepted the thrust of his tongue without resistance. Between their bodies, she pushed her hand downward until she cupped the hardening ridge of flesh at the juncture of his thighs. She pressed upward. Gently. Maddeningly.

"Maybe you shouldn't," Jonas said against her mouth. But Elizabeth's clever hand kept moving, rubbing. It was a wondrous torture. A perilous one for a man whose control had been leashed for so very long.

Pulling back, he found her laughing up at him, her face shining with a mixture of passion and delight. "Please," he said, capturing her hand to still it. "Let's take it slow."

She wiggled her fingers against his crotch. "That slow enough?"

He groaned. "Too fast, unless you want to be left behind."

"Well, that's not what I had in mind, exactly...." She stepped away, took his hands and tugged him toward the broad, flat rock they had vacated earlier.

Halfway there, she dropped his hands and then, rather defiantly, her shirt. She blushed crimson, but kept her gaze steady on his. Jonas tugged his knit shirt over his head and reached for the buckle of his belt. Her smile was pure, teasing seduction as she eased the straps of her bra down her arms.

Then something cracked in the woods at his back.

Elizabeth gasped. Jonas hauled her close to shield her from prying eyes. He looked over his shoulder, seeing nothing in the trees. But soon there was another crack, farther away but still distinct, like someone stepping onto dried, fallen timber.

Snatching Elizabeth's shirt off the ground, Jonas settled it around her shoulders. She turned her back to put her bra in place and shrug into the shirt. When she twisted round again, she muttered, "Did you see anything?"

"Nothing. You?"

"No, but..." She darted a quick look to the left.

Jonas whirled to follow her gaze. "What is it?"

She shook her head. "It's just this feeling. I've had it several times since we started up here. It's like someone's watching."

He scanned the surrounding forest again. There was silence except for the wind. Nothing out of the ordinary appeared to move. Not even a rabbit or a squirrel or a deer. "Perhaps we should go," he said, glancing at Elizabeth.

She was buttoning her shirt. "Do you think someone could have followed us?"

"Why?"

"For the same reason someone called me and broke into my room. To frighten me away."

Scowling, he did another quick survey of the trees and dense undergrowth that rimmed the meadow where they stood. There was nothing, except a growing sense of unease.

Jonas remembered from newspaper reports that Tracy Hensley had been chased off this land by someone in a strange costume when she was searching for forensic evidence with which to identify Charlie Avery's bones and piece together the details of his death. Then her husband, Sheriff Judd Hensley, had been injured in a fall over the cliff. There had been talk that he was pushed. But in the eighteen months or so since then, during which Jonas had become interested in exploring this place, he had never seen anyone or anything suspicious. He wasn't going to tell Elizabeth about Tracy's and Judd's experiences here. Not yet, anyway.

"It was probably just some kid who was getting an eyeful," he suggested.

"That's not very comforting," Elizabeth said, flushing as she tucked her shirt into her jeans. "In a few more minutes…" Her color deepened as she glanced toward the rock where they had been headed when the noise interrupted.

Jonas snatched his shirt from the ground and slipped it on, silently cursing their intruder. Given a few more minutes, Elizabeth would have been naked in his arms. He would have been inside her, filling her, stroking her, finding a release for the hard ache that still gripped his loins. One by one, erotic images clicked through his head. The sun on Elizabeth's skin. Her hands sliding through the hair on his chest. Her mouth…

He slammed the door on that last tempting fantasy as he picked up his backpack and pulled out an insulated jug of water. Though tempted to gulp it down and pour the rest over his heated body, he just took a sip and held it out to Elizabeth instead.

She took it, drank and wiped the moisture from her mouth with the back of her hand. Never once did her troubled gaze fall from his.

"What is it?" he asked.

"I was just thinking it might have been for the best that we were interrupted."

"You could be right."

Disappointment flickered briefly across her features before she grabbed the camera case she had left on the rock. Jonas took her arm before she could turn toward the path. "I said you *could* be right. Not that you were."

"It's just—"

"Stop it," he said, lifting fingers to her lips. "Didn't it feel right?" At her nod, he closed the space between them. "It's going feel just as right when we're alone, with a nice, firm bed. . . ." He leaned close. "And there'll be no possibility that anyone will interrupt us. We can take all the time we want."

She closed her eyes while his finger traced a line from her mouth, down her neck, to beneath the top button of her shirt. Then he pressed his lips to the hollow at her throat, murmuring, "We'll take lots of time, Elizabeth. All the time we need."

Her trembling sigh affected him as strongly as a caress. He didn't want to take time. He wanted to find some rudimentary shelter and plant himself deep inside her. He wanted it fast and hard. He wanted her. Unfortunately, the nearest shelter he could think of was his Jeep, and it was a good half-hour hike away.

"We'd better go," he said, stepping away with great reluctance.

Though she only nodded in reply, she gripped his hand as they began to retrace their steps to the creek. The climb down the low point in the cliff was silent and without incident.

Except for Jonas's own growing sense that they were being watched.

Was he simply reacting to what Elizabeth had felt earlier? Or was this real? After they crossed the creek, he glanced over his shoulder.

Elizabeth caught his eye and whispered, "So now you feel it, too?"

"Yeah."

He stepped up their pace as they followed the creek and then skirted the edge of the pastureland. It was difficult to hurry once they were back in the trees, and soon Jonas's sense of urgency began to fade.

When they climbed into the Jeep, he paused before fitting the key in the ignition. "We were imagining things, weren't we?"

Elizabeth still looked concerned. "I don't know. I kept expecting to look over my shoulder and see someone . . . or something."

But Jonas was feeling foolish. The only person who might have been following them was some randy Cheyenne teenager getting his jollies from watching him and Elizabeth make out. Jonas was so sure he was correct that he made a right turn not too far past the Kincaid ranch.

Elizabeth looked surprised. "Where are we going now?"

"Homer Gilmore's place."

"You don't think we should go back to town?"

"I'm positive there's nothing to be alarmed about."

"I hope you're right."

No one was home at Gilmore's dilapidated shack. Even if the old hermit was about, Jonas wasn't sure he would come out for them. Jonas had talked to Homer a few times, and the man had cleaned up and seemed more lucid since his daughter had moved back to town and married, but he was known to keep his distance from strangers.

Back at the intersection of Homer's rutted drive and the road, Jonas nodded northward. "If we drive up there, we'll see the area where they found Homer wandering around with rocks in his pockets, babbling about aliens. Want to go?''

Hesitating only a moment, Elizabeth nodded. The road was clearly little used, and after a short distance, they came to an overgrown driveway with a rusted mailbox leaning to one side of the entrance. Just past it, Elizabeth suddenly asked Jonas to stop and back up.

He complied, and she pointed to the box. "What are those letters on the side? Does the first one look like a *B?*"

Jonas couldn't make them out until they got out of the Jeep and scrubbed some accumulated dirt from around the faded letters. Then they were clear: *B-A-X.*

Elizabeth peered up the drive. "Lily Mae told me that the Lexine Baxter who supposedly ran off with Charlie Avery grew up on a ranch. You think this could be it?"

"I haven't heard of any Baxters since I moved here."

"The Kincaids bought this land after Lexine's father died and she couldn't be found."

"Doesn't appear they did much with the place."

"Except the grazing land, I'm sure. And maybe the sapphires."

Startled, Jonas repeated, "Sapphires?"

"The first Baxter who settled here was prospecting for sapphires. Supposedly there was a mine."

"Were these people wealthy?"

"At one time, according to—"

"Lily Mae, of course," Jonas supplied. "Did she happen to say where this mine was?"

"She wasn't certain."

"How convenient."

"I'm sure we can check it out. There'd have to be some records about it or notations in the town history. Surely sapphire mines aren't that common."

"Want to go see if the house is still standing? There might be a clue about Lexine."

Though she was curious, Elizabeth found herself extremely reluctant to go any nearer. There was a chilling *emptiness* about the place that gave her the shivers. She might have overcome them if she'd felt there was really anything of value or interest to be found here. But it had been thirty years since Lexine had disappeared. What clues could remain that she and Jonas would be able to discern?

"Let's just go," she said. "There's something creepy about this place."

But Jonas continued to stare up the drive, murmuring, "Sapphires."

"What are you thinking?"

"Just that it's strange the Kincaids would let this place go. This ranch house could have been rented out, you know."

"So maybe the Kincaids were trying to hide something."

"About the sapphires?"

"And Lexine Baxter and Charlie Avery."

Elizabeth shook her head. "I'm not following you."

"With Lexine Baxter out of the way, the Kincaids were able to buy this place, land she would have inherited from her father."

"So?"

"So maybe the Kincaids killed her."

"And Charlie?"

"Maybe he was just in the wrong place at the wrong time."

The scene he proposed played itself out in Elizabeth's mind all too easily.

"Let's go explore," Jonas suggested.

But Elizabeth still resisted, and he acquiesced with little argument. That feeling of being watched was with her again. It followed her as dense forest soon closed in on the sides of the road. The afternoon was beginning to fade.

Shadows were deepening beneath the trees when Jonas abandoned their quest of Homer's rescue site and turned back toward town. Elizabeth was secretly relieved, though she wasn't sure why. Perhaps it was just her well-honed instincts kicking in, but she sensed trouble of some sort.

They were still well out of Whitehorn when Jonas pulled the Jeep to the side of the road and drove down a short trail. The road was still visible through a screen of trees, but there was a grassy area beside the trail and a small lake in the distance.

"You think this looks like a good place for dinner?" Jonas asked.

Elizabeth glanced around. "Here?"

"I'm starved, aren't you?"

"Yes, but—"

"Come with me."

From the back seat he produced a picnic hamper and cooler. Opened, they revealed a blue-checked tablecloth, which Jonas spread on the grass and filled with containers of chicken and pasta salad, bread and cheese, fruit and a bottle of wine. As a final flourish, he lit two candles stuck in fat wooden candlesticks and placed them in the center of the bounty.

Elizabeth stared first at him and then at the picnic. "This is why no one will ever mistake you for a Montana cowboy, no matter how long you live in Whitehorn."

He employed a corkscrew with expert ease. "You don't think there are cowboys who like a good zinfandel?"

"They're few and far between. And they also don't cook like this."

"Neither do I. Supper comes directly from the Hip Hop. Melissa even packed the basket, I'm afraid."

"At least you're as resourceful as a cowboy."

"It's my Texas upbringing. We do things in a big way." He took two wineglasses from the hamper and filled them.

"Crystal, no less," Elizabeth murmured.

"Of course. Try this wine and then tell me it doesn't go with the sunset over the mountains."

Raising the glass to her lips, she turned in the direction he pointed. The sun was spreading its last rays over the peaks to the west, painting the sky in streaks of orange, purple and violet. The air was clear, the colors vibrant and yet soft, like images photographed through a tinted lens.

Close to her ear, Jonas whispered, "There's a table waiting, *madame*. Best seat in Montana for dinner."

He was right. Everything was the best—food, wine, conversation. They ate and drank and talked, while evening shadows deepened over the landscape. A few cars drove past on the highway, but Elizabeth hardly noticed. They could have been all alone in the world—just her and Jonas and the stars that began to glimmer overhead.

While the candles burned down, dripping wax on the tablecloth, Jonas told her about mountain climbing in Alaska, skiing the French Alps, deep-sea diving off the coast of Mexico. He had been everywhere, it seemed, tried almost every daredevil sport he could find. Speedboat racing, surfing, jumping from airplanes.

"There's a rush," he said, leaning toward her. "When you step out of that plane and there's nothing to catch you, nothing but wind . . . my God, you feel like you're flying. My friends and I . . ." Laughing suddenly, he stopped himself. "This must all be awfully boring, like watching someone else's home movies."

Elizabeth, who had stretched out on the blanket and propped her head on one hand, shook her head. "Are you crazy? You've had such an exciting life."

Highlighted in the flickering glow from the candle, his face went still. The mobile lines beside his mouth seemed deeply carved, underscored by the long evening shadows. He sat back, out of the direct light, and was silent.

"Jonas?" Elizabeth sat up as well, wondering at his reaction.

He reached for the food containers and opened the cooler. "We should be getting back. I'm sure you're tired, especially after last night."

She watched him toss the remains of their dinner haphazardly into the cooler while she debated how she really wanted this evening to end. Earlier today, when they'd been headed for lovemaking up on the Cheyenne's sacred ground, she had behaved with a boldness that had surprised her. But she had liked watching Jonas look at her body. As for his kiss, his touch...

There was really no reason to keep debating how she wanted to spend the rest of this night. Hoping to strike just the right balance between lightness and seduction, she said, "I'm not tired at all, Jonas."

He paused.

Before he could reply, she rushed on. "I'm not tired, but earlier today, you did say something about a nice, firm bed."

"Elizabeth—"

"A firm bed and lots of time," she repeated. She held out her hand, praying it wouldn't tremble.

He stared at it for a moment, then looked at her, his dark eyes glimmering in the soft candlelight. "You're sure?"

"If someone hadn't interrupted earlier, you'd be saying, 'Again?'"

He took her hand and smiled, and the shadows lifted from his features.

By mutual, unspoken consent, they blew out the candles, tumbled the rest of the things into the cooler, hamper and back seat and were soon on the road.

This highway looked different at night. More deserted, with more unexpected curves. Elizabeth much preferred driving to being a passenger, so she was straining forward to see the road unfold before them when she noticed Jonas glance in the rearview mirror.

He muttered, "What in the hell?"

There was barely time for Elizabeth to look back before a car bore down on them from behind. Jonas pushed hard on the accelerator and swerved to the left across the other lane, but the car behind—driving without headlights—followed. Jonas tried to pull back to the right, just as they headed into a curve.

Elizabeth heard the squeal of tires. Only they weren't the Jeep's. It was airborne.

Up and off the shoulder of the road.

Down an embankment.

Into a tree.

In the frozen, black moments that followed, over the hiss of the crumpled radiator, Elizabeth heard tires squeal again, then the revving of a powerful engine. She was able to twist around enough to see lights moving away.

"Going west," she muttered to Jonas. "Remember they were going back toward the mountains."

But Jonas didn't answer. He was slumped over the steering wheel.

Claws of fear gripped her belly as she struggled to get out of her seat belt. "Don't be dead," she kept saying over and over. "Please, Jonas, don't be dead."

Somehow, she got free of the belt and pulled him back from the wheel. The night was dark as the devil's cape, as her mother would have said, so Elizabeth couldn't see much of anything. But when she touched Jonas's forehead, her hand came away wet.

"Blood," she said, holding her fingers close to her face. "Blood, Jonas."

She let go of his arm. His body slipped to the side. *Lifelessly.*

Elizabeth shook as she dragged him upright in the seat again. Tears of panic blinded her.

Then Jonas groaned.

He wasn't dead.

The steady common sense that had guided Elizabeth most of her life took over. Jonas needed her help, not tears. Most of all, he needed a car to drive by and see them in this ditch. Soon.

But the Jeep's headlights were out, and nothing happened when Elizabeth pushed and pulled any of the knobs or dials she could locate in the dark on the dashboard.

She made a fumbling examination of Jonas to make sure there were no obvious breaks or cuts other than the one on his forehead. She felt nothing, so she turned to rummage in the glove compartment, where she found a flashlight. She flipped it on, gasping at the blood running down Jonas's face.

"Head wounds always bleed a lot," she told herself, trying to stay calm.

On the floor behind their seats, she found Jonas's backpack and the thermos of water. On the seat was the tablecloth they had thrown in the car. It wasn't clean, but it would have to do for a bandage. She wet one end and cleaned the blood away from his eyes and cheeks. With a vicious jerk, she tore off the other end, folded and pressed it to the cut. He stirred slightly, then slumped back in the seat.

The pressure seemed to slow the bleeding, but he was unconscious and needed medical attention in a hurry. The minutes ticked past. Fifteen. Twenty. Holding the bandage on Jonas's head, Elizabeth sat staring at her watch. She couldn't just sit here and hope that someone would drive by and see them. She had to do something to make sure they wouldn't be missed.

After wrapping the makeshift bandage around Jonas's head, she forced her door open and scrambled on wobbly legs up the embankment to the dark highway. There were no car lights to be seen in either direction. But someone had to come along. Someone other than whoever had run them off the road.

This time they just might finish the job.

Eight

The woman's voice was gentle, as was her touch. She reminded him of a place. A house where starched curtains swung at the windows in a breeze that smelled like new-mown hay. Where laughter floated up to a second-story window. And in the distance there was a pounding. A hammer, he supposed. Down at the barn...

"Home," Jonas murmured with yearning, as he opened his eyes. But instead of a bedroom in an East Texas farmhouse, he saw a woman's face. He blinked, and she came into focus. Elizabeth. Her pale face, smudged by dirt on one cheek, was framed by bright, blinding lights. Pain, like a hammer, pounded through his head. He shut his eyes, but the pounding continued.

"We're at the hospital," Elizabeth whispered. "Do you remember getting run off the road?"

His eyes flew open. He remembered the car behind them, the spin into the curve, sailing through the air. "We hit something."

"A ditch and a tree."

"But you're okay?"

Her fingers stroked his cheek. "I'm fine, but you've got a dent in your noggin."

"Noggin?" he repeated, smiling. "I haven't heard that word since—"

"Miss Monroe?" a deep voice interrupted.

Elizabeth straightened, and Jonas slowly turned his head toward the voice. A man stood at the end of the bed or gurney or whatever it was that Jonas was lying on. A tall man with black hair and dark eyes, who seemed vaguely familiar.

"Sheriff Hensley," Elizabeth said.

"How's he doing?" the sheriff said, nodding at Jonas.

Struggling to sit up, Jonas replied, "I'm fine." But the whirling of the room in front of his eyes belied the words.

Elizabeth took his arm. "I don't think you should sit up."

Ignoring her and conquering his dizziness, Jonas pulled himself to a sitting position. His shirt was off, but thank God they had left his jeans on instead of putting him in one of those damned emasculating hospital gowns.

"Your shirt was pretty bloody," Elizabeth explained. "And you should lie down."

"No way."

The sheriff chuckled, an understanding look on his face. "I can't stand to be flat on my back in these places, either. You never know when someone's going to come in and stick you with something."

Elizabeth glared at him. "Did your deputy tell you we were forced off the road?"

Frowning, Sheriff Hensley pulled a small notepad from the pocket of his dark brown uniform shirt. "Yes, Miss Monroe, my deputy called me at home on a Friday night and told me you were pitching a fit down here at the hospital."

"Someone ran us off the road. Deliberately."

"She's right," Jonas agreed.

The sheriff's eyes narrowed. "You're sure about that?"

Slowly, because it was difficult to concentrate with this pounding in his head, Jonas told him what had happened. When he was finished, Sheriff Hensley just stood looking at them both, tapping a pen against his pad.

Elizabeth made an impatient sound. "Well?"

Ignoring her, the sheriff said to Jonas, "At least your story matches what she told the deputy."

Jonas heard Elizabeth suck in her breath, but before she could unleash an angry tirade, he took hold of her hand. "She and I were in my Jeep together when this happened. Of course our stories match."

Sheriff Hensley hesitated for a moment. "Well, now... you see, Mr. Bishop, Miss Monroe here—"

"Is just a nosy, pushy reporter who likes making trouble," Elizabeth completed for the man.

He gave her a long look. "I didn't say that." But Jonas could tell it was what he thought.

"I'll agree she's pushy," Jonas told him, squeezing Elizabeth's fingers when she protested. "But everything happened just as we said. The car's lights were out. It was dark, and it all happened so quickly I can't tell you a make or model."

The sheriff scratched his head, and before he could say anything more, another man appeared in the doorway behind him.

Nodding to the sheriff, Dr. Kane Hunter moved with quick, efficient movements across the room. "How's the head?" he asked Jonas as Elizabeth stepped aside.

"Hurts."

The doctor, whose Native American heritage was clearly imprinted on his features, chuckled. "It should. You've got a slight concussion." He pulled a small light from his pocket, shone it in Jonas's eyes and made some notations on a chart. With brisk competence, he asked some questions about Jonas's general health.

"What about that cut?" Elizabeth said. "He bled a lot. And he was out for so long." Only then did Jonas put his hand up to feel a bandage on his forehead.

"We took a couple of stitches," Dr. Hunter replied. "But it should be fine. He's going to have an ugly bruise in addition to the cut, but he's really okay. It could have been worse. You did the right thing by getting some pressure on the cut soon after the accident."

Brown eyes solemn, she glanced at Jonas. "I'm just glad someone come along when they did."

"Who?" Jonas asked.

"They're from the reservation," Elizabeth replied.

"Jackson and Maggie Hawk," Dr. Hunter said as he scribbled something across the bottom of the chart and set it aside. He went on to explain that Jackson was the Northern Cheyenne's tribal attorney and his wife was a special consultant who coordinated tribal matters with the federal government.

"They were on their way home after a meeting in town," Elizabeth told Jonas. "They saw me out on the highway waving the flashlight around and helped me get you here. You kept coming to and fading out on the way here. I didn't expect you to remember."

"I'll have to call and thank the Hawks for their help," Jonas said.

"I'll give Maggie and Jackson your gratitude when I see them tomorrow," Dr. Hunter offered. "My wife and daughter and I are going over to their place for a celebration." He told Jonas he would ask a nurse to give him some pain medication to take home and to see him if he had any unusual symptoms over the next few days.

At the door, the doctor turned back. "Jonas, you should have someone with you tonight. If you can't, you should stay—"

"He won't be alone," Elizabeth said firmly, taking Jonas's hand again. Dr. Hunter waved goodbye and was quickly gone.

Sheriff Hensley cleared his throat.

Jonas looked at him. "I don't know what else we can tell you, Sheriff."

"Miss Monroe told my deputy this wasn't her first call to the police today."

"That's right," she said. "Last night—"

"I know about last night," the sheriff interrupted. "I spoke to Detective Calloway at the Whitehorn Police Department. He's going to drop by to talk to you before you leave."

"Oh, joy," Elizabeth muttered.

"Before he does," Sheriff Hensley continued, clearly pretending not to hear her, "can you tell me what you were doing up that way tonight?"

Elizabeth spoke before Jonas could. "Just driving."

The sheriff's brow knit.

"I spent the afternoon showing Elizabeth some of the area," Jonas said, pointedly not looking at her. There was no reason to lie, but no reason to tell the whole truth unless asked. They had been trespassing on private property, after all. "We went over to Beartooth Creek and did some hiking, then drove up near Homer Gilmore's place."

"Any particular reason why?"

"It's beautiful country," Jonas explained smoothly.

The sheriff looked at him, then at Elizabeth, then closed his notepad before turning to go. "I'll see you again before you leave."

When he was out of the room, Jonas said, "Get me my shirt, and let's go."

"I think the nurse has to—"

"I'm ready to go." He didn't mean to bite her head off, but for nine years he had managed to live in this town and avoid more than the most casual contact with the local law-enforcement officials. Now they were surrounding him, and he didn't care for the close scrutiny. It brought back some bad memories. "I want to go home."

With no further argument, Elizabeth retrieved his blood-splattered shirt, his billfold and watch from a plastic bag on a nearby table. Jonas slid off what he had determined was an examining table and momentarily swayed. He was woozy enough that pulling his shirt over his head proved a time-consuming task. When he'd settled it in place, he found Elizabeth watching him with concern.

"I think you need to take it easy," she said softly.

"I will when I get home."

She hesitated, chewing on her bottom lip. "Do you think we need to tell Hensley and Calloway about being followed today?"

"We told the sheriff about the car."

"I mean earlier."

"We're not sure we were followed." And telling anyone about a vague suspicion would merely bring them even more attention, something Jonas could do without.

"But Jonas, we were run off the road. We could have been killed. Someone is desperate to keep me and you from putting together the pieces of whatever's going on."

"We don't know that being run off the road has a thing to do with anything else. For that matter, we're not even sure there's anything that needs piecing together. It could have been a bunch of teenagers out for a joyride and taking stupid risks."

He could see she didn't buy that theory, but she said nothing else and followed him as he made his way gingerly out of the room. Besides the pain in his head, he had a few other aches as well. A nurse met them halfway down the hall, clucking over Jonas being up so soon. Since Dr. Hunter had released him, however, she could do nothing but give him the promised pain medication and point them toward the cashier's window at one end of the emergency-room lobby. Sheriff Hensley was at the other end, talking with a muscular man dressed in jeans and a faded denim shirt.

"That's Calloway," Elizabeth said just before the two men turned their way.

Jonas muttered a curse under his breath and went over to settle his bill with the cashier. He'd been hoping they would escape before Calloway showed.

Though Elizabeth thought the sheriff was taking what had happened today too lightly and she didn't look forward to dealing with Calloway again, she wasn't sure why Jonas seemed so anxious to avoid the lawmen. He'd done nothing wrong. The driver's license found in his wallet, which the sheriff's deputy had asked to see earlier, had caused no comment. Neither had his car registration. Though he had drunk some wine during their picnic, it wasn't enough to impair his judgment, and the subject of alcohol hadn't been mentioned by the deputy. So why was Jonas acting like a nervous felon?

Maybe because he was.

She tossed that notion aside almost as fast as it came to her. It didn't fit the few things she did know about the man and went against all her instincts. But she went on instant alert as Hensley and Calloway approached her.

The sheriff spoke first. "It seems that you've managed to ruffle a few people's feathers around town, Miss Monroe. Dr. Hunter said his wife had mentioned you. Then there's Melissa North, Rafe Rawlings...." Lines fanned out beside his eyes as he squinted at her. "Can I ask you what's going on?"

She squared her shoulders and looked him in the eye. "As I told you when I visited your office yesterday, I'm investigating some of the things that have been happening here for a possible story."

"Maybe you ought to just let things alone," Calloway suggested.

She swung her gaze to him. "I don't really want to." Despite backing off on writing anything about Rafe and despite her recognition that this town reminded her of home, Elizabeth still wanted to get to the bottom of things around here, if only to discover who had threatened her and hurt Jonas.

Calloway folded his arms, his frown deepening. "There might be someone who doesn't want you nosing around."

"So now you believe I'm being threatened," she replied, letting just a hint of sarcasm enter her voice. "You didn't this morning."

With a shrug, the detective glanced toward the cashier's window, where Jonas stood. "Kind of hard to dismiss a Jeep that looks like your boyfriend's does right now."

"My *friend's* Jeep," Elizabeth corrected, put off by his tone more than his description of Jonas. "I also know how it looks, and I'd like to know that some effort will be made to find out who ran us off the road."

"You can be assured that every effort will be made," the sheriff replied in even tones. "But you've got no description of the car. You say it came out of nowhere and disappeared toward the mountains. Do you know how many secondary roads there are that cut through those hills?"

"Probably a lot."

"So I'm sure you'll understand me when I say I'll do what I can."

Elizabeth nodded. To expect anything more would be unreasonable. There really wasn't much to go on.

"Meanwhile," Calloway added, "you can do some things for us, Miss Monroe."

"Leave town?" she suggested.

The detective shrugged. "If that's what you want to do."

She bristled. "It's not, and I have every right—"

"Okay," Sheriff Hensley said, putting out a hand as if to restrain Calloway. He looked at Elizabeth. "Miss Monroe, you can stay in Whitehorn as long as you want. And I can't really stop you from writing most anything you want, as long as it's not a pack of inflammatory lies."

"I wouldn't do that."

He held up a hand again. "I'm sure you wouldn't. But I would encourage you to consider that someone apparently doesn't like you or some of the questions you've been asking."

"Then something must be up."

The two men exchanged a guarded look. Calloway said, "Off the record, I'm beginning to think you might be right, Miss Monroe."

"But let us handle it," the sheriff said with an unexpected smile. "I wouldn't want you hurt."

"She won't be," Jonas said, stepping up to Calloway's side. "I'll see to that."

Elizabeth wasn't used to anyone speaking for her. "Jonas—"

"Could we just go?" he said curtly.

He was injured and wanted out of here. Elizabeth understood, so she swallowed the rest of her protest. It galled her, however, to see the flare of satisfaction in Detective Calloway's eyes.

The three men talked for a moment about where Jonas's vehicle had been towed and where he could pick up an accident report for insurance purposes. Looking at them, Elizabeth was struck by a similarity she might never have seen otherwise. They were all dark-haired, all supremely fit. Jonas was just as tall as the two officers, though his lean build contrasted with Calloway's defined muscularity and Hensley's broad-shouldered strength.

But it wasn't really a physical likeness that hit her. It was a bearing. An aura of self-containment. A masculine confidence that she realized suited this place they called home. Whitehorn, Montana, was a town of individualists. And these three fit in. Even Jonas, whose smooth sophistication she had once thought set him apart. This was a place where strong, silent types were the rule instead of an exception, where mavericks who didn't run with the herd were readily accepted.

Elizabeth mulled that over while Calloway gave them a lift to where she had left her car parked near the library earlier that afternoon. Jonas was in obvious pain, but he kept telling her she didn't need to stay with him. She ignored him, and by the time they got to his house, he was so exhausted he actually leaned on her as they climbed to a large, square bedroom on the second floor.

Poe and Raven sniffed Elizabeth anxiously and sat on the bed beside Jonas. Wincing, Jonas stroked the dog with one hand while he lowered his head to the other. The cat rubbed against his side.

"You need to get undressed and get to bed," Elizabeth ordered.

He attempted a weak laugh that ended with another wince. "This is not exactly the context in which I thought you'd be saying that to me tonight."

Stepping close, she gently trailed her fingers through his tousled hair. "There's always tomorrow."

He slipped his arms around her waist, resting his head low against her belly as he groaned. "You're a real optimist, aren't you?"

Elizabeth smiled and went to the spacious bathroom nearby to get him a glass of water with which to take his medication. When she came back, his clothes were in a heap beside the bed. He was sitting naked on the edge, his head in his hands again.

She stopped, momentarily nonplussed to see him sitting there so calmly, unconcernedly unclothed. Then, telling herself that he was injured, that men didn't have hangups about nudity like most women did, Elizabeth simply crossed the room and held out the water and the pills. He took them, but when he handed the glass back and turned to slide under the covers, she couldn't help but look, *really* look at him. At his nice, wide shoulders and strong legs. At the light dusting of dark hair that tapered downward from his chest, bisecting his flat belly and broadening again just where...

Elizabeth wrenched her gaze away, glad that only the bedside lamp was on so Jonas couldn't see her flush of embarrassment.

He groaned, and she looked at him again. "Are you okay?"

"Sure," he murmured, his eyes closed. "You can go, Elizabeth. I don't need..." The sentence went unfinished.

She waited a few moments, then bent close. His breathing was already deep and regular, signifying sleep and not the unconscious state he'd been in after the Jeep's plunge off the highway.

Straightening, she found two pairs of nonhuman eyes watching her every move. "You want food?" she asked Jonas's housemates.

Raven only cocked her head to the side, while Poe jumped off the bed with typical feline grace. Elizabeth followed him downstairs, with Raven bringing up the rear. She found their dishes and food in the kitchen, then checked the front door to make sure it was locked. Finally she returned to Jonas's bedroom.

It was a masculine room, with large, square furniture that looked new rather than antique like most of the pieces downstairs. The lines were simple. The Oriental rug on the broad-planked floor was muted in design and color, at least what she could see of it in the light from the fat brass lamp that still burned beside the bed. The bedspread, pooled on the floor where Jonas had tossed it, was a deep wine. Two well-cushioned chairs near the bed were upholstered in a dark brocade that matched the swags over the long windows.

The nearby bath was much more luxurious than the bedroom. Elizabeth imagined another bedroom had been taken over to provide the space for this bath. A long, gray, marble-topped vanity stretched along one wall. A whirlpool tub was set under a window, while the glass-walled shower stood in the very center of the room. The fixtures were gold. The floor was a smooth, glossy, black-marble tile.

But as weary, dirty and disheveled as Elizabeth felt, she wouldn't have cared if the shower was a hose hooked over a wooden stall. She stripped, bathed, then wrapped herself in a heavy white terry-cloth robe she found hanging on a hook behind the door.

Though her muscles ached from the hike and the jolting they had taken in the accident, she felt refreshed. Jonas slept on while she pulled the two chairs closer to the bed. Both were roomy, soft and comfortable, and she imagined she would sleep there just fine if she put her feet up in one and rested her back against the other.

Or she could get in bed with Jonas.

She was considering that when Raven came in, jumped on the bed and stretched out beside her master with a proprietorial air. Jonas turned over, groaning, and Elizabeth decided there wasn't room for her, even in that king-size bed. But the doctor had said he needed someone with him all night, so sleeping in another room was out. She was thinking about settling down in the chairs when the open door to the hallway caught her eye. She glanced at Jonas. He was breathing like someone deeply asleep. She might not ever have a chance like this to explore.

She felt guilty, no doubt about it. Nosy reporter though she might be, Jonas was more than just a mystery to her now. Should she be spying? She asked herself that several times as she opened doors to what appeared to be empty rooms on the rest of the second floor. His room was the only one furnished. That struck her as strange. But as she told herself her curiosity should be satisfied, she spied another door at the end of the hallway. Behind it, she found a darkened, narrow staircase.

Elizabeth hesitated, glancing back down the hall. Poe crept around the door from Jonas's room and stood looking at her. A censorious look, she thought.

"You're right," Elizabeth whispered to the cat. "I shouldn't go up."

But Poe had other ideas. He darted past Elizabeth and up the stairs.

She stared up into the darkness where he had disappeared. Now what if there was something up here that the cat wasn't supposed to be into? Like rat poison, perhaps? She needed to go get him. Reaching along the wall, she flipped on a light and climbed the stairs.

The comfortable, book-lined study was nothing like the bare attic she had been expecting. Poe was giving himself a bath in a worn leather chair in front of a small fireplace. A row of filing cabinets stood under one low-ceilinged eave. A computer sat on a long, cluttered work station near a window, while a phone, fax machine and more papers covered the top of an antique mahogany desk nearby. The room smelled like Jonas, like pipe tobacco and old leather.

Elizabeth knew she should turn around and leave. She shouldn't advance toward the computer work station or look at any of the papers there. But she did, anyway. She didn't touch anything. She simply stood, trying to read computer printouts that described a number of women whose names weren't familiar. Character sketches for his book, she decided. At the bottom of one of the sheets was a detailed narrative about the way the woman was murdered.

The explicit explanation made her shudder and turn away. Over at the desk, she again examined some papers without touching them. Her own name seemed to leap off a page peeking out from under another. Heartbeat accelerating, she picked it up.

The arrangement of the page looked just like the character descriptions near the computer. There was her name, an age followed by a question mark—he was off by a year—then a brief description of her, including height and build, color of hair and eyes. At the bottom there were a few words and phrases. *Curious. Annoyingly perceptive. Not easily fooled. Tempting.* That last word was crossed out. Then came the sentence, *She'll be hard to throw off the trail.*

Elizabeth chewed at the corner of her mouth for a moment, then crossed back to the computer to look at the character sketches headed by other women's names. In the space where each of their murders was detailed, her page was blank. She could feel her pulse pounding as she stared down at that white space. Then she threw the papers down.

"I'm being stupid," she told Poe, who was watching her from the chair. "He's not a murderer. Or anything else but a writer." All that that paper proved was how much he'd been thinking about her. Which was kind of nice. Especially that word he had crossed out. *Tempting.*

Well, she knew about temptation. That's what had led her up here, but she was leaving before she found something else that upset her. The only temptation she wanted in relation to Jonas was what he offered with his kisses. Somehow, some way, she had to shut down her reporter's instincts and wait for him to share his secrets with her. And if he didn't...

"I'll face that when it happens." Turning her back to Poe, she started toward the stairs and promptly stubbed her toe. With a small yelp of pain, she limped around for a moment before looking down to see what she had tripped over. It was a box with a prominent publisher's name printed on the side. And it was open.

She paused for only one brief, soul-searching instant. Then she knelt and pulled the box flaps apart. The name Gerald Tucker, printed in bloodred letters, stared up at her from four identical book jackets. Gasping, she seized one and sat back on her haunches. Though she read mainly nonfiction and usually for research, even she recognized this author's name. No details. Just the name. *Jonas's pen name.*

Her fingers traced the raised letters of the name, then the rest of the jacket design. The background was black, with one colorful feather such as might adorn an Indian's headdress. Blood dripped off the feather's end. At the bottom was the title in white.

On Sacred Ground.

It was the story he had told her about today, the one set on a reservation. His latest book. Bestseller *Gerald Tucker's* latest mystery. "I'll be damned," Elizabeth murmured.

She flipped the book over to see if there was an author photograph on the back. Nothing. A small biography on the jacket said only that he lived in the western U.S. But why would Jonas hide this? His books had been reviewed in enough publications and had landed on enough bestseller lists that she recognized the name. He should be proud. Beyond that, he had the sort of looks, demeanor and, from what she had heard of his athletic exploits, background to be a public-relations department's dream come true. He should be on Letterman, for heaven's sake, promoting this book.

Instead, he was hiding out in Whitehorn.

More puzzled than ever, Elizabeth opened the book, scanned the copyright page to see if Jonas's name was anywhere. It wasn't. Then she turned to Chapter One and began to read.

Jonas awoke with a jerk. The room was dim, with thin streams of sunlight coming through the slats of the blinds. For a moment he stared up at the familiar ceiling. Then he frowned. Something wasn't right. Lifting a hand to his head, he touched a bandage, and last night came streaming back.

The accident. And Elizabeth. Here in his house.

He sat up. Pain pierced his temples and a fog descended on his vision. While he was blinded, he felt a cold, wet nose push against his arm. He opened one eye to look at Raven. But instead of staring adoringly back as usual, the dog had her attention focused elsewhere. On Elizabeth. Asleep in the chairs beside the bed with Poe in her lap.

And the latest Gerald Tucker mystery was open on the chair arm.

One short, four-letter word summed up the situation for Jonas. He was in up to his chin now. Elizabeth had found the box of books that had arrived yesterday just before he had left to meet her. She had probably gone through the house and found out everything about him.

He stared at her, wondering if what he saw was really who she was. Curled up in the chair in his robe, with one hand under her cheek and one long, slim leg bared to his gaze, she looked like a sweet, sexy angel. A woman whose body and mind he would like to explore to his heart's content. And a reporter with a well-honed talent for ferreting out secrets.

She stirred, and the robe slipped in front, revealing half of one breast. Jonas remembered yesterday, his mouth on her tightly budded nipples, her hand caressing his erection. The memory made him hard. And the last thing Elizabeth had said last night had been a promise about what tomorrow—which was today—would bring.

Pushing the sheets back, he swung his legs over the side of the bed and groaned as his muscles protested. Raven jumped off the bed as well, landing with an indelicate *plop*. Poe stretched in Elizabeth's lap, jumped down, and the two scampered out of the room. In the chair, Elizabeth opened her eyes. She looked at him, blinked, then sat up, trying to tug the front of the robe together.

"So you know," Jonas said, nodding at the book.

She passed a hand over her face. "You're famous."

"Gerald Tucker's famous. I'm just a writer."

"But you and he are one and the same."

Jonas shrugged. This was an argument he had with his agent and publisher on a regular basis. Only his agent knew who he really was, and if he told, Jonas had promised to move far away, stop writing and never make another dime for him.

"The book is astounding," Elizabeth said quietly.

"Glad you like it." His reply was less than polite.

"You should have told me."

"And deny you the pleasure of discovery? I wouldn't do that."

She had the grace to look ashamed. "I shouldn't have looked around."

"No, you shouldn't have."

"But I don't understand why this has to be a secret."

"Because I want it secret."

"Then I won't tell anyone."

"Yeah, sure." Suppressing the groan that seemed to come with every movement, he pushed himself up off the bed. Only when he was standing and Elizabeth was staring up at him did he remember how very naked he was.

He was also hard as a brick. Growing more so with every moment that she looked at him.

And she seemed to look at him for a very, very long time. Then she stood, slowly letting go of the front of his robe so that it fell open down the front.

Jonas tried not to be distracted by the view, by her hot, intense regard or by the traitorous stirring of his sex. He was angry with her for snooping around his house. It was unethical, damn it. He hadn't invited her here. She was an unprofessional little...

Her hand against his chest broke his chain of thought. She looked up at him with melting, dark-chocolate eyes and whispered his name. He didn't move while she ran her fingers down his body, all the way down, to the hot, velvet tip of his sex. She took him in her palm, even as she raised her mouth to his.

He forgot about his anger, forgot a head that ached like seven kinds of hell, forgot muscles that screamed in protest. He just kissed her and let her stroke him.

Her face was flushed when she stepped back, and her color deepened when she pushed the robe off her shoulders and let it fall to the floor. She was all cream and gold and rose. Pale skin. Pink nipples that tightened as he brushed the back of his hand across them. A thatch of honeyed curls at the juncture of her thighs.

With a groan that had more to do with his arousal than pain, he pulled her into his arms. The contact assuaged his need to feel her close, but only exacerbated his growing pressure for release. His shaft throbbed hard and heavy against her soft belly, and as they kissed, she rubbed against him. It was a sublime agony that had to end or he'd lose his grip.

He drew away and slipped his hand down their bodies, to the moist cleft in her mound. One touch, and she pressed down, all wet and warm and eager.

What Jonas wanted to do was swing her back on the bed, fill her in one stroke. There was only one problem. Aroused though he was, his sore and protesting muscles weren't exactly up to swinging.

Maybe she read his mind. Or maybe she was just as ready as he was. Whatever the case, she was the one who eased him back on the bed. She knelt over him, then straddled his hips, taking him inside her body in one smooth, slick glide. She began to move. Jonas groaned again and closed his eyes.

Concerned, Elizabeth stilled. "Are you okay?"

"No."

"What's wrong?"

"You stopped moving." His dark eyes glinted up at her, tilted at the corners.

In retaliation, she arched her back, knowing her breasts lifted high and proud, tantalizingly close but just beyond his reach as she threw back her head and pushed down. Then she moved her body in one slow, circular motion that tore another groan from him and brought his pelvis up off the bed to strain against hers. His hands went to her hips, his strong fingers guiding her movements.

Leaning forward, she felt him pulse inside her; she felt him breathe and move and sigh. She had never experienced this oneness, this being so in concert with another person that she could anticipate his next motion. So connected, on every level, that she could feel the ripples of sensation as they tore through his body and spilled into her own. It wasn't just physical. It went higher, deeper than that.

When he climaxed, he looked straight into her eyes, whispering, "Elizabeth." She felt as if he had looked into her heart.

And when her name left his lips, her own completion began—like a sudden rainstorm, sheet after sheet of intense, downpouring response. As she plunged, swirling in the passion, she remembered what Jonas had said last night about jumping out of a plane, when there was nothing to catch you but the wind. She hadn't been able to imagine the sensation. Not until now. Only it wasn't the wind that had caught her. It was Jonas. He had caught her, made her feel safe enough to fly.

There was a name for what had just happened between them. And it wasn't sex. It wasn't lovemaking. It was trust.

With a last, trembling sigh, she slipped to Jonas's side. He turned and gathered her in his arms. For several moments, they just lay together, their breathing returning to normal.

But too soon he pulled away. He lay on his back, not looking at her. Their closeness, so clear just an instant before, disintegrated like so much magic dust. She could feel his distance.

Elizabeth pulled the sheet up over her body and turned on her side to study Jonas's profile. "What's wrong?"

He looked at her, his dark eyes stormy. "What do you know, Elizabeth?"

"Know?"

"About me. What else did you discover last night when you were prowling through my house uninvited?"

Nine

Elizabeth stared into Jonas's intense, angry gaze for a couple of moments, then sat up, clutching the sheet over her breasts.

"What do you know?" he repeated, pushing himself up on his elbows.

"Nothing."

"But you went through my study."

Feeling even more guilty than she had imagined she might, she told him how she had gone exploring after he was asleep last night, had found his study and some of the character sketches on his desk. "When I tripped over the box of books and looked inside, I knew you were Gerald Tucker. *On Sacred Ground* is the book you told me about yesterday."

"You didn't have to open the box."

Gaze faltering from his, she pleated and unpleated the sheet with her fingers. "You're right. I shouldn't have, but the temptation was too great."

"Then you looked around some more, didn't you?"

"No."

He paused, then said tightly, "I don't know whether to believe you or not."

Elizabeth looked up in surprise. "I'm not a liar, Jonas. I particularly wouldn't lie to a man I'm involved with. God knows I've been lied to enough in my life to know how much it hurts."

It wasn't clear if he accepted that or not because he sat up and turned his back to her.

As calmly as she could, Elizabeth slid off the bed and went around the end to retrieve the robe she had dropped. She slipped it on and headed for the bathroom, not looking back at Jonas. If he thought she was lying, the best thing she could do was get her clothes on and get out of here.

When she reached the door, he said, "There are just some things that are private, Elizabeth. Like a person's home, his personal things..."

"I know that," she said, pausing in the doorway but not turning around. "I am very sorry I violated your privacy. But my curiosity—"

"Yes, your nose for news."

Angered by his sarcasm, she wheeled to face him. "It has nothing to do with that."

"Then why were you prowling?"

"Because I knew we were going to sleep together, that we are becoming involved. And I just wanted to know..." She lifted a hand, then let it drop back to her side. "I wanted to know something more about you."

He sat as he was, hands clenched on his spread knees, glaring at her.

She took a step forward. "I wish you could trust me."

"I was beginning to."

"But what about this?" She pointed to the bed. "Isn't what just happened between us as trusting as it gets between two people?"

He pushed a hand through his hair. "Elizabeth, this was—"

"Don't say it had nothing to with trust," she interrupted, "because it did for me. I haven't done this so very much in my life, Jonas. Not because I didn't have opportunities, but because I couldn't open myself like this to someone I didn't care about, someone I didn't trust. Damn it, Jonas, this was important, special...."

He stood, reaching for the jeans he had discarded last night. "I didn't say it wasn't important to me, either. I've been alone a long time. I stopped being casual about who I slept with a long time ago."

"Thank God for that much," she said bitterly. "At least I know I didn't make love, with no protection, with a man who is promiscuous."

Looking startled, Jonas glanced up from zipping his jeans. "I'm so out of practice that I didn't even think of protection."

"And I was so foolish—"

"Don't say that." He came toward her, moving slowly, putting a hand to the bandage on his forehead. "Although it was a stupid chance we took, I can assure you I'm healthy." He paused, frowning. "But in terms of birth control—"

"Don't worry about getting trapped with a baby," she snapped, turning away. "Believe me, I'm the last person to do that to anyone."

His hand reached under her elbow and brought her around to face him again. "That isn't what I was thinking."

"Why should I believe you? You don't trust me—"

"Damnation, Elizabeth, you went through my things."

"And I'm sorry," she said again, struggling to remain calm. "It was wrong, and I'm terribly, terribly sorry. And I won't tell anyone about Gerald Tucker. I don't know why you think it has to be a secret, but you have my word that I won't say anything, write anything, tell anyone. Now why can't you believe me?"

"Because I've trusted unwisely before."

"So have I."

He walked away. "You don't know what I've been through."

When she'd found the books last night, Elizabeth had imagined she'd stumbled across the key to Jonas's mystery. He was obviously hiding something more, however, or else he wouldn't be so upset now. But she simply couldn't believe his secret was so awful. At the same time, she understood how betrayal and dishonesty could color your reactions to other people. Maybe if Jonas understood all that she had been through in her own life, he would trust her with his secrets.

Taking a deep breath, she said, "The first eighteen years of my life were just one big lie, Jonas, so I do know why it's difficult for you to trust anyone."

He stopped his pacing near the window. "What are you talking about?"

"Just before I graduated from high school, I found out that my older sister was really my mother. The people I called my parents, who had raised me, clothed me, fed me, but never quite loved me, were really my grandparents."

Jonas stayed where he was, silent.

Elizabeth attempted a laugh that failed miserably. "It was so funny, you know. Growing up, I always wondered what was wrong with me. Father was this really warm and loving man to most people, especially to everyone in his congregation. He was a minister, you see. And my mother..." She shook her head, as if that would clear some of the bitterness she felt. "Mother was always there for everyone in town who needed her. She was so kind and gentle. But she was cold to me. So cold." To her dismay, her voice broke on the last word.

"Elizabeth, don't," Jonas protested.

Bringing herself under control, she motioned for him to be quiet. "I want to tell you this, Jonas. I've never told anyone, but I want to tell you. Because I trust you, you see. I trust you with this dark, terrible secret—"

"But it's not so terrible."

"It was to me," she exclaimed. "To me it was hell growing up in that silent, cold house and not having a clue as to why I didn't fit in."

"How'd you find out the truth?"

"My sister—my *real* mother, Julie—came for a visit that spring just before my graduation. She told me."

"But why after all that time?"

"She said she hated lying to me."

Jonas crossed the room to her again. "Why did she let them keep you in the first place?"

Elizabeth knotted and unknotted the robe's sash as she offered the only explanation that she had been able to come up with. "Julie was only fifteen, and the boy who fathered me denied he had ever touched her. Mother and Father were devastated when she finally came to them. She had done this terrible wrong, brought shame to them, failed them. So she went along with everything they said to do."

In flat, deliberately emotionless terms, Elizabeth explained how her parents had pulled up stakes, left a church in Kentucky and went away until she was born. When her father looked for a new congregation, he presented himself as a family man with two daughters, one sixteen, one a baby.

Jonas looked confused. "I don't understand. Wouldn't it have been easier to let you be adopted?"

Pushing her hair back from her face, Elizabeth said, "Of course it would have been easier. And better for me. But they saw me as their responsibility. Raising me was their penance, perhaps, for having failed my sister... mother. God, I've never known what to call her, how to think of her, ever since I learned the truth."

"Where is she now?"

"She's been married a long time. Her husband and kids don't know the real story about me, as far as I know. I haven't seen her or them in a long while."

"And your parents?"

"They're gone."

"So you never laid this to rest."

"Yes, I have. I faced it a long time ago."

His look was disbelieving as he reached out and took her hands in his. "Then why are you trembling?"

"Because I want you to understand that I do know what it is like to have your trust shattered." She struggled to bring the point she was trying to tell him back into focus. "The three people I should have been able to count on the most, my family, lied to me about who I was. Mother said she lied to protect me and Julie. But I knew that wasn't true. She and Father lied to protect themselves, to make sure no one saw the chinks in the family honor. And after something like that, it's difficult to trust again. So I know where you're coming from, Jonas."

Her fingers squeezed his. "I won't let you down. Whatever you want to tell me, I can be trusted."

Jonas wanted to believe her. It would be such a release to lay bare the blackest part of his soul. But he couldn't do it today any more than he could have yesterday or the day before. He wasn't ready. Allowing Elizabeth into one corner of his life hadn't changed his desire to leave his past buried.

And yet he had to admit there *was* a difference now. Despite the way she had discovered the secret about his writing, he at least *wanted* to trust her. There now existed the *possibility* of telling her the whole truth about himself.

But he couldn't do it yet. She must have seen that in his face, for the look of expectation in her eyes dimmed to disappointment.

"I'm sorry," he murmured. "As I told you, Elizabeth, I've been alone so long that sharing anything about myself, especially the painful parts of my past, is difficult, to say the least."

"I know that, but—"

He silenced her with a touch to her cheek. "But I do want to share with you. I want..." He paused and slipped his hand through her shining cap of hair and cupped her neck. "I guess I don't know exactly what I want. This is all very new."

"To me, too."

"We've moved really fast."

She nodded, her gaze flickering toward the bed.

"Regrets?"

Her chin lifted. "No."

"Not for me, either." He smiled. "So why don't we let everything kind of slow down, let it develop?"

"That's exactly what I want." She rushed on, adding, "I don't have to know all your secrets, Jonas. That's not what this is about at all. Becoming..." She hesitated, then plunged on. "Becoming *involved* doesn't mean I need to know every nuance of your life."

"Doesn't it?"

She looked confused.

"In my experience, involvement usually calls for revelations of some sort or other."

"I can't imagine what revelation you might make that would change my opinion of you."

"Day before yesterday your opinion was that I was a pain-in-the-butt guy who was interfering in your pursuit of a story."

She smiled teasingly as she slipped her arms around his waist. "That may still be true, but you have other aspects to your personality."

He chuckled. "Oh, really? You may expound on that topic."

She pressed a gentle kiss to his throat, then lifted her mouth to meet his. "Many, many sexy aspects," she murmured.

He kissed her and reached for the tie of her robe. "I sort of like your aspects, too."

"You'll have to point them out to me."

"I plan to, one at a time." He nuzzled her neck, then drew away. "Maybe in the tub?"

Considering what they had just done together in his bed, how boldly she had grabbed control and taken her pleasure, he was amazed that she could still blush scarlet. But he liked being amazed by her. And he wanted to amaze her, as well.

In the tub, sore muscles and all, he worked very *hard* at being as amazing as possible. If the water they splashed on the floor was any measure, he succeeded. If he'd had any doubts after that, Elizabeth was vocal in expressing her total satisfaction.

They spent most of the day in bed, sleeping and making love, getting up only when hunger called. When it was nearly dark, they went out long enough to make pit stops at the drugstore for the protection they had ignored all day and to the grocery store to make sure they wouldn't starve. Then Elizabeth checked out of the Amity Boardinghouse. Jonas supposed the couple who ran the place thought the two of them were scandalous. He didn't care. He just wanted Elizabeth with him for as long as she wanted to stay. She said she had another week and a half of vacation. They didn't talk about what would happen after that.

They didn't talk about the mystery in town, either.

Or his past.

Or even his writing.

During the three long, lovely days they hibernated together in his house, they talked about music, about politics and art, about religion and baseball and the correct way to determine a spaghetti noodle's readiness for serving. There were a million and one subjects to cover, and Jonas suspected they were only getting started.

Sometimes they didn't talk at all. They sat in silence on his back deck, looking at the mountains. They took Raven for a walk at twilight through Whitehorn's quiet streets. They cuddled in front of the fire after dinner, listening to his vintage collection of Beatles' albums. And they lay together in the still, dark hours before dawn, not sleeping, just holding each other.

Taken altogether, those days were the most unforced, happy ones Jonas could remember since he was a young man just out of Texas. Or maybe he had never had days like this, because there had never been anyone in his life who fit him the way Elizabeth did. Sexually, they generated fireworks. Companionably, they were in sync enough for harmony, with just enough differences to continue creating the sparks that made conversation interesting. She eased into his life with so little effort, he almost forgot that he didn't deserve a decent woman like her, almost forgot to be wary of her.

On Tuesday, their idyll ended. Jonas had to make arrangements to have his Jeep looked at by his insurance company. He had to work on his book or fall so hopelessly behind he would never catch up. And that evening, he had a work session with the committee that was going to run the puppet theater at this weekend's Pioneer Days festival. Jonas had helped design and build the theater several years back.

"You built a puppet theater?" Elizabeth asked in amazement when he told her where he needed to go after dinner.

"Not alone, of course."

"But I'm amazed you would get that involved with the festival."

"I mix and mingle occasionally."

"But a puppet theater?" She still didn't quite believe him.

"Come with me and see. We have to repaint some of the background to fit the new play we're planning to present."

"So you're a puppeteer, too, not just a set designer."

"Sort of."

She went with him that night, feeling somewhat anxious. Since the incident with Moriah Hunter and Melissa Avery North last week, she'd figured she was viewed as the enemy in town. There was a stir of sorts when she appeared with Jonas in the high school gymnasium, where workers were busy with the puppet theater and other projects for the festival. She recognized many people there— Raeanne Rawlings; Jessica McCallum, with little Jennifer in tow; even Sheriff Hensley with his family.

After nodding to them all, Elizabeth volunteered to do whatever was needed to get ready for Saturday. She was assigned to help a bubbly, pretty blonde named Lori Bains, who was to repair some rips in the puppet theater's red satin draperies. Lori was unabashedly friendly, putting Elizabeth at ease. As they carried the curtains over to a group of chairs on the side, Lori confided she was pregnant with her first child and didn't particularly want to paint.

"All those fumes," she said, handing Elizabeth a needle and thread. "No matter what anyone says, they just can't be good for the baby."

Before Elizabeth could agree, a tall, blond hunk in jeans and Western-style shirt broke away from the painters and came toward them. Lori introduced him to Elizabeth as her husband, Travis.

Barely sparing a nod for Elizabeth, he asked Lori, "You okay, honey?"

His wife smiled indulgently up at him. "I'm just as perfect as I was when you asked ten minutes ago."

Travis looked a little embarrassed. "I'm driving you crazy, aren't I?"

"Yes, but I love it." Lori lifted her lips to accept his kiss and sighed contentedly when he rejoined the others. "He's been a little overprotective since I became pregnant."

"You seem very happy," Elizabeth murmured, feeling unaccountably wistful. Her gaze sought out Jonas among the workers busy near the theater's background sets. As if he knew she was watching, he turned and smiled. Her heart gave an odd little flutter as she smiled back.

Beside her, Lori laughed softly.

Elizabeth flushed at the blonde's knowing grin and concentrated on threading her needle.

"Looks like your stay in Whitehorn has yielded more than a story."

Surprised, Elizabeth looked up. "So you know I'm a reporter."

"Most everyone in town knows about you."

"You were so friendly I figured you didn't."

"Look," Lori said matter-of-factly. "I don't particularly want our town portrayed in a big-city newspaper as some sort of oddball place, but I don't think you can be faulted for asking some questions. A lot of us have been thinking there's been a string of weird events around here lately." She nodded toward the gymnasium doors. "Why, just think about her, for example."

Elizabeth followed Lori's gaze to where a table for coffee and soft drinks was being set up near the entrance. Mary Jo Kincaid was directing several older gentlemen in the effort. In her pale pink skirt and matching ruffled blouse, she was a real contrast to the predominantly blue-jeaned crowd.

"You think Mrs. Kincaid is weird?" Elizabeth asked Lori.

"Just tragic." Lori sighed. "She seemed devoted to her husband, and when he died so suddenly...well, all of us at the hospital felt so sorry for her."

"You work there?"

"I'm a midwife and go there with some patients."

"And you were there when he died?"

Lori nodded. "Mary Jo went into shock. And who can blame her? Everyone, even the doctors, thought he was going to pull through."

So Lily Mae was right, Elizabeth thought. There was some controversy about Dugin's death. A dozen questions flashed through her mind, but she fell silent as Lori began repairing a curtain hem.

During these last few days with Jonas, the town's mysteries had diminished in importance. And maybe that was for the best. Maybe Jonas was where Elizabeth should be concentrating. After all, it wasn't every day that a woman fell in love.

Was it love? Elizabeth set to work mending a small tear in a curtain while her mind raced. She had known Jonas for only a week. So how could it be love? There was so much she didn't know about him. How had he become wealthy? What had he done before becoming a novelist?

By looking at the copyright dates in all the Gerald Tucker mysteries in his house, she had surmised that he had begun publishing six years ago. A book a year since then—a fabulous book a year, judging by what she'd read so far. But he'd said he'd moved here and bought the house nearly nine years ago. The remodeling and furnishings had required money, lots of it. Had he been publishing under another pseudonym before that? She told herself to be patient, that Jonas would answer all her questions in due time. But patience had never been one of her virtues, especially when her curiosity was so aroused.

And yet there was a part of her that said what she didn't know about Jonas didn't matter. His secrets and the amount of time they had been together were superficial compared to the strong connection she already felt to him. The things she did know were incontrovertible truths. That his mind was quick and his company never dull. That his smile made the rest of the world retreat. That his touch could set her on fire. That he was patient enough to have bottle-fed an abandoned kitten. That he was loyal enough to have defended this town when he thought her pursuit of a story threatened it. That he was generous enough to spend valuable writing time painting trees on the plywood background of this puppet theater.

But was any of that enough basis for love?

She looked up from her sewing and sought him out again. He was at the edge of the crowd, kneeling to talk to little Jennifer McCallum. The child had apparently gotten away from her mother and wanted to help with the painting. Jonas was trying to charm a paintbrush out of her small, chubby fist. Elizabeth couldn't hear what he was saying, but he made Jennifer laugh—a high, sparkling giggle that carried above all the noise and activity.

Watching Jonas with that child, Elizabeth stopped questioning whether she was really in love with him. There were no doubts. She simply was.

And she wanted him to know it. Right now.

Following impulses seemed to be the rule rather than the exception with her these days. Elizabeth murmured an excuse to Lori, set the curtain aside and headed to where Jonas was now talking to Jennifer's mother. The little girl surrendered her paintbrush and began playing peekaboo with Sheriff Hensley's toddler, who was in a stroller nearby.

Jessica McCallum gave Elizabeth a sunny smile as she approached. "The story you wrote about Jennifer in the *Free Press*'s Sunday magazine was just wonderful."

Elizabeth blinked. Her absorption in Jonas had been so complete, she had forgotten the story would run this past weekend. She hadn't even seen the paper, something unheard-of in her career. If that didn't prove this was love, nothing would.

Jessica dropped her voice and glanced at Jennifer. "I'm glad you followed our wishes and emphasized the joys of adoption over the more sensational aspect of how she was left on a doorstep. You didn't gloss over anything, you just didn't play up the fact that she was abandoned. We're grateful."

Pleased, Elizabeth replied, "I think the way you and your husband and Jennifer have become a family is the most interesting part of the story. I'm glad you liked the way I handled it."

Jessica touched her arm. "Thanks for doing such a nice job."

She went after her daughter, who was now pestering another group of workers, and Elizabeth glanced up at Jonas. "You look surprised. Did you think I'd find something headline-grabbing to write about that little girl?"

"Maybe," he murmured. "And maybe I shouldn't really be surprised that you didn't."

"Oh, dear," she said in mock horror. "That almost sounds like you trust me."

"Could be." He grinned and dropped a hard, fast kiss on her lips.

Someone called for his help before Elizabeth could say the words that were overflowing her heart. So she saved them for later that night, after they'd made love and were still wrapped together in the middle of his bed, with the moonlight spilling through the windows and the sheets tangled around their bodies.

Jonas, who had been stroking his hand through her hair, went very still.

"I do love you," she said again, and told him all the reasons why.

A lead balloon of apprehension filled Jonas's chest as he listened to Elizabeth sing his praises. She was putting him on a pedestal where he didn't belong. He knew he should tell her the truth, that once upon a time in a decadent world, he had lived an obscenely selfish and reckless life. No kindness, large or small, that he did for others now could make up for what he had done before. Nothing could bring someone back from the dead.

Elizabeth's hushed voice broke into his reverie. "You're awfully quiet. Say something."

He wet his lips, tried to say the words he knew were right. They wouldn't come.

"Jonas?" Her tone was anxious now.

"I don't deserve you," he finally said, forcing out the words. "I don't deserve this."

"There are no strings attached to my feelings, Jonas. So don't think you have to reciprocate."

"It's not that." With a sigh, he turned on his side and looked at her. Moonlight touched her features, gilding one side of her face and the satiny skin of her shoulder with a pale, golden glow. He couldn't make out her expression, but could feel the tension in her body.

"What is it?"

He closed his eyes and tried to find the answer. Finally, lamely, he said, "I'm not all you think I am."

"Then who are you, Jonas? Tell me so I'll understand."

Now was the time. After offering him her love, she had asked a simple, direct question. Not giving her an answer was really the same as lying to her. Elizabeth had been lied to and betrayed enough in her life. Those closest to her had hurt her the most. He knew how that felt. He also knew she wouldn't tolerate his lies.

And yet he kept his silence. He was so damned afraid of her disillusionment with him that he couldn't do the right thing, the honorable thing, which was to let her know exactly what kind of man she was professing to love. He was afraid the truth would send her running. At least this way he had her here. After the cold years of solitude, he had her warmth. And he was selfish enough to want to keep it, at least for a while longer.

So instead of answering her, he fitted his lips to hers. He kissed her with all the yearning of a man who wanted to be what the woman who loved him needed and wanted. He kissed and stroked her creamy breasts, her soft belly, the moist delta between her thighs. She opened for his intimate questing, moved against his probing tongue, climaxed in a shattering outpouring of passion.

Minutes later, when she reached for him, offering the same release, he merely pulled the covers over them both. "Just sleep. Just let me hold you while you sleep."

Elizabeth cuddled against him, spoon fashion, and he relaxed into sleep before she could even close her eyes. She kept thinking that he hadn't answered her question.

The unknown, which she had decided was so unimportant, loomed large and frightening in the dark.

"Who are you, Jonas?"

The question came at her from the shadows, then echoed in her head and through her dreams.

Fears fled in the light of day. But the real world didn't. Early the next morning, Elizabeth was yawning and making coffee in the kitchen when Jonas and Raven came in from their run.

Jonas tossed a copy of the *Whitehorn Journal* on the island. "Take a look at that. One of the town's mysteries is solved."

Staring up from the front page was a sketch of a young woman. Underneath was the headline Car-bombing Victim Identified.

"The woman who was blown up in that car a while back," Elizabeth murmured.

"One and the same," Jonas answered. "The article says the state police and the FBI have been checking dental records of women reported missing ever since the bombing. Nothing turned up. Then one of the TV newscasts in Billings ran a special program on unresolved crimes. A sketch of Whitehorn's mystery lady was included."

"You mean they hadn't run a sketch before?"

"I think they did. But no one stepped forward with any information. And anyhow, the first sketch was based on details given by the guy whose car blew up."

"He was a private investigator," Elizabeth said, scanning the article. "Nick Dean."

Jonas nodded. "This woman was hitchhiking when he picked her up just outside of town. And even though he worked with a police artist to sketch her, it evidently wasn't a good likeness."

"And the bombing left her body in bad shape?"

"Yeah. The authorities finally called in a specially trained artist who used a computer program to reconstruct a likeness of facial features based on skull structure, et cetera."

"And the computer likeness, coupled with Nick Dean's recollection, provided a much clearer image of the woman's face." Elizabeth looked down at the picture again. The young woman, identified as Marie March, had been a twenty-four-year-old waitress from Billings. A friend recognized her from the sketch. Her identity had been confirmed late yesterday afternoon through medical and dental records.

The article went on to say that more than three years ago, after giving birth to a daughter out of wedlock, Marie left her friend, with whom she was living, with plans to return to Chicago, where she had grown up. The friend tried to dissuade Marie, who had no living family and who hadn't been well since before her baby was born. Marie left Billings, however, promising to write. She never did, but the friend had no reason report her missing. Marie seemed to have dropped out of sight after that, resurfacing over a year later in Whitehorn. There, she had the misfortune to get into a car with P.I. Nick Dean. While he escaped serious injury, she was killed.

Elizabeth looked up at Jonas. "No one knows why the car blew, do they?"

He frowned, rubbing his chin as he leaned against the counter. "Seems like I remember that the P.I. uncovered a Native-American-artifact-smuggling operation. I assume the explosion had something to do with that.''

"It says here that Dean started out investigating Charlie Avery's death.''

"And someone tried to blow him to smithereens,'' Jonas said thoughtfully. He raised an eyebrow at Elizabeth. "Do you think someone didn't want him to find out about Charlie?''

"Or they wanted Marie March dead.''

"Why?''

"That's the real question.'' Staring down at the newspaper article again, Elizabeth tried imagining why anyone would want a young unwed mother dead. With the facts she had, she came up empty. The logical explanation was exactly what Jonas had said, that Nick Dean was supposed to die instead of Marie. That was the only way this death connected with anything else.

Silently, she ran through Whitehorn's series of strange events. She had to start thirty years ago, with Charlie Avery's death and the disappearance of his young girlfriend, Lexine Baxter. Then there was Rafe Rawlings, found in the woods. Then little Jennifer found on the Kincaid's doorstep three years ago...

Three years ago?

A glance at the article about Marie March made Elizabeth's mouth run dry. "Jonas. Oh, my God, Jonas.''

"What is it?''

"A little over three years ago Marie March had a baby daughter.''

"So?''

"So Jennifer McCallum was found three years ago in April.''

Eyes widening, he stared at her. Then he shook his head. "You're reaching, Elizabeth. This friend of Marie March's said she went to Chicago.''

"Then why did she end up in Whitehorn eighteen months later, *without* her baby?"

"There could be a hundred reasons."

"But doesn't it strike you as a strange coincidence?"

"Maybe," he agreed. "But maybe you're still just overanxious to find a connection among all these events."

Grabbing the newspaper, Elizabeth made a dive for the telephone and punched in directory assistance. "Billings," she answered, when the operator asked for the city. She gave the name of the woman in the article who was listed as Marie March's friend. In a matter of moments, she had a number and was dialing again.

"What are you doing?" Jonas asked.

"Checking this out. Seeing if this woman can identify anything about Jennifer."

He took the phone out of her hands, breaking the connection before it could ring. "Why do this, Elizabeth?"

"To find out."

"But what about Jennifer?"

"I think she deserves to know if Marie March was her mother. Someday this might answer some real questions for her."

He looked at her for a long moment. "I guess you'd understand about her needing to know the truth, but what about her parents, the McCallums? What if some unknown family member comes forward and wants to claim Jennifer?"

"The article said there was no family."

"They might crawl out of the woodwork."

Elizabeth paused, biting her lip, then she reached for the phone again. "I think learning the truth outweighs the risks."

Jonas stepped back, knowing it wasn't a risk he would take, but hoping Elizabeth was right.

"Miss Corbett?" she said into the receiver. "This is Elizabeth Monroe, a reporter for the *Denver Free Press*. I'd like to talk to you about Marie March. Specifically about her baby daughter. What can you tell me about her?"

Ten

Nessa Corbett was a buxom redhead with a voice made gravelly by too many years of too many cigarettes. A bartender at the restaurant where Marie March had worked, she was old enough to have been the young woman's mother. Jonas suspected Nessa's life hadn't been all sunshine and roses. Maybe that was why she had taken Marie under her wing and given her a place to live before and after her baby was born. Marie had come to mean a lot to the older woman. Nessa, a woman who probably didn't cry easily, did so when she realized Jennifer was most likely Marie's daughter.

During the phone call with Elizabeth, Nessa described Marie's baby as a tiny, blue-eyed blonde, born two weeks to the day before Jennifer was found on the Kincaids' doorstep. "She had the sweetest, most angelic little face," Nessa said. "I took one look at her and fell in love." That comment was strikingly similar to what everyone had said about Jennifer as a baby.

After talking with Elizabeth, Nessa agreed to make the hour-long drive from Billings to Whitehorn to talk face-to-face. Jonas, who at that point still had his doubts about the connection between Marie and Jennifer, went with Elizabeth to meet Nessa at a fast-food place off I-90 outside of town.

When he saw the one photograph Nessa had of Marie holding her baby, he began to think Elizabeth was on to something. More than the sketch in the paper, the photo captured Marie's delicate beauty. Something about her eyes made Jonas think of the little girl he had teased only the night before at the school gymnasium. Moreover, the baby in the photograph looked a lot like the baby picture of Jennifer that had run with Elizabeth's article in the Sunday magazine section of the *Free Press*. It was when Nessa compared the pictures that she cried, convinced Marie's child and Jennifer were one and the same.

Jonas and Elizabeth took Nessa to Sheriff Hensley, who studied the photographs before he agreed to talk with Nessa. Elizabeth and Jonas were asked to wait in the lobby. After some thirty minutes, Sterling McCallum came through and went behind Hensley's closed door. He soon emerged, grim-faced, and exited the building.

Hensley appeared, but would only tell Elizabeth that he would explain everything later. It was some time later before he allowed Nessa to come out. Joining Elizabeth and Jonas in a corner of the deserted lobby, the tearful woman told them that Jennifer had been found with a small antique cameo brooch pinned to her blanket, the same cameo Marie was wearing in Nessa's photograph.

"No one told me about a cameo," Elizabeth muttered as she jotted down notes.

Jonas understood the reasoning. "Why release something to the press that only the person who left her could identify?"

"That poor baby," Nessa said, wringing her hands. "Why would Marie leave her baby with strangers? She knew I would help her."

"Maybe they weren't strangers," Elizabeth offered.

That was exactly what Jonas was thinking. But what connection could a waitress in Billings have to the wealthy, powerful Kincaids? Unless, of course, Dugin Kincaid had had an affair with Marie and gotten her pregnant. That's what everyone in town had hypothesized when Jennifer was found. Perhaps for once the gossip was right.

"Do you know who fathered Jennifer?" he asked Nessa.

The woman, who looked exhausted, sagged back in her chair. Her hand shook as she pulled out a cigarette. "Marie found out she was pregnant right after she started working with me. She was still seeing the guy at the time, she said, but he never came around when I was there. It seems like she told me his first name once. I've been trying to think of it ever since I identified Marie."

"Does the name Dugin Kincaid ring a bell?" Elizabeth asked.

Nessa shook her head.

"But did the father know Marie was pregnant?"

"When she told him about the baby, he gave her money for an abortion and split. Marie said it was good riddance, but I didn't believe her. I think he hurt her real bad. When she was so sick, I begged her to call him. But she wouldn't talk about it."

Elizabeth frowned, staring down at her notepad. "So Marie had a difficult pregnancy?"

"It wasn't just the pregnancy," Nessa replied, before taking a drag on her cigarette. "I think there was something bad wrong with her. About a week before Jennifer was born, Marie came home from the doctor looking real upset. She cried all night. I tried to get her to tell me what was wrong, but she wouldn't. She was tight-lipped that way, didn't want no one feeling sorry for her. But now I wish..." Her voice trailed away as new tears filled her heavily made up eyes.

Elizabeth reached out and patted Nessa's arm. "You were a good friend to her."

Dabbing at the mascara that flowed down her cheeks, Nessa nodded. "I never had a child, but Marie was such a sweet little thing, I wished she was my daughter. She'd never had nobody care for her, growing up in foster homes the way she did. That's why she wanted that baby so bad, so she could do right by her.''

Jonas was puzzled. "It doesn't really make sense that someone like Marie would abandon her daughter to strangers.''

Nessa agreed. "For someone who grew up all on her own, Marie believed in family.''

Looking at Elizabeth, Jonas could see her thoughts had returned to the same place his had been before. Could Jennifer be related to the Kincaids?

"I had some hopes for a family, too,'' Nessa continued, sighing. She gave Jonas a weary smile. "I wanted Marie and that baby to stay with me. I was going to be a grandmother, or at least act like one. I was looking forward to it.''

"Then why weren't you worried about Marie when she didn't write you?''

The woman shrugged, lifting the cigarette to her mouth once again. "Much as I thought she was different, I was pretty used to people leaving me.''

Her jaded outlook was sad. But the saddest part to Jonas was that he knew exactly how she felt.

Elizabeth seemed stuck on another point. "Didn't you hear about Jennifer being abandoned three years ago?''

Nessa ground her cigarette in the ashtray nearby. "I honestly don't remember. If I did hear about it, I didn't connect it with Marie's baby. I thought they were in Chicago. If I'd had any inkling, I would have come forward then.''

"Do you want Jennifer now?''

Jonas gave Elizabeth a sharp look. What in the hell kind of hornet's nest was she trying to stir up with that questions? Jennifer had a good home, and Nessa Corbett had no claim on her. Some kind of off-the-wall custody battle might make good headlines, but it wasn't what anyone needed.

Before Nessa could answer, the door across the waiting room opened. Sterling McCallum stepped in, his solemn-looking wife at his side, daughter Jennifer in his arms. Jonas was stunned. What possible reason was there to bring the child down here now?

Nessa stood, murmuring, "Oh, my," as she started forward.

Elizabeth hung back, surprising Jonas. This afternoon he had seen the reporter in her reemerge after lying dormant for the past few days. She had been rabid in pursuit of this scoop.

But she stayed beside Jonas as Nessa crossed the lobby and stopped in front of the McCallums. The redhead lifted one work-worn hand toward Jennifer, who regarded Nessa with her customary sunny smile. No one moved. Not the McCallums. Not the clerk behind the desk. Not Sheriff Hensley, who had emerged from his office.

To her credit, Nessa didn't do anything to upset Jennifer. In a clear, steady voice, she said, "My, but you're as sweet looking as your mother."

Her smile growing wider, Jennifer looked at the only mother she knew. "Mommy's pretty."

"Very pretty," Nessa agreed. She dropped her hand back to her side. "And your mommy and daddy are very lucky to have a pretty little girl like you."

Jonas didn't realize he was holding his breath until he heard Elizabeth exhale beside him. He wasn't sure what either of them had been expecting. Nessa didn't seem the type to cause a scene, but he had been surprised by people before. He still had to wonder at what the McCallums had been thinking to bring Jennifer here.

Sterling McCallum shifted his daughter from one hip to the other. "Come on, sweet stuff," he said to her. "Let's go back to your dad's office and see if there's some candy hiding in my desk for you."

When he and Jennifer were gone, Jessica stepped forward, a hand outstretched to Nessa. "When my husband told me about you, and about Marie March being our daughter's birth mother, I knew we needed to bring Jennifer down here to see you. I felt like you'd want to see her."

Nessa took Jessica's hand. "I did. Thank you. A lot of people might have been afraid to let me see her, afraid of what I'd do."

"But Sterling said you were fond of her mother," Jessica explained. "He said he thought you were a good person, and I always trust his judgment. So I wanted you to see her right away, to see how happy she is."

"And she is, isn't she?" Nessa said, dabbing at the tears that were running down her face again. "Marie would be glad she's so happy." Jessica patted her shoulder, talking softly as she led the woman to a chair nearby.

Beside Jonas, Elizabeth turned away, murmuring, "Jessica McCallum is a lot braver than I am."

"Maybe she's just confident. Can you imagine anyone thinking that that child belongs with anyone other than the only parents she's ever known?"

"But what if a father turns up?"

"After what Nessa said about him? Even if he's not the person we're both thinking he might be, the man Marie told Nessa about doesn't sound like someone who'd be eager to take responsibility for a young child."

"But like you said this morning, a creep could come calling, making trouble for the McCallums."

Frowning, Jonas folded his arms across his chest. "That's something you should have thought about a while longer before you started all this."

Elizabeth stared up at him. "You're angry with me, aren't you?"

Anger wasn't the right word. *Uncomfortable* or *uneasy* were better choices. For several days he had chosen not to think about her being a reporter. He had pushed aside the knowledge that her specialty was digging up dirt and fitting pieces of puzzles together. Maybe he had foolishly deluded himself into thinking she had miraculously turned off the curiosity that fueled her professional engine. But he had seen how quickly she pounced on the idea of Jennifer being Marie's child, how she had worked the angles and followed it through. She was good. One day she might do the same thing with some bit of information he dropped. And then what? Would he be a story, just like Jennifer? Would she write down his facts and his reactions in her little notepad?

"Jonas, I think finding out about Jennifer was the right thing for everyone concerned," she stated now.

"So do I," said a voice from behind them. They both turned to face Jessica, who added, "I'm glad to know the truth."

But Elizabeth's expression was still apprehensive. "Maybe I should have called you first, Jessica, but I didn't want to upset you needlessly if my hunch turned out to be wrong."

"I think you handled it just fine," she assured her.

"You're a very generous woman," Jonas said with admiration.

Elizabeth studied him for a moment before turning back to Jessica. "Jonas thinks I was just pursuing a story. But it wasn't only that. I..." She paused, then plunged on. "I wasn't raised by my birth mother, either, and I just tried to think how Jennifer might feel one day, how she might wonder about the people who brought her into the world."

Jessica's smile was pensive. "This way she'll have some of the answers."

"About her mother, anyway," Jonas said.

The outside door opened, admitting a man in a well-tailored suit, who strode to the desk. After giving him a glance, Elizabeth lowered her voice. "Jessica, do you think Jennifer could be Dugin Kincaid's child?"

"Dugin's?" Jessica repeated, looking surprised. "He denied it emphatically when Sterling first investigated the case."

"Could he have done anything else?" Jonas wondered aloud. "He was about to get married."

"That's true," Jessica admitted.

"Maybe it should be checked out," Elizabeth suggested.

Jessica cocked an eyebrow. "How?"

"DNA or blood tests."

Nodding, Jessica said, "Those have already been ordered, to make absolutely certain Marie March was Jennifer's mother." She glanced toward Nessa, who sat staring off into space. "Although I don't need any tests. I think we have enough proof."

"But we don't know about Dugin," Jonas interjected. "Since he died under unusual circumstances, there must have been an autopsy performed. Surely tissue and blood samples were taken and stored by the coroner."

"I'm going to go suggest all this to Sheriff Hensley," Elizabeth said, turning purposely toward the desk at the end of the room.

"And I'd better go with her," Jonas muttered to Jessica. "She tends to rub the sheriff the wrong way."

The tall, anxious-looking man who had come inside a few minutes earlier was also at the desk, also demanding to see the sheriff. The clerk said Hensley was tied up with a long-distance phone call and suggested he sit down and wait.

But the man was impatient. "Tell the sheriff this is an urgent matter. I need to talk to him about this woman." He held up a copy of the *Whitehorn Journal* and pointed to the sketch of Marie.

While the clerk rang through to Hensley's office, Elizabeth and Jonas exchanged a look. She said to the man, "Did you know Marie March?"

He fingered his silk tie, looking uncomfortable. "Not exactly."

"And what does that mean?"

"Why do you want to know?"

"I'm a reporter with the *Denver Free Press*."

The man's face and neck turned deep red. "I can't talk to you." To the desk clerk, he demanded, "I want the sheriff. *Now.*"

With elaborate courtesy the clerk replied, "He's still on a call, sir."

"Then tell him who I am. I'm Hiram Bascom, the Kincaids' lawyer. That name used to get some results around here."

Elizabeth said, "Mr. Bascom, does whatever you know about Marie March have to do with the Kincaid family?"

Bascom ignored her and pounded a fist on the desk. "Good lord, doesn't Sheriff Hensley have anything more to do than run up long-distance phone bills? I have some information and some questions about this March woman—"

The clerk began a protest that Elizabeth interrupted with an excited, "What information, Mr. Bascom?"

"Can she harass me this way?" Bascom demanded.

"Ma'am, please," the clerk said wearily to Elizabeth.

She paid no attention, moving close to the lawyer, invading his space. "Was Dugin Kincaid Marie March's lover?"

"Not Dugin!" Bascom sputtered. Then he fell back a step, emitting a sound that was a cross between a squeak and a groan.

Elizabeth swooped in for the kill. "If not Dugin, who?" Her eyes widened. "Was it Dugin's father? Jeremiah?"

From behind Jonas came a gasp. He wheeled around in time to see Nessa rise from her chair.

"That's it!" she said. "Marie said her baby's father's name was Jeremiah."

Beside her, Jessica paled. "Jeremiah Kincaid is Jennifer's father?"

A vein had popped out on Bascom's perspiring forehead. "I didn't say that. You can't quote me," he told Elizabeth.

But Jonas knew she wouldn't have to. The man's face said it all. And tomorrow it would be front-page news.

Turning from a chart she had tacked up on Jonas's study wall, Elizabeth murmured, "That's two of the town's mysteries solved today."

Jonas, who was seated in his leather chair in front of a small, crackling fire, nodded but said nothing.

Elizabeth perched on his chair arm. "What are you thinking?"

He shrugged. "Just that old Jeremiah Kincaid would've been pretty unhappy about that lawyer tipping his hand."

After trying to deny that Jeremiah was Jennifer's father for several minutes, Bascom had crumbled. He had revealed that soon after Jeremiah Kincaid died, his law firm received a letter from Marie March, claiming that she was the mother of Jeremiah's child. She said she would be coming to Whitehorn to get her child and would expect a provision to be made for both of them by the Kincaid family and estate. She also said she had been ill for quite some time, or else she would have sued for support before Jeremiah's death.

The letter had puzzled the attorney, particularly the part about Marie returning to Whitehorn to get her child. Postmarked Chicago, the envelope had no return address, so he had set it aside, expecting Marie to appear soon after. It wasn't the first time a woman had tried to slap Jeremiah with a paternity suit, he said, so he wasn't unduly alarmed. But when Marie didn't come to Whitehorn, Bascom almost forgot about her. This morning he'd seen the article in the paper, remembered her name and begun to wonder if someone was going to show up with her child to file a claim against the Kincaid estate. Bascom had come over to the sheriff's office to see what he could find out, but he had bungled his attempts at secrecy.

Elizabeth sighed. "You'd have thought someone as rich as Jeremiah Kincaid would've had a real shark as his attorney."

"You went after him like pretty much of a shark yourself."

The sharpness in Jonas's tone caught Elizabeth off guard. Before she could formulate a reply, he got up and added a small log to the fire. His profile was serious, his jaw set.

"Are you upset with me?" Elizabeth finally asked, when the silence had stretched a little too long for her comfort.

"Of course not."

"But ever since this afternoon, you've been so quiet."

"I guess I'm thinking about the McCallums."

"They seemed to take all this rather well." This afternoon, Elizabeth had stayed at the sheriff's office until Hensley announced that rushed blood tests made it ninety-nine percent certain that Jeremiah and Marie were Jennifer's parents. Then Elizabeth, accompanied by Jonas, had gone by the McCallums' place to see if they wanted to make a statement. Jessica had gone one better, granting an exclusive interview, which Elizabeth had faxed to her editor from Jonas's study just a half hour ago.

"The McCallums are in shock," Jonas said.

"But I'm sure it will be okay," Elizabeth insisted. "Jeremiah's dead. You heard Mary Jo Kincaid say that Jennifer belonged with the McCallums."

"Yes. I heard Mary Jo." Turning his back to the fire, Jonas hooked his thumbs in his belt and frowned. "Did you think she was weird tonight?"

Elizabeth found something about Mary Jo Kincaid to be weird, *period,* but she couldn't put her finger on exactly what it was. While they were at the McCallums', Mary Jo had appeared in a filmy, seafoam green frock, tearfully dabbing at her eyes with a lacy handkerchief. She said Jennifer should be in the only home she had ever known, with the McCallums; that she was sure Jeremiah and her beloved Dugin would agree.

Though she had dutifully noted Mary Jo's touching statement, Elizabeth found the tears a bit much. Something in the woman's clear, carefully enunciated words hadn't rung true. There was a coldness underlying her very proper tone that had sent a chill up Elizabeth's spine. Why, she didn't know, she told Jonas, but Mary Jo Kincaid's voice had given her the creeps.

"For me it was her eyes," he murmured. "Her eyes were hard, despite the tears."

Frowning, Elizabeth turned back to the chart tacked to the wall. It contained all of what she called the "White-horn mysteries," dating from Charlie Avery's death all the way up to today's revelations. "Maybe we should add Mary Jo to this list," she told Jonas.

"I thought you weren't doing stories on the town."

"After what happened today?"

"Today was probably the end of all the mysteries that can be linked together. None of that other stuff on your chart is related."

"I don't think—" The ringing of the phone cut off Elizabeth's protest. "That's probably my editor." She headed for the desk, picked up the receiver and, as she suspected, heard Ted's voice.

She answered a series of rapid-fire questions first. Then she turned the conversation to the story about Jennifer she had sent in this afternoon, and the follow-up she had done tonight. Jeremiah Kincaid had been a big enough player in Rocky Mountain states' politics that the story would be picked up by news services throughout the region. She listened to Ted's comments with a widening smile.

"My, my," she said finally. "This little nothing of a town has turned into pay dirt, hasn't it?" Looking across the room at Jonas, she saw him turn back to the fire. He seemed tired, as well he should at nearly midnight, after the sort of day they'd had today.

Forcing her attention back to her editor, she quickly outlined some of the other mysteries. Ted was incensed that someone had threatened her, broken into her room and run her off the road. But he was even more angry that she hadn't called to tell him. He had conveniently forgotten that he had ordered her not to call. As she went on, the possibility of a lost sapphire mine caught his attention. He said he had just read an article about sapphires being used in highly advanced medical technology. Elizabeth promised to do some checking about the mine and to be careful. She hung up before Ted could start in on another round of questions.

Jonas continued to stand with his back to her, staring down at the fire. Finally, she crossed the room to his side.

"I suppose your editor was excited," Jonas said.

Knowing he was still opposed to any more stories about the town, she deliberately tried to play it down. "He was concerned about the break-in, the threats and the accident."

Putting a hand to the small bandage that still covered the gash on his forehead, Jonas nodded. "I didn't hear you tell him about me."

"I didn't." That wasn't exactly true, but it was close.

"Why not?"

Elizabeth looked up to find Jonas studying her with narrowed eyes. "My personal life is my own."

"I thought you told me that this guy, Ted, is a close friend."

"He is."

"So why not tell him about me? Didn't he want to know why he was calling you at a different number than the Amity Boardinghouse?"

She wasn't sure why Jonas was being so intense about this. "When he asked where I was staying, I said a friend's."

"And he didn't question that or ask about me?"

He had, but Elizabeth had been evasive. If Jonas hadn't been standing right here, however, she might have told Ted all about him, asked Ted's advice about falling in love so quickly, especially with a man of mystery. But she didn't really need to ask. She knew Ted would preach caution and restraint. And it was far too late for either. Besides, there wasn't anything Ted could say that she hadn't thought of herself.

"Ted is my editor," she told Jonas. "Not my keeper. He's probably glad that the paper isn't footing the bill for my hotel any longer."

Jonas looked skeptical.

Elizabeth turned away, changing the subject. "I remembered I hadn't put the missing sapphire mine on this chart." She started toward it, but Jonas caught her hand.

"Let's forget it tonight, okay?"

"Just let me write down—"

The rest of her sentence was lost as he spun her into his arms for a deep, lingering kiss. "Isn't that more interesting than sapphires?" he whispered against her mouth.

"Definitely. Except that I can't write about this."

He kissed her again. "Maybe you should."

"And what would I say?"

"Something about chemical reactions," he said, reaching for the edge of her cotton sweater. In one smooth motion, he pulled it up and over her head. "You could write about how my chemicals react to your chemicals." Expertly, he unclasped her bra. "Especially when you're like this."

Elizabeth shivered as his fingers skimmed across one breast and then the other. "What are your chemicals doing right now?" she asked.

"Solidifying." He pushed her bra straps down her arms, sent the garment to the floor, then reached for the snap of her jeans.

Playfully, she ducked away. "I don't know if I want to conduct this interview while you're fully dressed and I'm not."

He shucked his shirt in record time, and unbuckled his belt as he crossed the room toward her. "Is this more like it, Miss Monroe?"

"Get rid of the boots," she said, pointing at his feet.

After shedding shoes and socks, he advanced a few more inches. "I have a feeling this interview could turn into something up close and personal."

"Do you?" Ducking under his outstretched arm, she retreated toward the desk. Jonas watched while she shed her jeans and finally stood before him in nothing but her white bikini panties. When he started forward, she shook her finger at him. "Now, now, Mr. Bishop. You have to answer a few questions."

"Why don't we get naked first?"

"Because I want to hear about your chemicals."

"They're about to make me burst through this zipper."

Chuckling, she lowered her gaze to his crotch. "That sounds interesting. You'll have to show me."

He did.

Excitement curled through her belly. Her nipples tightened. She grew moist between her thighs. Though Jonas hadn't moved, she could almost feel him touching her, filling her.

"What do you think?" he asked as he dropped his pants and kicked them out of the way.

"Most impressive," she finally managed to say.

"So how are your chemicals?"

"All aquiver."

He grinned and came toward her, his eyes sparkling. "Sounds intriguing. You'll have to show me."

She pushed her panties down her legs, dropping them at his feet.

He looked from the crumpled scrap of material to her, his smile widening. "Maybe our chemicals ought to mingle."

Feeling the edge of the desk against her backside, Elizabeth said, "What a wonderful idea." She slipped onto the desk.

Jonas held out a small foil packet.

"My, but you came prepared," she said, taking it from him.

"Just call me hopeful." He stepped close. "I came up here hoping you'd be interested in a feature about our comingling chemicals."

"Oh, I'm interested." She opened the packet and then slowly, teasingly, unrolled the condom up his hard length.

Sighing, he said, "I'm counting on you to write this ending just right, Miss Monroe."

"We'll do it together," she whispered, opening to him.

Without preamble, he let her guide him into her body. She was so ready, she didn't need any preparation. She wrapped her legs around him, moved against him, rose to meet his deep, welcome thrusts. And when she began to climax, he picked her up, holding her tight to his firm, strong body, until he, too, began to shudder in release. He eased her back to the desk, pushing deeper into her.

For the first time since their first few, unprotected couplings, Elizabeth wished there was no barrier between them. She imagined Jonas planting a child in her womb.

And the image stunned her. She had never wanted children, never wanted to take a chance on inflicting a lonely, miserable childhood like her own on someone else.

But at this moment, with Jonas filling her, as they danced this basic, ancient mating dance, she wondered what it would be like to feel his baby in her belly, to hold his child to her breast.

Maybe it was those thoughts that made her move against him again, even before his orgasm was complete. Her muscles contracted, gloving his body with tight little pulls. Murmuring her name, he started to retreat, but her legs gripped him firmly. She caught him to her for a long kiss while her pelvis ground against his in a circular motion. She felt him growing hard again.

"Wait," he whispered. "We need to use another—"

She trapped his protest with her lips. He stretched inside her.

And they danced again.

Later that night, Elizabeth lay beside Jonas in bed, wondering at her boldness, at what she had done. Even though their protection had quite obviously become ineffective during that second time, she probably wasn't pregnant. The time of month was all wrong.

But what if that didn't matter?

What if a child was growing inside her right now?

Turning on her side, she pressed a hand to her stomach. What if she was having a baby with a man she still knew so little about? A man whose name probably belonged on that chart of mysteries she had tacked to the wall? She vacillated between fear and excitement, hardly sleeping at all.

But in the morning she realized the real reason for her jumbled emotions. Her period came. And with it came a dark sense of foreboding. She tried to shake her depression during breakfast with Jonas, but couldn't. Finally, she left for the library to do some research on sapphires. She didn't tell Jonas exactly what she was up to. He had made it clear enough last night that he didn't want to discuss any stories she was doing on the town. Their lovemaking had been a distraction, a successful and altogether pleasurable attempt to derail her thinking. He had done the same thing the night before, after she had told him she loved him.

And why was that?

From the beginning, she had known Jonas was hiding something. Or was hiding *from* something. Did it have anything to do with what else was happening in this town? Since she didn't believe he even belonged here, it was hard to imagine him linked to any of the other mysteries.

Pausing beside her car in the drive, Elizabeth glanced up at the third-floor windows. She couldn't see him, but she knew Jonas was watching her. Again that sense of impending disaster swamped her. She wondered if her natural desire to uncover stones would lead to a discovery she would regret about the man she loved.

Eleven

"Are you feeling okay, dear?"

Glancing up from her study of a local history text, Elizabeth found Lily Mae Wheeler regarding her with a concerned expression.

"You look so pale," the woman continued. "True love hasn't blown off course, has it?"

Elizabeth summoned a smile. "True love?"

"You and that dashing Mr. Bishop."

"I guess we're the talk of the town."

"Up until we found out about Jeremiah Kincaid being Jennifer McCallum's daddy." Teardrop crystal earrings swung against her cheeks as Lily Mae darted a look around the secluded corner of the library. "Why don't you come with me and we'll talk?"

Elizabeth hesitated only a moment before gathering up her notes and following the older woman through a door marked Staff Only. Her research into a possible sapphire mine at the old Baxter ranch had proved fruitless so far.

Not only was Elizabeth's mind more on Jonas than on her work, she also hadn't located much information. The librarian on duty had been unable to find some of the historical documents on the Whitehorn area that Elizabeth had found listed in the card catalog. Elizabeth had asked for them this morning. When they weren't immediately located, she'd gone over to the sheriff's office to see if there was any new information about Jeremiah Kincaid, Marie March or Jennifer. She had even visited Jessica and

Jennifer at home. Since Jonas was working, she'd had lunch at the Hip Hop.

When she returned to the library, the staff was in an uproar over the missing documents. Since these books, ledgers and maps were held in a special collection not to be taken off the premises, their disappearance was a serious matter. The search was complicated by the fact that the library was busily preparing for a used-book sale in conjunction with this weekend's Pioneer Days festival.

Elizabeth mentioned the missing materials to Lily Mae as they descended a cool, dim stairway to the basement.

"Yes, everyone's in a tizzy over those missing books," Lily Mae agreed, pushing open a door to a brightly lit workroom. "If you ask me, some volunteer probably reshelved them in the wrong place. It gets so busy around here with story hours and special teas and book sales that it's hard for us volunteers to get everything done. We're not college-educated, paid librarians, after all."

From her tone of voice, Elizabeth suspected Lily Mae had been questioned about the missing documents. Elizabeth thought anyone might be forgiven for thinking of the bleached blonde as a ditz. The way she could ramble on about nothing was one thing, and it wasn't everyone who would choose such a clingy and bright red-and-gold pantsuit for volunteer work at the library.

Lily Mae motioned for Elizabeth to take a seat near a long table where she said she was sorting through books for the sale. "If you need any information about the history of the town, maybe I can help you."

"I wanted to find out more about that old sapphire mine you mentioned."

"Well, I've told you all I know about that. But I have a friend..." The faint blush on Lily Mae's cheeks and the fluttering of her false eyelashes indicated the person might be more than just a friend. She giggled girlishly. "He's a history professor and knows just about everything about this part of the country. He might be able to help you.''

Elizabeth took down his name, pausing when the surname sounded familiar. ''Is this Professor Roper any relation to Sheriff Hensley's wife?''

''He's Tracy's father,'' Lily Mae said. ''And such a fine, fine man. A widower, too. Lost his wife about four years ago, and—''

''That's too bad.'' Elizabeth cut in before the woman could warm up to the subject. She directed the conversation in another direction. ''What's everyone saying about Jeremiah Kincaid?''

Lily Mae pressed a hand to her ample bosom. ''It's really something, isn't it? Although, of course, I wasn't too surprised. Jeremiah was always quite a ladies' man.''

''But Marie March was a little young for him.''

''He liked 'em at any age.'' Lily Mae chuckled. ''And from what I hear, Jeremiah never lost his edge, if you know what I mean.'' She winked.

A hastily cleared throat brought Elizabeth's and Lily Mae's attention to the door. The harried head librarian stood just inside, her lips pursed. ''Lily Mae, I really need you to finish sorting and tagging these books.'' She looked at Elizabeth. ''And no one but staff is supposed to be down here, you know.''

''Don't blame Lily Mae, please,'' Elizabeth said smoothly. ''I begged her permission to look through these books. I'm going to be working in the puppet theater this weekend during the festival, and I didn't want to miss out on any real finds in the library booth. I just adore book sales, especially when the money goes for a good cause, like a library.''

''Yes, well, I suppose it's all right,'' the woman said as she stepped aside for a man dressed in jeans, a Western-style shirt and cowboy hat to come inside with a box full of books. ''Lily Mae, these are from the Kincaid ranch.

Just leave them alone until I can look through them. There might be something of value. Miss Monroe can pay you for whatever books she wants."

"Yes, ma'am," Lily Mae replied, just an edge of sarcasm in her voice. When the librarian was gone, she muttered, "Some people around here are sure impressed with themselves today."

That earned laughter from Elizabeth and even a grin from the cowboy, who quickly brought in three more boxes from the Kincaid ranch. He placed them right beside the boxes of books stacked up for the sale.

"My, but Mrs. Kincaid is being generous," Elizabeth commented.

The cowboy nodded. "She's redoing the ranch library, ma'am." He tipped his hat and left.

"I hear she's redone every room out there," Lily Mae said with a faint sniff.

"You don't think she should?"

"It's her house, of course. But the house was a real showcase for Western art and Native American artifacts. I can just imagine how she's covered it in pastel chintzes and flouncy florals."

Thinking of the widow Kincaid's pale, feminine wardrobe, Elizabeth imagined Lily Mae was right.

The older woman sniffed again as she pulled a stack of books from a nearby box and stuck price tags on the spines. "Mary Jo may have fooled the Kincaid men, but not me."

"In what way?" Elizabeth asked, checking over the books as well.

"Her age." Lily Mae emptied one box and then delved into another. "That woman's not nearly as young as she wants everyone to believe."

"How can you tell?"

"Honey, puhlease. I know enough about trying to look young to know when someone else is hiding her age. I bet

Mary Jo Plumber Kincaid has had an eye job, a nose job, a chin tuck and maybe even some enhancements in other departments.''

Elizabeth laughed. "You may be right, but it's no crime to try and stay young."

"Especially when looking young and pretty helps you land a rich husband."

"You don't think Mary Jo was in love with her husband?''

Lily Mae paused to consider the question for a moment. "I really don't know," she said finally. "She was awful torn up when Dugin died. But when I think back on how she zeroed in on him from the first . . ."

As Lily Mae recounted Mary Jo Kincaid's arrival in Whitehorn, Elizabeth listened halfheartedly and sifted through the books that were being tagged. Her professed love of books was no lie. It was something she and Jonas had in common, from the look of the crowded shelves throughout his house. Her own apartment was jammed with books she'd had no time to read, and already she had found a stack of promising volumes here.

Glancing up, Elizabeth saw that Lily Mae, who was talking as energetically as she was unpacking and tagging, was emptying the boxes from the Kincaid ranch. Elizabeth started to protest, but then glanced down at the book she held. It fell open to reveal faded but still-legible handwriting. A very feminine, flowing script.

Elizabeth flipped to the first page. It was a journal dated nearly fifty years before and belonging to someone named Julia Kincaid. Maybe there was something of value here. She saw that Lily Mae was unearthing other volumes just like it. Moving quickly, with only a slight feeling of guilt, Elizabeth mixed the slender, gold-embossed books with others that she selected at random. Only when no more journals were taken from the box did she call Lily Mae's attention to the mistake she was making.

"Well, my goodness," Lily Mae said. She pulled price tags willy-nilly off books and stacked them back in the box. "I guess I'd better move these Kincaid boxes over to the side."

"I'll do it," Elizabeth offered. After dragging the boxes to another part of the room, she found it easy to do a quick perusal of their contents. Lily Mae wasn't paying the slightest bit of attention. She was rattling on about how Dugin Kincaid had grown up in the shadow of his handsome, perfect older brother, who was killed in Vietnam.

"His death just about did their mother in," Lily Mae added.

"What happened to her?"

"Julia passed away about fifteen years ago."

So Julia Kincaid had been Jeremiah's wife. Maybe her journals would shed some light on a few things. Elizabeth still wondered if the sapphire mine might have been the reason the Kincaids bought the Baxter ranch. Lexine Baxter's disappearance and Charlie Avery's death might well have been connected to that land purchase.

Casually, trying not to betray any excitement, Elizabeth counted the volumes she wanted to buy. Lily Mae didn't even glance at the books as Elizabeth stacked them in an empty box. She just added up the cost, took her money and waved goodbye, saying cheerily, "I'm glad we had this little talk. The roses are back in your cheeks."

Not one person stopped Elizabeth as she climbed back up the stairs and left the library with her box of books. She was beginning to see how easily someone could have taken documents from the local history collection.

What she didn't understand was why.

Shadows were lengthening outside when Jonas came downstairs and found Elizabeth asleep on the sofa in his library. From the rug in front of the sofa, his pets looked up at him with slumberous eyes, as content with Elizabeth as they had ever been with him. A book was open at her side; other books and papers were scattered on the floor and the low table near the sofa.

He paused for a moment to study her—the mussed honey hair, the faint flush on her cheeks, the pink lips that seemed to be lifted at the corners in a smile. She looked sweet and innocent, like a young girl taking a nap. If he bent over and kissed her, he knew just how she would taste and smell, just how she would sigh, how smooth her skin would be. He was already more acquainted with her than with any woman he had ever lived with. Just one week of being Elizabeth's lover had taught him more than a lifetime of experiences.

He was in love with her. Truly in love for the first time in his life.

Funny how certain he was. He had spent most of his life running away from love, away from the safety and security such tender emotions had provided in the East Texas farmhouse where he had grown up. He'd had such wonderful examples in his parents. They had loved each other so well. Why had he ever imagined there should be more in life than that? To be happy, all a man needed was a woman who loved him, someone he trusted, children to raise, work that he loved.

Unfortunately, his priorities had been so screwed up that he had chosen the work first, and with it the fame and fortune and high life that only Hollywood could offer. He'd chosen wrongly. He had never known a good woman's love or respect. And though his parents were the only people who had always loved him, he had lost their respect in the end. Before both of them died—his father two years ago, his mother fourteen months before that—he had seen the questions in their eyes, the wonder that they could have raised a son whose life could go so wrong. Then, as now, Jonas wasn't able to provide an answer.

He also didn't know what he was going to do with this love for Elizabeth. In her, he saw the same questions his parents had asked. And she didn't even know his story. Not yet. If he had his way, she would never know. The trust she said she had in him would never be tested; he would never fall from his pedestal.

This morning he had sensed the unease in her, the questions that hovered behind everything else she said to him. Like a coward, he had retreated to his study, hiding in his work as he had done ever since moving to Whitehorn. The quality of whatever he had written today was probably questionable. He'd kept thinking about Elizabeth, wondering where she was, what resources she might be tapping to discover his secrets. God, how he wanted to believe she wasn't investigating him.

She stretched now in her sleep, her eyelids fluttering open as he touched her hand. Looking up at him, she smiled. "Hello."

Shooing Raven and Poe away, Jonas sat down on the edge of the sofa. "Hello, yourself."

"It's late. I hope you got some work done."

"Some." Jonas picked up the book at her side, turning it around so that the word *Journal* was faceup. "What's this?"

Yawning, Elizabeth sat up and told him about her visit to the library, the missing historical documents and her filching of these journals from under Lily Mae's nose.

Jonas frowned. "You probably got her in trouble."

"Why? The head librarian had no idea what was in those boxes."

"But you took something that wasn't for sale."

Now it was Elizabeth's turn to frown. "For God's sake, I didn't commit a crime."

"Some people would call it stealing." Jonas got to his feet, flipping through the book and not looking at Elizabeth.

"You wouldn't have a problem with it if I weren't a reporter."

"You're probably right."

"But Jonas." Elizabeth slid off the seat and stood, thrusting a hand through her hair. "These journals are fascinating. Everyone's talked about what a bigger-than-life person Jeremiah Kincaid was. Well, his wife found him to be just a man, a very fallible man."

She went on to tell him that Julia Kincaid had written first of her hopes for her marriage to a young and handsome Jeremiah Kincaid. But by the time her second son, Dugin, was born, she had given up on marital happiness. Jeremiah was unfaithful at every turn and didn't bother much about hiding his indiscretions. Julia had been mortified at first, but then she had decided to look on the bright side of her marriage. She had two boys whom she loved and everything money could buy.

Each diary covered nearly four years. By the end of the second one, Julia emerged through her weekly entries as a strong-willed woman who liked her privileged life and was willing to overlook her husband's infidelities to keep it. She'd said she would leave him if he made too much of a fool of himself over some woman, that she would make sure he paid through the nose, with money and a huge scandal. Julia's family was not without resources, and she promised to bring Jeremiah down should he ever go too far. Toward that end, she had retained the services of a private detective to keep tabs on him.

"That's how Julia found out about Clint Calloway," Elizabeth said, picking up another of the journals.

"The detective?"

"He's Jeremiah's son."

Jonas stared at her, stunned. "How can that be?"

Elizabeth tapped a page of the journal. "Jeremiah had an affair with Clint's mother."

"At least according to Julia Kincaid."

"She wrote that Clint's mother came to her...." Elizabeth flipped through the journal. "It's right here. His mother came to Julia, with Clint, thinking she could convince Julia to divorce Jeremiah."

"And marry her."

"I'm sure that was the plan."

"And what did Julia do?"

"Told her to leave. Threatened Jeremiah about what she'd do if he ever publicly claimed the child or if he kept up the affair."

"That still doesn't prove Clint really is Jeremiah's son."

Elizabeth sifted through the papers and books on the table, finally pulling a faded newspaper clipping from one of the journals. "This was Jeremiah and Julia's oldest son, Wayne, the one who died in Vietnam. I want you to look at this photograph, look really hard and think about Clint Calloway. There's a resemblance, Jonas. It's not anything obvious if you're not looking for it. But look at the nose, the set of the mouth, the hairline."

He wasn't sure, but he thought she was right. It did seem as if the handsome, supremely masculine lines of young Wayne Kincaid's features were echoed in Clint Calloway's tough, strong face.

"I wonder if Calloway knows," Jonas murmured.

"Probably. It wouldn't surprise me if half the town knows."

But Jonas disagreed. "That's not something that wouldn't have been discussed, especially after Jeremiah and Dugin died. Wouldn't Clint be entitled to part of the Kincaid fortune?"

"You would think so."

"I don't think Calloway knows," Jonas murmured.

"I guess I'll find out."

He paused, staring at her. "You're going to ask him?"

"Of course."

"And what if he doesn't know?"

Her gaze skittered away from his. "Just like with Jennifer, that's a risk I'll take."

"Calloway doesn't strike me as someone who would welcome Jeremiah as his father."

"But he does seem like someone who would welcome the truth."

"You don't really know if it's the truth," Jonas protested. "All you've got to go on is the journal of a woman who's dead and a vague resemblance between two men. That's not proof."

"Maybe Clint has proof."

"But what if what Julia Kincaid wrote was a fantasy? What if you go telling him this based on the suspicions of a jealous wife?"

"I don't think she was that sort of woman."

"No matter what sort she was, I doubt she would be excited to know you're reading her private diaries."

"The point is that I *have* read them. They paint an interesting portrait of a wealthy and influential family. A family with *three* sons. Two wealthy and pampered. A third illegitimate and unclaimed."

"And maybe that's the way it should stay."

"But it's a fabulous story. Surely the novelist in you sees the drama, the emotion in it."

"These are real people, Elizabeth. Not made-up characters. If you write this story, a story I doubt Julia Kincaid ever wanted told, you'll be playing with these people's lives."

She looked torn. "I hear what you're saying, Jonas. I understand. But I don't know if it's a story I can walk away from."

"But you got hold of that information through treachery."

Elizabeth regarded Jonas with a scowl. "You make me sound like a state spy."

"Reading those books the way you have is the same as spying."

"I see it as a journalist taking advantage of an opportunity. If no one wanted them read, why were they kept after her death? And why would Mary Jo Kincaid donate them to the library?"

Turning away, Jonas drew in a deep breath and released it slowly. "This isn't something we will ever agree on, Elizabeth. I hate the media. I hate their methods, their intrusiveness, the way they justify themselves."

She was silent for a moment, but her voice shook when she spoke. "Why do you say *their?* You're talking about *me.* My methods, my intrusiveness. Do you hate me?"

He faced her again with a quick denial. "Of course I don't. I just wish you weren't—" He bit off the words before they could escape.

But Elizabeth said them for him. "You wish I weren't who I am."

"That's not true."

"But you hate what I do. You hate something that I love. I don't know why…." She held up her hand when he started to speak. "I'm not asking you why. I promised myself I wouldn't ask you anything about yourself again. But you hate something that's a part of me, something deeper than just a job or a career. A journalist is more than what I am. It's *who* I am—"

"Yes, I know." He cut in harshly. "I know that very well."

"But you want me to give it up."

He did. With all his heart, he wanted to take that part of Elizabeth that questioned everything, that looked for the flip side of every issue, that dug beneath the surface, that didn't accept the easy answers. He wanted her passion, her sweetness, her strong spirit and her tender heart. He loved her for those qualities. It would be so nice if he could pick and choose among her characteristics, deleting those that had led her to journalism. And yet what would that leave? Only part of the special woman she was.

"I could do it," she said, stepping toward him. "I could give it up. For you. Only for you."

He rocked back on his heels. "You have no idea what you're saying."

"I love you, Jonas. That's the most important—"

"Don't say that," he protested. Tossing the journal back to the sofa, he took hold of her shoulders. "You don't know what you're saying. You've never given up something that's part of you. I have. And it's like cutting away a section of your soul. You can't do it. I know you *couldn't* do it. Not even for me."

He would never ask her for that. Not ever. Much as he wanted to.

And so here they were. Their identities—hers so clear, his still hidden—stood between them like a rock wall.

Her brown eyes darkened to near black as she stared up at him. "What are you saying to me, Jonas?"

Emotion roughened his voice. "I'm saying you are who you are."

"But the way you feel—"

"And I'm who I am."

"So where do we go from here?"

Because he didn't know, he simply shook his head.

She stepped into his arms, burying her face against his chest. "I love you so."

He wanted to tell her the same. Not saying those words to her took every bit of control he had. He couldn't, however. He couldn't split himself open that way, lay himself bare should she let him down. Should? He almost laughed at his choice of words. The more correct term would be *when* she let him down. And wouldn't she? Hadn't everyone?

Elizabeth went still in his arms, then backed away, her features set in tight lines. "I'm making a idiot of myself, aren't I? What you'd really like is to be rid of me."

"God, no!" The exclamation was torn from deep inside Jonas.

"But you obviously don't feel the way I do. You just stand there, and you don't tell me..." She bit her lip.

He grasped her shoulders again, urgency twisting through his gut. "I don't want you to leave. Not yet. Since I met you..." He took a deep breath, and his words were slow, halting. He had never felt so inadequate with the English language. "I've never known anyone like you, never felt...and what I want is for us to be—to be together, somehow...."

Elizabeth could see the desperation in his gaze, feel it in his touch. The words he couldn't seem to find were there, just beneath the surface. For some reason he couldn't say them. For some reason he wouldn't tell her. Familiar frustration surged inside her, but she forced it back. She finally just put her arms around him.

"I'm sorry," he whispered brokenly, stroking her hair.

She squeezed her eyes shut, fighting tears. She wouldn't cry for what he couldn't say. What he offered would have to be enough.

They said nothing more that night. Not about love. Or journalism. Or what they were going to do when Elizabeth had to return to her job and her life. She knew it was cowardly of her to hide from confrontation. But the sense of foreboding with which she had started the day deepened that night.

The barriers separating her and Jonas were firmly in place.

Elizabeth felt them acutely. Because of them, she even lied to Jonas. The head librarian called her the next morning, frantically trying to locate some missing books from the Kincaid boxes. It seemed the ranch hand who'd delivered them had picked up one box by mistake, and Mary Jo Kincaid wanted the books back. Elizabeth pretended innocence. She went so far as to assure the librarian that she had prevented Lily Mae from making such a mistake. The librarian was so upset that Elizabeth imagined Mary Jo was pitching a fit. And that made Elizabeth suspicious. What more could be in those journals that she hadn't yet read?

Knowing Jonas's opinion on the subject, she didn't tell him what her call was about, even though he studied her as if he suspected. He said nothing, however, and worked upstairs while she pressed on with her reading. She thought about phoning Clint Calloway to set up a meeting, but she put it off, eager to see if there was something else she should pursue instead.

The telephone rang again that afternoon. Jonas took it in his study. Then he raced down the stairs, calling Elizabeth's name.

She met him at the door to the library. His face was ashen. "What is it?" she demanded.

"Jennifer McCallum," he said breathlessly. "She's gone."

Twelve

Gone.

In the hours that followed Jonas's announcement, Elizabeth was to reflect often on the inadequacy of the word. How could those four letters express what had happened to Jennifer McCallum? For that matter, how could one three-year-old girl simply be *gone* from the preschool story hour at the library? *Gone,* while story leader Mary Jo Kincaid's back was turned. *Gone,* while Jennifer's mother was tutoring a student in the library's literacy project. Most of all, how could the police simply tell her devastated parents Jennifer was *gone?*

But she was. As if into thin air. Elizabeth had been around enough criminal investigations in the past to know when the cops were bluffing and when they didn't have a clue. By Sunday morning, when most of the citizens of Whitehorn turned out to search for Jennifer instead of attending church, Elizabeth was certain the police were stumped.

Everyone was hoping Jennifer might have just wandered away. Elizabeth found it hard to believe a little girl could walk down Whitehorn's main street and make it out of town without anyone noticing. But stranger things had happened. The alternatives were even more frightening. If someone had taken Jennifer, hurt her...

Elizabeth got a grip on her runaway speculations. The police were saying little, but she was sure all the usual avenues had been checked and rechecked, just in case this was a stranger abduction. Bus station. Airport. Car-rental agencies. The problem was that if someone had grabbed Jennifer and put her in a car, there were a lot of wide open spaces around Whitehorn. Kidnappers could have taken her anywhere. A child molester could have, as well.

Murmuring a prayer that Jennifer was simply cold and hungry and trapped somewhere close, Elizabeth tried to focus on the somber group of volunteer searchers who were receiving instructions from Sheriff Hensley and the police chief.

There was Hensley's wife, Tracy, looking grim as she listened to her husband. Pretty Lori Bains was manning a coffee urn, her handsome husband at her side. Rafe Rawlings was near the front of the room. His wife, Rae-anne, was moving through the crowd with Melissa Avery North, passing out doughnuts. Melissa's husband, rancher Wyatt North, was standing beside Cheyenne tribal leader Jackson Hawk and his wife, Maggie, who had brought a contingent from the reservation. Beside them was Dr. Kane Hunter, his wife Moriah and a slender, dark-haired teen-ager who Lily Mae had told Elizabeth was the Hunters' daughter. Even Moriah's reclusive father, Homer, was here. As was Nessa Corbett, who had driven in yesterday from Billings.

Lily Mae pointed out many of the townspeople Eliza-beth hadn't met, and she was struck by how similar the men were, with their strong features and stern expres-sions. Their women, too, standing straight and close to their sides.

She jotted down impressions and the names Lily Mae gave her. Private Investigator Nick Dean with his preg-nant wife, Sara Lewis. Ranchers Luke and Maris Rivers. Ethan Walker, with his wife, Judge Kate Randall Walker. And then there was Clint Calloway. Watching his tight, controlled features, Elizabeth wondered if he knew it was his half sister for whom they were all searching.

Standing a little to the back, his arms crossed, was Jonas. Instead of looking at Sheriff Hensley, who was speaking, his eyes were fastened on the group of reporters, representing print, radio and television, that was clustered to one side.

News of Jennifer's disappearance, coming so close after the revelation that she was Jeremiah Kincaid's daughter, had spread like wildfire through the whole region. A child vanishing in a busy library was one thing. A child who could possibly inherit millions was something else again.

Hensley finished his instructions, and the group began breaking apart, heading for the areas he and the police chief had assigned. Elizabeth spied Jessica McCallum with Mary Jo Kincaid near the platform at the front. Jessica looked pale but composed. But her face darkened when Elizabeth approached.

"I don't want to talk to you," she said in a clear but shaky voice.

"Jessica," Elizabeth said, stopping in surprise. "I just want to know how you are."

"I'm sorry," the distraught woman replied. "I'm very sorry I let you do those articles about Jennifer."

Elizabeth was puzzled. "I don't understand."

"Don't you see?" Mary Jo cut in, blue eyes glittering. "You wrote those stories. Everyone saw them, saw who Jennifer was. That's why she's gone."

Falling back a step, Elizabeth looked at Jessica. "You don't believe that, do you?"

Jessica put a hand to her forehead. "I don't know what I believe right now. I just know my baby's gone. She's gone, and because I let you write about her, print her picture, it could have been anyone who took her. Anyone."

The note of hysteria in her voice shook Elizabeth, as did the accusation in her face. Hers and Mary Jo's. And everyone else who was standing around, staring at them.

Interfering little fool, Mary Jo thought, glaring at the reporter. *She had been nothing but trouble since coming to town. She set everyone's tongues to wagging, made everyone ask too many questions. She had dug up the stuff about Jeremiah being Jennifer's father. She had caused this whole ruckus. When Mary Jo had bought her bus ticket to come back to Whitehorn, she had known she'd face a lot of trouble, but never once had she figured on the complications caused by this nosy reporter. God, but she couldn't wait to get out of here, to get out of these stupid, frumpy clothes, to be done with all these people.*

Clint Calloway broke through the crowd, taking Jessica's arm. "Come on. You shouldn't be here. Let me take you to Sterling. He's at home—"

"Yes," Jessica interrupted, her gaze spearing Elizabeth. "He's at home waiting for the ransom call."

"A ransom I'll cover," Mary Jo added defiantly. *Lord, what a great actress she had become.* "We'll get that little girl back. She's my family, too."

Glancing furtively around, Clint managed to quiet both women and lead them toward the exit. But not before he skewered Elizabeth with his own blazing glance.

Everywhere she looked someone turned away from her. Only Lily Mae reached out to clasp her hand and whisper, "Don't take it personally. Everyone's just real upset. You're not to blame."

Elizabeth knew in her gut that if she hadn't done the stories about Jennifer, someone else would have. Once Marie March's identity was determined, someone else would have put two and two together and come up with Jennifer's parentage. Some smart cop like Calloway or Rawlings. Or Kincaid's lawyer. Or the McCallums themselves. This wasn't her fault.

And yet she felt her face flame and her heart begin to pound. Avoiding the glances thrown her way, she turned, looking for Jonas.

She found him standing as he had been, arms folded, as far from the other reporters as he could get. And he, too, was looking at her with a question in his gaze.

Walking toward him, she lifted her chin. "Don't look at me that way."

He lifted one dark eyebrow. "What way?"

"Like what Jessica McCallum said was true."

Instead of commenting, he just took her elbow. "I'm supposed to search near the house. Are you coming with me, or just covering the disappearance for the paper?"

She ignored the underlying sarcasm in his tone and tucked her notepad in her purse. "I'm coming, of course."

They searched all day, pausing only for a bite to eat and for Elizabeth to fax an updated report to her paper. If Jonas disapproved, he said nothing.

A cool rain began to fall around dusk. Little by little, the searchers straggled into the gym for coffee and sandwiches. No one had found a trace of a little girl in bright pink pants and a polka-dot shirt.

Maybe because Elizabeth was as disheveled and dispirited as the rest of the searchers, no one looked at her as they had this morning. Several people gave her statements, pleading with whoever might have Jennifer to bring her home.

The sheriff asked everyone but those who knew the area well to leave for the night. He would put out a call if it was necessary to search farther afield tomorrow.

At Jonas's house, Elizabeth grabbed a quick shower, then wrote a story, weaving in observations about the searchers, about a community that had banded together to find a precious child. She faxed it in and called Ted.

Then she put her hands over her face and sobbed.

Jonas found her crying in his study. Setting aside the mugs of coffee he carried, he gathered Elizabeth in his arms. When she didn't stop crying and didn't respond to his comfort, he sat down in his leather chair, pulling her into his lap.

Finally, when the storm of tears began to subside, she pressed her face to his chest. "I'm sorry. I didn't mean to fall apart."

"It's okay. It's been a tough couple of days."

Elizabeth sat up, brushing a hand through her hair. "All day long, everywhere I looked, I kept thinking I'd see her. And then I'd pray I wouldn't see her, that we wouldn't find her...*left* somewhere to—" she swallowed, battling new tears "—left somewhere to die."

"That's not going to happen," Jonas soothed. "Someone's going to ask for money."

"But they should have done that by now."

"Maybe they have."

"Then why were all of us out there looking? Hensley wouldn't have done that if he knew she had been kidnapped for ransom."

Tenderly wiping some of the tears from her cheeks, Jonas said, "I guess you're right."

With a ragged sigh, she snuggled back against his chest. "This would be so much easier if I didn't know her. If she was just some little girl—"

"But every little girl belongs to someone, is known by someone."

"You're right, of course." She was silent for a moment before whispering, "What if she were our little girl?"

The very idea of him and Elizabeth having a child was enough to squeeze Jonas's heart. And if she were missing as Jennifer was... He hurt all over just thinking about it.

Perhaps Elizabeth read his mind, for her arms tightened around him. "I guess now I know what Ted was telling me when he sent me up here two weeks ago. He said I needed to get my humanity back. I just wish my lesson didn't have to come like this." She raised her head again. "They're going to find her, aren't they?"

Jonas pulled her against him once more. "I hope so, Elizabeth. I pray so."

But he knew they were both well aware that life had no guarantees.

They sat that way for so long that Jonas lost track of time. Elizabeth fell asleep. But he continued to hold her, thinking that maybe, just maybe she really did have the compassion to understand who he really was. Maybe if she knew the truth, she wouldn't see him as just another story. After all, she hadn't approached Clint Calloway yet, had she? And she had cried over Jennifer's disappearance. The hard-nosed reporter who had brought down half of Denver's city government and caused a congressman to weep on national TV, had cried over a missing child.

Maybe it was time to trust her completely.

When Jennifer is found I'll tell Elizabeth the truth, he promised himself.

After two more days of searching, Sheriff Hensley called off the volunteers. He wouldn't tell Elizabeth or any of the other reporters who were camped out in town if a ransom request had been made. He said he thought Jennifer had been taken out of the area. He asked people to keep their eyes open, of course, but the rest of the formal search would be carried out by trained law-enforcement officials. Detective Calloway was put in charge of the case.

Again Elizabeth wondered if Calloway knew exactly who Jennifer was. His relationship with her would be a poignant sidebar to this story. But more than that, he might want to know. The knowledge that he was looking for his blood kin might lend an urgency to his search.

She deliberated for a full night over confronting Calloway, just as she worried over discussing the matter with Jonas. There had been new tenderness between the two of them since the night she had cried in his arms. And yet nothing was resolved. As he had said, they were each who they were. Elizabeth didn't particularly want to argue journalistic ethics with Jonas anymore, just as she didn't particularly want to walk away from this story about Calloway being Jeremiah's son and Jennifer's half brother.

In the end, she went that morning to find the detective without mentioning it to Jonas.

Calloway was at the sheriff's department, of course, and he didn't particularly want to speak with her. But Elizabeth, professing to have information about Jennifer, persisted until he saw her alone. Then she told him about the journals and what they revealed about him. From the look of shock and rage on his face, she knew he had been in the dark until now.

She left him the journals that pertained to him and walked away, saying she would wait for his statement before filing a story.

He found her at the Hip Hop that afternoon, having coffee with a television reporter and a cameraman from Missoula who were covering the search for Jennifer. In fact, the whole café was filled with media types just waiting for a break in the story. They all fell silent as Calloway strode in and began passing out a statement. In it, he admitted to being Jeremiah's illegitimate son.

Elizabeth read the words, then looked up into the detective's simmering, blue-gray eyes. "Looks like you won't have an exclusive," he muttered, ignoring the pleas for comments from the rest of the reporters around them.

Two weeks ago she would have been furious. Two weeks ago she would have raced every reporter in the place for the nearest phone. But now she put out a hand in sympathy to Calloway. "You may not believe this, but I really do know what you're feeling."

"You couldn't."

"You can't see it now, but someday I think you, and Jennifer, will be glad to know the truth about your parents."

"Easy for you to say."

"I'll tell you about my own parents sometime."

"No, thanks," he snapped. "I've got a little girl—a *sister*—to find. You and everyone else here can print whatever you want about that thieving rat Jeremiah Kincaid and me, his bastard son. But all that matters is that I find Jennifer."

He turned on his heel and left everyone still clamoring for his attention. Halfway across the street, he dropped the sheaf of statements he still clutched to the pavement. They blew away in the wind.

Elizabeth managed a bittersweet smile. Big, tough Clint Calloway had been hurt by the truth of who he was. But he would survive. Just as she had survived since that long-ago spring when she had learned the truth about her own family. And if she hadn't learned any lessons from the knowledge then, she was learning now. She wasn't proud of hurting Clint, but she was proud of herself for the way she had handled it. Instead of barreling in and writing the story, she had waited. Maybe he had stolen her scoop, but that didn't matter. It was his life, after all. She was just writing about it.

Laughing out loud, she decided Ted would probably say her ambivalence about losing an exclusive meant she was sharing a little too much humanity. But she didn't care. She wanted to go home and tell Jonas what had happened.

She found him in his study, of course. Standing over the fax machine. Staring down at a piece of paper. When he looked up at her, his eyes were savage.

Her heart beat hard against her ribs. "What is it? Jennifer?"

He threw the paper at her. "Read it yourself. It's what you've been waiting for."

"What are you talking about?"

"It's all about me. From someone at your paper named Dawn."

Throat tightening, Elizabeth bent to pick up the paper. Even though her curiosity about Jonas's past had never abated, she had completely forgotten her call to Dawn about checking into his background. So much had happened since then—their being run off the road, becoming lovers, falling in love, not to mention the revelations about Jennifer and her subsequent kidnapping. It was because of the story on Jennifer that Dawn had even known where to fax her. Elizabeth had been communicating with the paper via Jonas's fax every day.

"Aren't you going to look at it?" Jonas demanded coldly.

She glanced down, then quickly back to him. "Why don't you just tell me what it says?"

"No!" He strode forward, grabbing hold of her hand and lifting the paper toward her face. "Read it, Elizabeth. Read every word out loud."

She snatched her hand away, tearing the paper in half. "Stop it. I want you to tell me. I was waiting for you to tell me whatever it is that's so awful that you're hiding from it."

"Waiting?" His laughter was filled with rage. "How could you be waiting when you had someone at the paper checking me out?"

"But that was before—"

"Before we were lovers?" he interrupted. "You mean to say you didn't plan that? I figured that was just part of the ruse, the way to get close, to get your story." He pushed his face close to hers, his features twisting in anger. "I hope it was good, Elizabeth. I hope my touching you, making love to you, was payment enough for this scoop."

"Shut up," she said, trying not to give in to the tears his bitterness brought to her eyes. "My sleeping with you, loving you has nothing to do with this." She threw her half of the offensive paper on the floor. "God in heaven, Jonas, you have to believe me."

He ignored her plea, bending to pick up the paper again. "Let's hear this, shall we? Let's see what your researcher has found." He fitted the two halves together. "'Jonas Bishop Tucker,'" he read.

Elizabeth gasped. "So Tucker's your real name, not just a pseudonym?"

"You may remember me. Jonas Tucker."

She shook her head.

"A film director," he said, not reading from the paper now. "They called me a *wunderkind*. I left college and went to Hollywood thinking I'd be a screenwriter. I lucked into some stunt work just before I would have starved to death. I got luckier still and directed my first picture when I was twenty-nine. Four more followed. All big action thrillers, each more expensive than the last. Big budgets. Big stars. I was hot. Very hot."

She was stunned, and she was also beginning to remember him. There had been a scandal. Someone had died.

"I had everything," he continued. "Money and fame. And power. Especially power. For someone who had grown up poor but decent, I really got off on that power. I believe I even thought I was immortal."

"You jumped out of planes," Elizabeth murmured, thinking of what he had told her about himself during their picnic supper just over a week ago.

"And fell off mountains and plunged down rivers and killed a man."

She sucked in her breath.

Jonas appeared so set and frozen that he didn't even glance at her. "He was just a boy, and he wanted to be part of my group, my circle of *friends*." The sneer he put into the word showed they were really anything but friends. "Peter Thompson was just a kid who wanted to be a big wheel, like I had wanted to be when I was his age. He wanted to make movies and be famous. He thought he had a part in my last film, but he didn't.''

Finally, Jonas looked at Elizabeth. "I laughed at him. I told him to go home to Oklahoma or Indiana or wherever he was from. I had let him believe he was 'in,' you know. And he had scurried around like some little mouse, doing me favors, taking my clothes to the cleaners, scoring drugs for my friends who indulged themselves that way, finding women for those who indulged another way." He closed his eyes, hands clenching into fists at his sides.

Elizabeth could see the battle raging inside him. "Jonas, don't—"

"But you wanted to know," he said, still not opening his eyes. "Well, know the truth. Not the tabloid lies. Know that Peter came to a party the night after I laughed in his face—laughed in his face when he asked when shooting would begin on the picture he thought he'd be in. That night, he came all the way up to the penthouse where I was living, and he climbed up on the railing of the balcony. Everyone was laughing. Even me, at first. Then I really looked at him, looked at him the way I hadn't looked at anyone in a long, long time. And I knew what he was going to do."

Putting a hand to her mouth, Elizabeth waited to hear what she knew had happened.

"I grabbed for him. I ran over and I grabbed him. Everyone, all my rich and useless friends, were laughing and laughing, but I grabbed for him. But he fought me. He jerked away. And he fell." Jonas opened his eyes and looked into hers. "He screamed my name all the way down. Thirty stories."

She held back her sob by force of will.

"So now you know. I killed him. Only not the way anyone said I did. Not the way the rags printed the story."

"But Jonas," she whispered around the lump in her throat, "you didn't kill him. He jumped."

"Not according to every paper that picked up the story."

"But responsible journalists—"

"Every newspaper and newscast in L.A., not just the tabloids, said that I was a murder suspect."

"They made a mistake."

"And compounded it every day for months."

"Because your profession put you in the spotlight."

"I was still a human being. Peter Thompson was a human being. I think we both deserved more than they gave us."

"Perhaps you're right."

"Perhaps?" The rage was back in his face, having replaced the flat, dead expression that had stolen over his features when he was talking about what had happened. "Just look," he said, holding out the fax again. "Look at what your own newspaper was able to drum up with their research. They've got all the lies. There were stories that said Peter and I were fighting over a woman. Over a man. That we were lovers. That I picked him up and threw him off the balcony. That I had been committed to an insane asylum. By the time the feeding frenzy was over, I felt as if I should be committed."

He turned his back on Elizabeth, wadding the fax into a ball and tossing it aside. "Even the truth they printed was hurtful. Every detail of my life was put out there for everyone to read. Every youthful mistake I had made. Every woman I had been involved with. My parents..." He shook his head. "My parents were so ashamed. They'd known before then that I wasn't leading a life they exactly approved of, but they hadn't thought I had sunk into degradation, either. Seeing it all spelled out was torture for them."

"But what happened when it was made clear you didn't do anything wrong that night?"

He wheeled back to face her. "That? That minor detail of truth rated little more than a mention on the late news, a paragraph on a back page. By that time, the woman I was with, whom at the time I honestly thought I loved, was selling stories about our personal relationship to the press. She had a colorful past I knew nothing about, so the two of us made good copy for a while. Till I disappeared."

"When you came here?"

"Eventually."

"And you've been hiding here ever since."

He frowned. "Hiding?"

"Using a false name, writing books under a pseudonym." She met his gaze straight on. "Hiding."

"I started a new life."

"But what kind of life? Based on lies?"

"Lies?" he repeated, flushing. "You have a lot of nerve talking about lies to me. After what you've been doing—"

"I haven't done anything. I didn't tell anyone about your Gerald Tucker alter ego."

"Because it wasn't juicy enough. You were just waiting for the real dirt, weren't you? The same way you've been fishing for dirt about the whole town." He stalked over and ripped her chart of "mysteries" off the wall.

She managed a mirthless laugh. "I thought your mystery might have something to do with all the rest."

"Of course it doesn't." He tossed the chart at her feet. "All these 'mysteries' are just things that happen to people, Elizabeth. There's no conspiracy. There's no big story. No link. Simply a lot of little people living their lives. That's what I came here to do. That's what I was doing until you showed up. That's why I wanted you out of here. I didn't want all the damned media attention focused on this town."

"Because you were afraid." Her voice broke on the last word.

"Yes, I was afraid," he proclaimed proudly. "I was frightened out of my mind that someone would see me, would bring up the nightmare that I had tried to put behind me." He paused to take a deep breath. "You see, Elizabeth, it's only been lately that I haven't fallen asleep every night with Peter Thompson's scream ringing in my head. Can you blame me for not wanting to relive those events once more?"

"No one sent him over that balcony but him. Not you. Not the media."

"But when he was dead, they sure circled in to feast on my flesh." He came toward her, eyes glittering in the fading sunlight that spilled through the windows. "Have you started your article on me? After living with me, going through my house, probably my computer, have you started writing the article?"

Her face burned as if he had slapped her. "I told you, Jonas. There's no story about you."

"But isn't it too good a story to walk away from? Aren't I just like that poor devil, Clint Calloway?"

Her expression must have betrayed her, for triumph flared in his face. "You didn't walk away from him, did you?"

She lifted her chin, not about to retreat, because she wasn't ashamed of her actions. "I told him about Jeremiah. He believed me and released the news himself."

"Bully for him," Jonas said. "Maybe I'll do the same."

Taking a step forward, her hand outstretched, she said, "You don't have to. If it means so much to you that no one know who you really are, I won't tell. I'll never tell."

"I don't believe you."

His harsh words made her falter. "Jonas, please—"

"I hope you have all the details you need for your story."

"There is no—"

"Because I want you gone."

There it was, that word again. *Gone.* So simple, so devastating.

"I wish you would listen to me, believe me—"

"Funny thing was..." A muscle jumped in his jaw. Elizabeth could sense the iron control he was imposing on himself. He cleared his throat, but his voice came out raspy and strained. "It's so funny, you know. Because I did believe you. I believed your whole story. About loving me, trusting me."

"That's because it's all true."

"Oh yeah?" He bit his lip, and she saw the tears in his eyes. "Well, if it's true, I guess I'll read it in the paper, won't I?"

With those final, bitter words, he left her standing there. He left the study and the house. He left her alone with her breaking heart. And since he didn't trust her, didn't believe her, he left her no choices. When he came back, she had to be gone.

And so she was.

Thirteen

Without Elizabeth, Jonas's house echoed in strange ways. The emptiness was so damn loud he couldn't sleep. He kept seeing that fax coming out of his machine. He kept remembering the moment when he had known, with absolute certainty, that she was no different from everyone else who had ever betrayed him.

He felt so stupid. Like a classic cuckolded male. She had crooked her finger, wiggled her tail, and he had fallen into her trap.

After the scandal that had changed his life, his mother had told him that people repeat their mistakes until they learn from them. Jonas had vowed then not to follow the same path. He had sealed himself away, not getting close to anyone. But he had forgotten the lesson when Elizabeth showed up.

She had played him for a fool. He had known even before they got involved that people always have their own agenda, that they are loyal first and foremost to themselves. Hadn't he been that way himself once? He had used people, abused them, taken what they'd offered, then tossed it back in their faces. No doubt if Peter Thompson hadn't killed himself right in front of his eyes, Jonas would still be the same selfish bastard.

But he wasn't the same.

A selfish bastard probably wouldn't have been vulnerable enough to fall for a pretty reporter with warm eyes, soft laughter and a winning smile. The man he had been wouldn't have appreciated her subtle beauty. Or the story she had told him about her parents. Or the way she had cried over Jennifer.

Was she just acting? Was anything she had said and done for real?

Maybe she was genuine, he thought. Maybe she really had cared. And maybe his refusal to tell her about himself, his inability to trust her, had been just one last blow for a woman who had been betrayed too many times before.

And maybe he was a bigger fool for hoping she might really love him.

On the third afternoon after Elizabeth had gone, Jonas stood at the window of his study, staring out at the town. His town. Where everyone knew his name, but no one really knew him. Where he was so desperately, completely alone.

Poe rubbed against his leg. Raven pushed her nose into his hand. And Jonas shut his eyes, remembering Elizabeth's laughter when the pets had jumped on the bed at a most inopportune moment. He remembered her scent, fresh as a Montana spring evening. He could actually feel her soft skin, feel her touch gliding up his body....

With a heavy sigh, he sat down and stared at the telephone. It hadn't rung in two days. The calls he had expected hadn't come. At his feet were newspapers from every major city in the western U.S. There was no mention of his name. In Elizabeth's paper, her only byline was a "nothing-new-to-report" update on Jennifer McCallum, run the day before yesterday. The information about Clint Calloway rated only a paragraph.

What was Elizabeth waiting for, he wondered? He felt sure the story of a reclusive refugee from decadent Hollywood would be a juicy enough tale to get into print, especially since he was now a bestselling author.

"Why doesn't she get it over with?" he demanded of his pets. The question built inside him, as it had been doing ever since she left. Finally, feeling as if he were about to explode, he went looking for Elizabeth.

She wasn't at the Amity Boardinghouse, or the Hip Hop. Melissa Avery North said she hadn't been in for days. At the police station, Clint Calloway said he thought she was gone, and good riddance. Lily Mae Wheeler, who stopped Jonas on the street, said Elizabeth hadn't even told her goodbye.

An irrational anger gripped Jonas. But the emotion was a welcome replacement for the hollowness that had filled his insides since he'd confronted Elizabeth and she had gone. He grabbed hold of his anger, clung to it. It propelled him home, where he paced up and down for hours.

Still angry, he packed a bag.

Furious, he drove to Billings.

Fuming, he caught a plane for Denver.

Elizabeth was back at the newspaper, in the cubicle that she had missed so much. But it felt so strange. She felt strange, like she had become someone other than the woman who had left here more than two weeks ago.

"So you're back."

Swiveling in her chair, she found Ted regarding her with a fond smile. "I'm here, anyway."

"You gave up on the story about the town."

She nodded. "Once the little girl was snatched, there didn't seem much point to the rest of it. I actually came home a couple of days ago." She looked down at her hands. "I know I didn't call in. I'm sorry—"

"No problem." Ted stepped into her cubicle and perched on the edge of her desk, crossing his brawny arms over his wide but firm middle. "When you didn't phone or answer my last call to your *friend* in Whitehorn, I figured you were home."

She shot him a grin. "I could have been dead in a ditch."

"I thought the *friend* would tell me if that were so."

"No, he wouldn't have known," she said, not even trying to ignore the subtle inflection in Ted's voice. He probably knew from the way she'd sounded on the phone that the friend she had met in Whitehorn was much, much more.

"You okay?" Ted asked.

"It was an educational trip."

"Those can be hard on a person."

She nodded. "I learned a lot about people, about myself. I think it'll show in the writing."

"It already has. Those stories about the search for the little girl—" he gave her a thumbs-up "—they're good stuff. Whether you intended to or not, you captured the heart of that town up there. All those people working together, trying to find her. It was good journalism."

"I'm glad you think so."

Ted gave her another intense look. "You sure you ought to be back at work?"

"I'm sure."

He hesitated a moment, then added, "You want to talk about him?"

She shook her head. She wasn't sure she was ever going to be able to talk about Jonas with anyone. Just thinking of him caused an ache that was as physical as any pain she had ever known.

"If you do..." Ted began, then he stood. "What the hell?"

Elizabeth spun around in her seat again and found Jonas in her cubicle doorway. She gasped. "What are you doing here?"

He didn't say anything for a moment. He just stared at her, looking slightly unhinged. His black jeans and white shirt were rumpled, as if he had slept in them. His skin was pale. His eyes were rimmed with dark circles.

Ted stepped forward. "Listen, buddy—"

But Elizabeth stood and caught his arm. "It's okay, Ted. This is . . . my friend from Whitehorn."

Ted frowned. "He looks like trouble."

Still staring at Elizabeth, Jonas said, "I just want to know when you're going to print it."

"I'm not," she answered. "I told you I wouldn't."

"Print what?" Ted asked.

Ignoring him, she continued, "Jonas, I'm sorry that people have treated you so badly that you can't trust me. But I said I wouldn't print your story. And I won't. I know you don't believe me, but I love you too much to do something that you don't want."

This time, Ted stepped away as Jonas moved toward her. "You don't love me."

"Why is that so hard for you to believe?" Elizabeth demanded.

"Because of who I am. What I've done."

"You did nothing."

He stopped just inches from her. "But I did. I wasn't a good person. I don't deserve your love." Though the words said one thing, the plea in his eyes said another.

The pain he continued to feel over an unfortunate young man's suicide was so real that Elizabeth could feel it, too. She reached out and took his hand. "I've been sitting here thinking how much I've changed," she said. "I'm not the same person I was two weeks ago. And you're not the person you were, either."

"You've changed me," he whispered.

"You changed yourself," she insisted. "You're not the person you were when all those terrible things happened. The Jonas I know is kind and strong and patient. His only problem is that he won't listen to me. He won't believe in me when I tell him that I love him."

He swallowed hard, his fingers gripping hers. "Not listening has always been my biggest problem."

"You need to work on it."

"Maybe you can help."

She felt a smile trembling on her lips. "You'll have to ask really, really nice."

Leaning close, he slipped his arms around her waist. "I've been going crazy without you," he whispered. "I flew in last night, telling myself I just wanted to know when you were going to write the damned story. And then I came around the corner and saw you here... and nothing else mattered. I need you, Elizabeth. I love you."

The words rippled over her like a breeze on a hot summer day. So welcome. She felt them all the way through her soul. "You can't imagine how much I've wanted to hear that."

He lifted a hand to her hair. "I'm so sorry for the things I said. The accusations I made."

"You were angry. You've been hurt before—"

"That's no excuse," he insisted. "If I hadn't been such an idiot, so afraid of someone discovering my secrets..."

"Well, they are *your* secrets."

"Right now I'd like to shout them from a rooftop. I may even confess to my publisher. They'd like me to do a book tour."

She framed his face with her hands. "Not without me."

Jonas kissed her then, kissed her with all the yearning and passion that had been building since she'd walked out of his house. And as they kissed, he imagined he heard cheers.

When he drew away, he realized the cheers were real. Everyone in the entire newsroom was standing around Elizabeth's half-open little office, clapping and cheering with enough abandon for a stadium of soccer fanatics.

"Just what I always wanted," he grumbled, grinning. "To be surrounded by members of the press while I propose to the woman I love."

Elizabeth smiled up at him, brown eyes crinkling at the corners. "It's what happens when you fall for a reporter."

Jonas caught her bright, sparkling laughter with another kiss, much to the delight of the assembled group.

They were still kissing that afternoon, when they caught the last plane to Billings. Elizabeth was going to cover the rest of the search for Jennifer. Jonas was going to tell everyone in Whitehorn exactly who he was. And besides, they both agreed, there were still some mighty strange things going on in that town. It would be nice if they could figure it all out.

Before they left for their honeymoon, at least.

* * * * *

MONTANA MAVERICKS

continues with

COWBOY COP

by Rachel Lee

Available in July

Here's an exciting preview....

One

"We have to work together. You don't have to *like* me."

Clint Calloway didn't even glance up when Dakota Winston spoke. His attention remained fixed on the small pile of matchsticks in front of him, and on the street below his window. She might have been talking to a deaf man.

"Look, Clint, it's apparent you don't like having me for your partner," she continued earnestly. "I guess I can understand that. You're an experienced detective and I'm just a rookie." A *female* rookie. The unspoken adjective seemed to vibrate in the air.

He still didn't respond, just reached out with one blunt fingertip to move a matchstick across the blotter on his desk, placing it in another group. Dakota had been watching him do that periodically since they had started working together two days ago. She couldn't imagine what he was doing with those matchsticks, and when she asked he wouldn't answer. All she knew for certain was that the end of each of them had been painted a different color. It was clear to her they represented something, but he wasn't going to enlighten her. That was just another of the man's frustrating characteristics, and he had quite a few of them.

The matchstick, tipped in red, joined a different pile. Then Clint turned his head and studied the street to his left. His cubicle was in the corner of the police station, and had two windows, the one right in front of him overlooking Center Avenue, and the other overlooking Coyote Path. Dakota figured that absolutely nothing on this corner of Whitehorn, Montana, escaped Clint Calloway's attention.

"Look," she said to Clint's back, "I'm a fast learner. Just tell me what you want me to do and I'll do it. If I mess up, I want to hear that, too. I really want to be a good cop."

No response. Her sense of frustration was overwhelming but there didn't seem to be anything she could do about it. If this man didn't speak a single word to her throughout the time they were paired she'd just have to live with it. She had too much to prove and was too new at this business to make a stink about anything a respected veteran detective might do. If she complained, she'd be labeled trouble, never mind that it was Clint's fault.

So she bit back any further words and tried to find another way to handle this. The only thing she could come up with was to shut her mouth and try to be the best damn cop this guy had ever worked with. It was a tall order for a rookie, and she knew it, but he sure wasn't leaving her any other alternatives.

The seconds dragged by. He moved another matchstick. Then slowly, he turned his head a little and asked, "Are you through?"

Her cheeks heated. "Yes."

"Then let's get some things clear here. I don't like you. I'm not *going* to like you. You can work your butt off trying to be a good cop, but you aren't going to make it. Women shouldn't be cops. They get too tangled up in their feelings and mess things up. This job calls for a cool head, not emotional reactions to everything."

"I—"

He cut her off ruthlessly. "I've been listening to your drivel, now you can listen to mine. What I think about women cops doesn't matter. Fact is, I got saddled with one and I have to put up with it or get fired. So I'm stuck with you and you're stuck with me. Just keep your mouth shut, do what I tell you and stay out of my way."

Anger blossomed inside her, but it was tempered by the fact that she had already suspected these feelings. Putting them in the open this way merely saved her having to wonder about it. He was a male chauvinist. Fine. He wasn't the first one she'd met and he wouldn't be the last. If his objection to her was simply that she was a woman, she could handle it, and prove him wrong in the process. She certainly wasn't going to slink away with her tail tucked between her legs.

"Great," she managed to say steadily. "I prefer to know where I stand."

"Now you know." His voice was deep and as rough as gravel, a sound that suited his appearance. Built solidly, he looked tough, invincible; the kind of guy you'd want beside you in a fight. She'd heard he'd earned his toughness as a kid on the wrong side of the tracks. She could only imagine what it had been like for him, but she was willing to excuse some rough edges as a result of it.

His gray-green eyes were stormy as they raked over her, and she found herself thinking that he had the raw, ragged good looks of a successful alley cat. There were faint scars on his knuckles, mementoes of any number of fist fights, she supposed, and his nose had an interesting little bend in it, probably from contact with someone's fist. An old scar bisected one of his dark eyebrows, giving him a satiric appearance.

The look he gave her was distinctly male, a man measuring a woman and evaluating her sexual attributes. Dakota had received plenty of those looks in her life and had learned to ignore them, but this time she felt an almost overwhelming urge to fold her arms across her breasts. Instead she pressed her fingertips into the sides of her thighs and resisted the urge to clench her hands into fists.

Act relaxed, she told herself. Don't let this guy know he can get to you.

Evidently it worked. His expression changed and he looked toward his desk. He pointed to a stack of thick manila folders. "These are our open cases. Start reading."

"I thought we were supposed to be working on the Jennifer McCallum kidnapping."

He made an impatient sound. "The kid was kidnapped a week ago. We haven't a damn thing to go on. No ransom demand has been made, and nobody saw a thing. Rule of thumb is that after forty-eight hours, the trail is ice and the kid's chances are slim. If we're going to accomplish anything at all now, we have to use our brains, Ms. Winston. If you have one, familiarize it with the case."

"Why you son of a—" She caught herself and bit the word off, glaring at him.

"If you can't stand the heat, get back in the kitchen." He pointed again to the stack of files. "Start reading. You'll be no damn good to me if you're not ready to work when the opportunities arise."

He swiveled his chair back to face his desk, pointedly dismissing her. Dakota clamped down on her anger, her teeth clenched so tightly that her jaw ached. Keeping her movements deliberate so as not to reveal the depth of her anger, she picked up the stack of files and carried them to her desk. Two days with Detective Clint Calloway and she was ready to commit murder.

But at her own desk, away from the source of her anger, she calmed down swiftly and began to think. She couldn't keep on getting this upset by his provocation or she was going to seriously mess up... which was probably what he was hoping for. Once she messed up, he'd be justified in asking that she be assigned to someone else.

And while that might be a whole lot more comfortable, the bottom line was that she didn't want to mess up, and she wanted to work with Clint Calloway. He had a reputation of being a maverick, almost a psychically talented investigator. That meant he knew tricks she wanted to know, that he had a way of viewing problems that could be really useful if she could learn it. Skills that could someday set her apart the way Clint Calloway was set apart.

So she had to hang on to her temper and endure whatever kind of hazing he gave her. She had to prove to everyone that she had what it took. Sort of a trial by fire. She'd expected this, of course. Women cops weren't rare by any means these days, but they still weren't entirely welcome, and would probably never be welcomed at all by some male policemen. She'd suffered from some of that attitude at the academy, and even a little of it in college when her classmates in Criminal Justice had learned of her desire to join law enforcement. She'd certainly suffered from it during her two years with the Miles City force. Clint Calloway as just a more forceful expression of an outdated attitude. She could handle it. She could handle *him*.

Reaching out, she snagged the first file, and began to read about the abduction of a three-year-old named Jennifer.